BLAZE

OF

SECRETS

Jessie Donovan

This book is a work of fiction. Names, characters, places, and incidents are either the product of the writer's imagination or are used fictitiously, and any resemblance to actual persons, living or dead, business establishments, events, or locales is entirely coincidental.

Blaze of Secrets
Copyright © 2013 Laura Hoak-Kagey
Mythical Lake Press, LLC
Second Edition

Cover Art by Clarissa Yeo of Yocla Designs.

ISBN 13: 978-0989733618

To my dad
For surviving all of my crazy adventures over the years and
never doubting me whenever I think of new ones.

And to Michelle Cuadros
Best friend, sister, and my first reader.
Someday we'll find you new hamsters, I promise.

Other Books by Jessie Donovan

The *Feiru*

The Feiru *(FEY-roo) are a race similar in appearance to humans, but with slight genetic differences...First-born children of* Feiru *mothers have the ability to manipulate elemental energy particles, which, until recently, had been undetectable to human scientists. What type of element they can control—fire, earth, water, or wind—and whether their ability is aggressive or healing in nature is determined by genetics. These* Feiru-*specific abilities are commonly referred to as "elemental magic" amongst their kind.*

...As long as the Feiru *continue to uphold the rules and regulations set forth in The Agreement, and hide their unique abilities and existence from humans, they will be allowed to govern over their own kind. If they violate The Agreement, the* Feiru *liaison offices of the various world governments will meet and devise a plan on how to handle the* Feiru *failures... The primary function of the* Feiru *liaison office is to prevent worldwide paranoia, no matter the cost.*

—Excerpt from the *Feiru* Liaison Training Guide, US Edition

CHAPTER ONE

First-born Feiru *children are dangerous. At the age of magical maturity they will permanently move into compounds established for both their and the public's protection. These compounds will be known as the Asylums for Magical Threats (hereafter abbreviated as "AMT").*

—Addendum, Article III of the *Feiru* Five Laws, July 1953

Present Day

Jaxton Ward kept his gaze focused on the nearing mountain ledge ahead of him. If he looked down at the chasm below his feet, he might feel sick, and since his current mission was quite possibly the most important one of his life, he needed to focus all of his energy on succeeding.

After all, if things went according to plan, Jaxton would finally see his brother again.

He and his team of three men were balanced on a sheet of rock five thousand feet in the air. To a human, it would look like they were flying. However, any *Feiru* would know they were traveling via elemental wind magic.

Darius, the elemental wind first-born on his team, guided them the final few feet to the mountain ledge. As soon as the sheet of rock touched solid ground, Jaxton and his team moved into position.

The mountain under their feet was actually one of the most secure AMT compounds in the world. Getting in was going to be difficult, but getting out was going to take a bloody miracle, especially since he'd had to barter with his boss for the location of his brother. In exchange, he had promised to rescue not just Garrett, but one other unknown first-born as well.

Taka, the elemental earth first-born of Jaxton's team, signaled he was ready. He nodded for Taka to begin.

As Taka reached a hand to the north, the direction of elemental earth magic, the solid rock of the mountain moved. With each inch that cleared to form a tunnel, Jaxton's heart rate kicked up. Jaxton was the reason his brother had been imprisoned inside the mountain for the last five years and he wasn't sure if his brother had ever forgiven him.

Even if they survived the insurmountable odds, located Garrett, and broke into his prison cell, his brother might not agree to go with them. Considering the rumors of hellish treatment inside the AMT compounds, his brother's hatred would be justified.

Once the tunnel was big enough for them to enter, Jaxton pushed aside his doubts. No matter what his brother might think of him, Jaxton would rescue him, even it if took drugging Garrett unconscious to do so.

Taking out his Glock, he flicked off the safety. Jaxton was the only one on the team without elemental magic, but he could take care of himself.

He moved to the entrance of the tunnel, looked over his shoulder at his men, and nodded. After each man nodded, signaling they were ready, he took out his pocket flashlight, switched it on, and jogged down the smooth tunnel that would lead them to the inner corridors of the AMT compound.

If his information was correct, the AMT staff would be attending a site-wide meeting for the next hour. That gave Jaxton and his team a short window of opportunity to get in, nab the two inmates, and get back out again.

He only hoped everything went according to plan.

~~*

Kiarra Melini stared at the small homemade shiv in her hand and wondered for the thousandth time if she could go through with it.

She had spent the last few weeks racking her brain, trying to come up with an alternative plan to save the other prisoners of the AMT without having to harm anyone. Yet despite her best efforts, she'd come up empty-handed.

To protect the lives of the other first-borns inside the AMT, Kiarra would kill for the first and last time.

Not that she wanted to do it, given the choice. But after overhearing a conversation between two AMT researchers a few weeks ago, she knew the AMT would never again be safe for any of the first-borns while she remained alive.

The outside world might have chosen to forget about the existence of the first-born prisoners, but that didn't make them any less important. Kiarra was the only one who cared, and she would go down fighting trying to protect them.

Even if it meant killing herself to do so.

She took a deep breath and gripped the handle of her blade tighter until the plastic of the old hairbrush dug into her skin. Just as she was about to raise her arm to strike, her body shook. Kiarra closed her eyes and breathed in and out until she calmed down enough to stop shaking. Ending her life, noble as her reasons may be, was a lot harder than she'd imagined.

Mostly because she was afraid to die.

But her window of opportunity was closing fast; the AMT-wide meeting would end in less than an hour. After that, she would have to wait a whole other month before she could try again, and who knew how many more first-borns would suffer because of her cowardice.

Maybe, if she recalled the conversation between the two researchers, the one which forebode the future harsh realities of the other AMT prisoners, she'd muster enough nerve to do what needed to be done.

It was worth a shot, so Kiarra closed her eyes and recalled the conversation that had changed the course of her life forever.

Strapped to a cold metal examination table, Kiarra kept her eyes closed and forced herself to stay preternaturally still. The slightest movement would alert the researchers in the room that she was conscious again. She couldn't let that happen, not if she wanted to find out the reason why the researchers had increased her examination visits and blood draws over the past two weeks.

Most AMT prisoners wouldn't think twice about it, since they'd been conditioned not to ask questions, but Kiarra had gone through something similar before. The last time her visits had increased with the same frequency, the AMT researchers had stolen her elemental magic.

Since then, no matter how many times she reached to the south—the direction of elemental fire—she felt nothing. No tingling warmth, no comforting flame. She was no different from a non-first-born, yet she was still a prisoner, unable to see the sky or feel a breeze, and forced to live in constant fear of what the guards or researchers might do to her.

Of how they might punish her.

Dark memories invaded her mind. However, when the female researcher in the room spoke again, it snapped Kiarra back to the present. The woman's words might tell her more about her future, provided she had one after her treatment.

She listened with every cell in her body and steeled herself not to react.

"Interesting," the female researcher said. "Out of the ten teenagers, nine of them still can't use their elemental magic, just like F-839. Dr. Adams was right—her blood was the key to getting the Null Formula to work."

It took all of Kiarra's control not to draw in a breath. Her serial number was F-839, and all of the extra blood draws finally made sense—the AMT was using her blood to try and eradicate elemental magic.

The male researcher spoke up. "They're going to start a new, larger test group in a few weeks and see if they can stop the first-borns from going insane and/or committing suicide. If we don't get the insanity rate below ten percent, then we'll never be able to implement this planet-wide."

"Don't worry, we'll get there. We have a few million first-borns to burn through to get it right."

Kiarra opened her eyes and embraced the guilt she felt every time she thought about what had happened to those poor first-born teenagers.

Because of her blood, not only had five teenagers already gone insane, but their insanity was driving an untold number of them to suicide.

And the researchers wanted to repeat the process with a larger group.

She couldn't let that happen.

They needed her blood, drawn and injected within hours, as a type of catalyst for the Null Formula to work. If they didn't have access to her blood, they wouldn't be able to conduct any more tests.

There was a chance the researchers might find another catalyst within a few weeks or months, but it was a risk she was willing to take. Stopping the tests, even for a few months, would prevent more people from going insane or committing suicide.

Kiarra needed to die.

I can do this. Think of the others. Taking a deep breath, she tightened her grip around the shiv's handle and whispered, "Please let this work," before raising the blade with a steady hand and plunging it into the top half of her forearm.

Kiarra sucked in a breath as a searing pain shot up her arm. To prevent herself from making any more noise, she bit her lip. Despite the AMT-wide staff meeting, a guard would come to investigate her cell if she screamed.

You can do this, Kiarra. Finish it. With her next inhalation, she pulled the blade a fraction more down toward her wrist. This time she bit her lip hard enough she could taste iron on her tongue.

While her brain screamed for her to stop, she ignored it and gripped the handle of the blade until it bit into her palm. Only when her heart stopped beating would the other first-borns be safe—at least from her.

An image of a little girl crying, reaching out her arms and screaming Kiarra's name, came unbidden into her mind, but she forced it aside. Her sister had abandoned her, just like the rest of her family. Her death wouldn't cause anyone sadness or pain. Rather, through death, she would finally have a purpose.

This was it. On the next inhalation, she moved the blade a fraction. But before she could finish the job, the door of her cell slid open.

Kiarra looked up and saw a tall man, dressed head to toe in black, standing in her doorway and pointing a gun straight at her.

Shit. She'd been discovered.

She wondered where she'd gone wrong. None of the guards should be wandering the halls. Everyone from the head warden to the maintenance staff was required to attend the monthly AMT meetings.

Of course, she had never seen any of the staff wearing black uniforms before. Maybe the AMT had increased security and the man was a new type of guard.

Whatever the slip-up, it would cost her if she didn't act before they could restrain her or drug her unconscious.

She swung the shiv upward, toward her throat, but between one heartbeat and the next, the man had pinned her arm, holding the shiv to the bed with his knee. He held a knife against her throat, the metal still warm from his body heat.

He leaned close enough that his breath tickled her cheek. "Toss away the blade, pet."

He increased the pressure against her throat, but not enough to draw blood. The blade was meant to be a threat, but to Kiarra, it might just be the solution.

She arched up toward the blade and felt it nick her throat. But before it could do any real damage, the man tossed the blade away and pinned her to the bed with his weight. Stunned dumb for a second, Kiarra didn't fight back as the man leaned close to her face and whispered, "Keep it up, pet, and you're going to get yourself killed."

None of the guards would talk to her like that, in a gentle, soothing tone.

Something was wrong.

Brushing the feeling aside, Kiarra adjusted her hold on the shiv she still clutched in her right hand. If she could get free, she might just have one last shot at success.

Channeling all of her anger and frustration from the last twenty-eight years, Kiarra smacked her forehead against the man's chin. The split-second distraction gave her enough time to wiggle her hand free and stab her blade into the man's bicep. He grunted but didn't move away like she'd planned. Instead, the man used all of his weight to pin her down while he plucked away her blade and tossed it across the room. As it clattered against the wall, a heavy sense of defeat caused her throat to close and tears to prickle her eyes.

Her only chance to save the other first-borns was gone.

Despite her resolve, despite her best effort, she had failed.

More people were going to die.

Without meaning to, she whispered, "You've ruined everything."

Pausing a second at her words, his eyes searched hers for answers. His green-gold eyes were curious and Kiarra almost believed he wanted to hear her story. Then he pulled out a zip tie from one of his pockets, maneuvered her hands together, and secured it around her wrists. She flinched as her cut was pressed tightly against her other arm, but she ignored the sting of pain.

Kiarra tried to pull her arms apart, but the plastic ties wouldn't budge.

She was trapped.

No, no, no. It wasn't supposed to be this way. She should be dead.

Instead, she was a gift all tied up and waiting for the guards. Once they found out what she'd done, they would punish her. Just like before.

Pain.

Blood.

Darkness.

Kiarra bucked and twisted, wanting nothing more than to get free. There was no way she could survive that nightmare all over again. "No, no, no!" she screamed before sobbing, "Please, just kill me."

The man gripped her chin hard and said, "Stop." His authoritative tone broke through her hysteria and made her pause. He continued, "We need to get the fuck out of here, to somewhere safe, but I can't do that if you fight me every step of the damn way."

Did he just say "we"? The strange black clothes, the soothing voice, the reluctance to harm her. It all made sense.

This man wasn't a new guard; he was an intruder, here to kidnap her.

Kiarra's heart pounded in her chest. How did an outsider know about the value of her blood? It didn't make sense. The AMT researchers kept their work under lock and key, both physically and electronically. What would this man do with her?

The situation had just gone from bad to worse.

Another man's voice came from the door, and Kiarra jumped when she heard the new man's accented voice say, "Boss, I've got him."

The green-eyed man turned and kept a grip on her hands with one hand while using his knee to keep her legs pinned to the bed. "And the others?"

The new position let her see the doorway, where another man was standing, dressed in the same black clothes with one major difference—he was all but dragging one of her cell neighbors along with him.

What do they want with him? Maybe her cell neighbor had his own secrets.

The man at the door said, "We're all ready to bust out of here if you are."

The other man's words snapped her back to what was happening to her. As much as she hated living in the AMT, her fate outside could be much worse, especially since she would no longer have any special protections like she did in the AMT; her blood was too valuable to damage her. In recent years, any researcher who harmed her was punished.

The green-eyed man adjusted his grip on her arms. She contemplated struggling to get free, but the muscles of his arms told her that overpowering him would be impossible.

Her stomach churned. What the hell was going to happen to her?

The man's voice murmured, "Right," before he stood, lifted her up, and hoisted her over his shoulder. Kiarra froze as her belly touched his shoulder.

Touching was strictly forbidden inside the AMT. She wasn't sure if she wanted to revel in the hard warmth or panic at the proximity of the strange man.

Before she could think too hard on the subject, the man moved to the door and out into the hallway. As she bounced against the man's back, Kiarra wondered what the guards would do to both her and the intruders if they were caught.

CHAPTER TWO

Jaxton tightened his grip on the woman tossed over his shoulder and hoped like hell the little tigress would behave. She seemed determined to die, and part of him wondered why.

But as the sound of boots and voices behind them grew louder, he focused back on his mission and pushed himself to run faster. Everything, including his brother's life, relied on them making it back to Taka's tunnel in one piece.

The woman over his shoulder moved, and he felt her push her arms against his back and lift her upper body. He was about to tell her to stay still when two guards appeared from around the corner up ahead, blocking their path.

Fuck. He had hoped to avoid a confrontation, but with guards both behind and in front of them, he didn't have a choice—they would have to fight.

He was about to signal his men to take position when the woman on his shoulder shouted, "The guards have tranquilizer guns."

The woman's warning held more than a little bit of panic; Jaxton believed she was telling the truth.

He thought of his options. The hallways inside this AMT were lined with steel, which meant that Jaxton and his team couldn't use guns since the bullets might ricochet. And if the guards were using tranquilizer guns, they'd take Jaxton and his men out before they could engage them in any sort of hand-to-hand combat.

He had only one option left—if they were to have any chance of escape, Taka, Marco, and Darius were going to have to use their elemental magic.

"No restrictions!" he yelled to his men, the signal for them to use their magic freely. Jaxton maneuvered to the side and was just about to lower the woman slung over his shoulder to the floor when he heard a gun go off.

The woman sucked in a breath before her body went limp.

Jaxton maneuvered her to the ground and plucked the dart out of her arm. He checked to make sure she was breathing—and she was—but he needed to deal with the guards before he could do anything else for her.

He stood up and counted a total of ten guards surrounding them. His men had eight of them in hand, so Jaxton focused on the two blocking the corner that would lead them to the tunnel.

One of the two guards had a strange-looking gun pointed at him. Jaxton reckoned that was what the woman had warned him about. He'd take out the tranquilizer gun first and worry about the second guard later.

He wouldn't risk a bullet ricocheting off the steel walls, so Jaxton drew out a pair of bolas from one of the pockets on his chest and swung them around a few times before letting them fly. They hit the mark and wrapped around the gun with enough force to knock it to the floor with a clatter.

With the tranquilizer gun out of the way, Jaxton gave a unique whistle to signal to the others that he was going to engage. After years of working missions together, he trusted his team to cover his back and protect the two rescued AMT prisoners on the ground.

He charged at the two guards blocking the corner. The first guard threw a punch, but Jaxton ducked the swing and danced to the right before punching the man in the soft area of the kidney. The man groaned, and Jaxton took advantage of the opening. He stepped back to the left and smashed his fist into the side of the man's face.

The man went down with a thud.

When the female guard glanced down at her fallen co-worker, Jaxton rushed toward her.

She noticed the movement and reached for something on her belt, but Jaxton was quicker. He used his weight to topple the woman off balance and they tumbled to the ground, rolling until Jaxton gained the upper hand and pinned the woman's shoulders to the ground with one arm.

Out of the corner of his eye, he saw her hand inch toward her belt. Jaxton leaned more of his weight onto the woman's shoulders, took a hold of her wrist, and squeezed. The guard winced and Jaxton plucked the object that looked like a stun gun from her utility belt and tossed it out of reach.

Marco's call of attack echoed down the hallway. Jaxton rolled away just in time to see a stream of water encircle the guard's lower body before freezing around the woman's legs, trapping her without doing the woman any lasting harm.

Sometimes having friends with elemental magic came in handy.

With his two targets out of the way, Jaxton jumped to his feet to check on the others.

His men were unharmed, as were the woman and his brother, but while all ten of the AMT guards were unconscious on the ground, there were at least two hundred guards inside this particular AMT compound and more could arrive at any minute.

They needed to get the hell out of here.

As if reading his mind, Darius had already tossed Jaxton's brother over his shoulder, so Jaxton scooped up the unconscious female inmate into his arms and started running.

A quick check assured him the woman's heart rate was a little slow, but not dangerously, and the wound on her arm had clotted thanks to the pressure of the other one against it. After all the trouble he'd gone through to get her out of the AMT, she had better bloody well not die en route. His boss, Neena, must have plans for her, and what Neena wanted, she got.

He heard some kind of commotion behind them just as they reached the tunnel entrance, where jagged rocks bent and twisted with the steel of the AMT walls. Darius ducked inside the tunnel first, and Jaxton followed suit. Marco and Taka would cover their retreat.

Of course, escaping the tunnel was the easy part; getting off the mountain was going to be tricky. After the amount of energy his men had already used confronting the guards, Jaxton hoped Darius would be able to concentrate long enough for their final trick.

Once they walked out onto the snow-covered mountain ledge, goose bumps rose on the woman's skin. Jaxton hugged her close against his chest as he moved to stand next to Darius. He glanced down to check; while cold, the woman was still alive.

Marco emerged from the tunnel and stepped to the side just as Taka slowly backed out of the hole, moving the earth as he went until the tunnel was sealed.

Since they were standing on a mountain ledge thousands of feet above sea level, the only way the guards could reach them now was from the sky.

Marco and Taka came over and took positions facing Jaxton and Darius, the four of them making a tight-knit square. Jaxton nodded at Darius to begin.

Darius kept one hand on Garrett's back, but raised the other to the east—the direction of elemental wind—and soon wind began to swirl around them, increasing in speed with each pass.

Jaxton's stomach did a little flip. He knew what was coming. But no matter how many times they'd done this before, he would never get used to traveling via elemental wind.

Category Five winds swirled around them, and soon a piece of the rock ledge cracked and the ground jolted under their feet. Yet because of training and practice, the men maintained their balance even as the section of rock was lifted into the air. The woman in his arms shivered, and Jaxton nearly crushed her against his body in an attempt to warm her. The trip across the chasm wouldn't last long, but he just hoped she'd survive the cold.

Chapter Three

Kiarra blinked a few times and tried to ascertain if she was still dreaming, but when the unfamiliar surroundings stayed constant, she knew the men in black had managed to escape the AMT.

After fifteen years in prison, she was finally free.

Part of her wanted to laugh at the highly improbable situation, while the other half wanted to cry tears of joy at finally escaping. Her future was far from certain, but, at least for now, no one was going to die simply because she was still alive.

And while she didn't want to get her hopes up, there was a small chance she might not have to die.

Tears prickled her eyes, but she took a deep breath to help get her emotions under control. She couldn't afford to fall apart right now, so she forced herself to rely on her most effective weapon: her logic.

She looked around the room, hoping to find something that would not only help her better understand her kidnappers, but maybe help her think of a way to escape.

The room was a small, mostly blue bedroom with a plush chair in the corner, two windows off to the side, and a mirror above a dresser. There were also framed pictures of far-off places scattered across the walls. The room was the opposite of her sterile, cold cell. One could almost call it homey.

But the most important difference from the AMT was that instead of fluorescent lights, sunlight streamed through the windows. Kiarra stretched her neck until she could see the clear blue sky outside. More than anything, she wanted to feel the warmth of the sun on her cheeks.

It'd been fifteen years since she'd last seen the sky or felt the sun on her face. The AMT had stolen those years from her, and while she'd never get them back, she would make the most of the freedom she had now.

Of course, how long her freedom would last depended entirely on her kidnappers.

She still wasn't sure what had prodded her to warn the men about the tranquilizer guns. Yet when it had come down to it, her gut had told her that taking her chances with the intruders had been the better of the two options. Time would tell if she'd made the right decision.

She tried to sit up, but material dug into her wrists and ankles, preventing her from moving off the bed. Considering her attacks on the man in her cell, coupled with her attempts to stab herself, it didn't surprise her that they'd put restraints on her arms and legs. At least they were material and not metal, like the ones inside the AMT examination rooms.

Thinking of the AMT brought back the researchers' conversation about using her blood for tests on other inmates. Were the men here going to do the same thing? To be honest, she had no idea why else they would want her. Ransom was useless since Kiarra's family had disowned her years ago, and the AMT would simply send enforcers to retrieve her rather than try to negotiate for her return.

Her only real concern was that the men might hurt her, especially now that she didn't have any special protections like

19

she'd had inside the AMT. There was nothing to stop them from beating——let alone raping—her.

Fear gripped her belly again, so Kiarra inhaled deeply and willed her mind to push aside the fear and approach the situation rationally. After years of waking up in strange examination rooms, and being poked and prodded for days on end, finding herself in restraints was no big deal. While she knew almost nothing about the men who'd broken into the AMT, freaking out about what they'd do to her would serve no purpose.

She needed to take advantage of the time she had now, alone in this room, to try and plan escape routes, especially since the longer she stayed here, the greater the chance that the AMT enforcers would find her.

Just as Kiarra calculated how far off the ground she was based on the height of the trees outside her window, someone knocked and opened the door, revealing the tall, lean frame of the green-eyed man who had broken into her cell. He was dressed in a set of new black clothes, with a nude-colored bandage wrapped around his left bicep.

She was going to pay for that.

The man noticed her gaze, looked down at his arm, and then back up again. "Take a good look at your handiwork, because I assure you it won't happen again."

His voice was deep and slightly lilting. She wanted to know what country he was from, but that was low on her list of priorities. If she were going to chance asking a question, she would think of something more useful.

The man continued to stare at her as if he was waiting for her to say something. *Fine.* He hadn't been rough with her back inside her cell, but she wondered if he would smack or verbally abuse her as the AMT staff had done in the past when she hadn't follow the rules or been complacent.

There was only one way to find out.

Kiarra gathered her courage and tried to keep her voice even. "You aren't the first to underestimate me."

She waited for him to strike her, like the AMT guards would've done, but he kept his distance and said, "What's your name?"

It looked like he wasn't going to hit her, at least for now. She answered, "F-839."

He growled, "Not your bloody serial number. Tell me your name."

Kiarra blinked and looked away. Each prisoner was given a serial number when they first arrived at the AMT and learned to respond to it. She couldn't remember the last time someone had used her actual name, and after so long, she wasn't sure if she wanted this stranger to be the first one to call her by it.

The act seemed intimate, as if the use of her name would transform her from a prisoner to a person with rights and opinions, and she wasn't sure if that was a good idea. She didn't know what the man wanted with her, and hope was a dangerous emotion for any AMT prisoner.

Kiarra had learned that lesson the hard way.

She looked back at the man. His eyes trained on her face, and she resisted a shiver. He wasn't looking at her with cool disinterest, as if she were nothing more than an experiment subject to be discarded when things went wrong. No, it was almost as if he acknowledged that she was a person, not something to be cataloged with a serial number.

The man maintained eye contact as he took a step toward her. Kiarra's heart raced as she battled her nerves to stay calm.

Inside the AMT, people had only come near her to punish her or to experiment on her, which had conditioned her to hate it, and she didn't have adrenaline or a life-and-death situation to override her fear.

And her commitment to logic only went so far.

The man was now only a few feet away and Kiarra clenched her jaw to keep from tugging at her restraints, determined not to let the man see how his closeness affected her. If she could keep herself calm during her experiment sessions, she could force herself to stay calm now too.

~~*

Jaxton saw a brief flash of fear in the woman's eyes and stopped moving. He didn't want to trigger panic in the woman and repeat the last hour he'd just spent with his brother. While this woman might be afraid, at least she wasn't screaming and thrashing about like Garrett had done when he'd first woken up. No matter what Jaxton had tried, Garrett hadn't calmed down until Jaxton had drugged his brother unconscious.

Between this woman's attempted suicide and his brother's behavior, Jaxton was starting to believe the rumors he'd heard of late. Something was going on inside the AMT, something they desperately wanted to keep secret from the *Feiru* public.

Taka had suggested that Jaxton question the first-born female and see what he could learn. Since Jaxton had, in effect, rescued the woman, he had a slight edge over someone like Taka, or even Darius, since they were complete strangers.

However, he wouldn't learn anything as long as the woman continued to fear him. She wouldn't even disclose something as simple as her bloody name. He needed to fix that.

He took a step back and leaned against the dresser, waiting to see how the woman would respond. When she relaxed a little, the increased space having a positive effect, Jaxton jumped on the change and decided to give a little tit-for-tat to get the woman talking. "Let's try this again. My name's Jaxton. Care to tell me yours, pet?"

The woman stared at him a minute before nodding to herself and asking, "Why do you call me 'pet'?"

"Would you prefer ducky? Or princess? Until you tell me your name, I'll have to get creative." She didn't so much as smile. He would have to try a different approach. "How about this: I remove your restraints, and then you tell me your name."

She raised her chin a notch and nodded. Jaxton uncrossed his arms and took a step toward her, but this time, the woman didn't flinch.

He made it to her bedside, turned down the duvet, and reached for the ankle restraints. The instant his fingers brushed her cool skin, her muscles tensed. Just like with his brother, this woman didn't like being touched.

The question was: why? While the most likely answer was the AMT staff had abused them, Jaxton secretly hoped that wasn't the case. The last thing he needed was the woman constantly afraid he was going to hurt her.

Not wanting to scare the poor chick any more than necessary, Jaxton managed to keep his anger at the AMT from showing on his face, just barely.

As he unbuckled the straps, he decided to distract her and encourage her to open up to him. "Considering your stature, you packed one hell of a head-butt earlier. Where'd you learn to do that?"

He glanced up at her face, but her expression remained blank. Where had the tigress from the AMT gone? He needed to find a way to draw her out again.

After pulling the blanket back over her feet, Jaxton moved up to her arm restraints and stopped just short of frowning at the frailty of her wrists. Clearly the AMT bastards hadn't fed her enough.

He undid the last buckle, took a few steps back, and waited. The dampers in the room would prevent the use of elemental magic, but judging from the woman's current emotional state, Jaxton didn't think he had anything to worry about.

The woman had her eyes closed and was doing some sort of rhythmic breathing, probably trying to fight some kind of meltdown. While he was afraid she might close in on herself and be unable to answer any of his questions, he needed to follow his own rule of successful interrogation: give a person time.

Once she finally stopped her deep breathing, she stretched her arms up over her head and opened her eyes. She rubbed her freed wrists and touched the bandage on her arm before she said, "Kiarra. My name is Kiarra."

Kiarra. The name suited her. While her accent was American, she defied the blonde-haired, blue-eyed stereotype with her short black hair, dark eyes, and olive skin. Most *Feiru* in America were a hotchpotch of ethnicities, and Kiarra looked to be no exception.

"Well, Kiarra, now the question is, if I leave you unrestrained, will you promise not to try offing yourself again? Blood is a bugger to clean out of the carpet."

Kiarra sat up slowly, wincing once or twice in the process. He remained silent, wanting to give her a chance to adjust, and watched as she pulled the blanket around her shoulders and wrapped it tightly around her body before she whispered, "I don't want to die."

Well now, that statement only birthed more questions.

Before he could ask her to clarify, there was a knock on the door and Darius peeked into the room. "Jax, someone's here to see you."

"Unless someone is dying or the world's about to end, tell them to sod off."

Darius opened the door a few inches more and said, "But *she* wants to see you." He waved in Kiarra's direction. "And talk to her."

Bloody hell. There was only one woman who earned both an emphasized "she" and had the ability to locate an undisclosed safe house.

They were about to receive an unsolicited visit from his boss, Neena Chatterjee.

Right on cue, her voice echoed up the stairs. "Jaxy darling, I'm tired of waiting. Ready or not, here I come."

~~*

Kiarra drew the blanket tighter around her body and wished the soft fabric would shield her from the world and give her a few minutes of privacy. Between the pounding in her head and the flitting caresses of Jaxton's fingers against her skin, she was close to a meltdown; she wasn't sure if she could handle meeting or touching another person.

As it was, Jaxton merely touching her feet and wrists had brought back memories of one of the AMT researchers and what he'd done to her. Luckily, one of her coping techniques—deep breathing with her eyes closed——had allowed her to focus back on the present.

She watched as the tall man with dark skin and warm brown eyes moved aside to let in a small woman with barely restrained curly black hair and golden brown skin. The woman strutted into the room as if she owned it, with a dark red duffel bag slung over her shoulder.

The woman stopped next to Jaxton and spoke, her accent more singsong than Jaxton's. "Jaxy, I'm a bit disappointed in your welcoming party." She gave a fake pout. "No cakes, no balloons, not even any gifts? Poor Kiarra deserves all of that and more."

Kiarra did a double take at the sound of her name and looked at the mirror above the dresser. It looked like a regular mirror, not like the two-way ones used in the AMT examination rooms. *How does this woman know my name?*

She wanted to ask, but hesitated. Jaxton hadn't struck her when she'd refused to answer him earlier, so maybe this woman would allow her to ask questions too.

Gripping the inside of the blanket, she looked at the curly-haired woman and forced herself to ask, "How do you know my name? Were you listening in?"

The woman tossed the duffel bag at Jaxton without looking and turned with a warm smile on her face. "Do you really want to waste two of your three allotted questions on such silly things?"

Kiarra frowned, her curiosity stronger than her caution. "Three questions? I don't understand."

The woman winked. "I'll give you a few freebies, since you're new around here." The woman took a step toward her and Kiarra gripped the blanket tighter, still uneasy but wanting to know what the hell the woman was talking about.

The woman continued, "I only grant three answers to a person at any given time. Because of my secret—and brilliant—abilities, too many people want to know trivial things, such as who will win a singing contest or what sports team will earn a championship title." She waved a hand in dismissal. "The three-question limit saves my sanity."

Jaxton muttered something in the corner, but the woman just blew him a kiss and said, "Jaxy loves me despite his attitude. He believes my three question rule is childish."

Kiarra glanced over at Jaxton. "Love" was the last word she would use to describe his expression.

She wondered at the relationship between the woman and Jaxton. The best she could tell, Jaxton was in charge of the men in black from the AMT. Yet he let this woman say and do as she pleased with barely a word in protest.

The woman took another step toward Kiarra, but just in case she really only had three questions, she looked in Jaxton's direction and asked, "Why do people seek out this woman for answers?"

The woman laughed. "Clever girl." She waved a hand at Jaxton, but never took her eyes from Kiarra's. "I'll handle this, Jaxy."

Jaxton started tapping his fingers against his arm. She nearly smiled at his irritation, but caught herself just in time; she hadn't felt the urge to smile in years.

As she met the woman's brown-eyed gaze, Kiarra wished she could unsettle people like this woman, using nothing but her words and attitude. But for now, all she had going for her was the threat of elemental fire.

At least, until someone called her bluff.

The woman touched her arm, but rather than tensing or bolting at the touch, a sense of calm came over her. It made no sense. She looked up with a frown. "Who exactly are you?"

"I'm Neena." The woman held out a hand. "And we need to have a little chat. How about we go downstairs for some girl time?"

She eyed the hand, but didn't take it. "Girl time" as a child had meant sleepovers and gossip. Kiarra wasn't interested in either. She wanted to know what these people were going to do with her.

"Neena, leave her be," Jaxton said. "She clearly isn't ready for a one-on-one with you yet."

Jaxton's words prickled. People had assumed things about Kiarra for far too long. True, given the choice, she would like nothing more than to be alone in her room for a few hours and sort out her thoughts. But for no explicable reason, she wanted to prove the man who had kidnapped her wrong.

Besides, the woman's presence had lessened her fear and uneasiness. Kiarra didn't want that strange calmness to disappear just yet.

She gripped the blanket tightly in her hands one more time before letting it drop to the bed. She reached out and took the woman's hand, feeling even more relaxed at the contact, almost as if she didn't have anything to fear from her. "Let's go."

Neena winked. "I knew you'd have a change of heart."

Neena pulled her off the bed and the pounding inside Kiarra's head, one of the aftereffects of the tranquilizer, intensified. She managed to stay upright despite the pain and allowed the woman to pull her out of the room and down the stairs.

28

Chapter Four

Neena didn't release Kiarra's hand until they reached the downstairs living room. Glancing around the room, there was a couch, a bookshelf, some end tables, and a large painting of some mountains, which was hanging over a cold fireplace. She eyed the fireplace and rubbed her arms against the chill in the room, wishing she'd brought the blanket down with her, something she never would've been allowed to do inside the AMT.

As Neena walked over to a large black bag on the far side of the room and rifled inside it, Kiarra wondered if Neena had been the one to discover her secret and send Jaxton and his men to break her out of the AMT. Neena looked innocent enough in her tight-fitting jeans, gold flats, and silky green top, but Kiarra knew appearances could be deceiving.

No matter how much the woman's presence calmed her, or how well they treated her, she needed to be careful. These people were nicer to her than the AMT staff—which, frankly, wasn't hard to do—but she was a long way from trusting them.

Neena extracted a beat-up book from her bag, held it up, and said, "Catch!"

Kiarra managed to catch the abused book and read the title: *DEFEND Rules and Regulations.*

Neena walked over and tapped the title with one of her perfectly shaped fingernails. "This darling has saved me many times, so take good care of her. She comes in handy when you want to skirt around the rules without breaking them."

She didn't want to waste any of her three—or was it now two?—questions, but right now, Kiarra had no idea what the woman was talking about. "What's DEFEND and why do I need to know about its rules?"

"That's two questions wrapped into one, but brilliant as you are, I'll humor you." Neena tapped the word "DEFEND."

"DEFEND," Neena continued, "stands for Defending Every *Feiru*'s Equality, No Discrimination. I know the name is a bit rubbish, but I had more pressing things to worry about at the time."

"At the time?"

Neena got a far-off look in her eyes. "Ah, the days of cajoling my first recruits." Neena shook her head and continued. "You and I are both part of the first-born club, my dear. Shortly after the Chatterjee clan rescued me from the AMT, I decided to turn my anger into something more productive. Hence, DEFEND."

Kiarra's heart skipped a beat. "You're a first-born?"

Neena gave a sympathetic smile. "Yes, and while I wasn't imprisoned as long as you, it took me a while to feel comfortable with myself again. I didn't become a leader overnight, but you will get there." She tapped a finger against her chin. "Actually, some claim I'm still not leader material. But they change their tune before long." Neena's eyes took on an evil glint. "I can be quite persuasive."

Kiarra hoped she never needed to be "persuaded" by Neena.

She didn't know the circumstances surrounding Neena's imprisonment and escape, but at least now she knew that others had come out of the AMT alive and stayed that way.

Maybe Kiarra could do it too.

Neena turned away from her to look out the window and Kiarra realized that Neena still hadn't answered the second part of her question. "Why do I need to find a way around the rules?"

Neena faced her again and winked. "That is for you to find out." Her face grew serious. "But make sure to memorize the basics of the book. We all make mistakes, but I won't tolerate deliberate harm to my organization."

Kiarra glanced down at the battered book in her hands. "But why would I need this book?"

Neena smiled. "Because, my dear, you are my latest recruit."

"What?"

"It's not going to make sense to you now, but it will in time." Neena tilted her head. "And you can't refuse, because not only do I know the secret of your fire, but also the one about your blood. I'll expose them both to the world if I have to."

Kiarra stopped breathing. "How do you know about that?"

Neena waved a hand. "It doesn't matter. Besides, if you agree to work and train with DEFEND for three months, I'll make sure my people protect you. No doubt the AMT enforcers are already coming after you by now."

Kiarra was worried about the AMT enforcers, but Neena's offer was little more than blackmail. If she refused, or tried to escape, and word got out about her lack of elemental magic, Kiarra would spend the rest of her life inside a research facility.

A breeze brushed against Kiarra's cheek and the sense of calm from earlier returned. She looked up at Neena. "I don't really have a choice, do I?"

"You always have a choice, my dear. But whether you decide to take the correct path or not is up to you." Neena scooped up her bag, pulled out a phone, and looked at it. She clicked her tongue. "I'll give you fifteen minutes to make a decision. Come upstairs when you're ready."

Before Kiarra could muster up another word, Neena was gone.

Without Neena's presence, the strange calmness that had come over Kiarra disappeared, and the reality of her situation sank in. She was exposed, in a strange house full of strange people, one of whom was threatening her with blackmail.

Part of her wanted to take the easy way out and finish what she'd started back in her cell in the AMT, and kill herself. But as she looked out the window across the room, taking in the trees and bushes in the yard, she realized how much she wanted to live now that she'd had a taste of the outside world again. Neena's offer might be the only chance she had to do that.

Besides, who knew—maybe after her training Kiarra would even find a way to help the other first-borns from the outside.

She didn't trust Neena, but if things went bad, she could always end her life later. As long as she acted like she wanted to live, and put in a little effort toward her training, they'd never suspect her Plan B, if it came to that.

Decision made, Kiarra took a deep breath and stood up. As she made her way up the stairs, she tried not to focus on the fact that she was merely trading one prison for another.

~~*

Once the two women left the room, Jaxton wondered how much Neena was going to disclose to Kiarra. The rules of

DEFEND were very clear: only Neena or Aislinn—the other co-founder and co-leader of DEFEND—were allowed to talk about the organization with outsiders. Occasionally, they gave permission if neither of them could logistically meet with someone, but those exceptions were rare.

Neena and Aislinn were very protective of their creation.

Not that he could blame them. DEFEND had started with just the two of them, but after years of sacrifice and hard work, it was now a worldwide operation with growing clout. DEFEND was the only grassroots *Feiru* organization that had a chance of taking on the powerful AMT Oversight Committee and changing the status quo.

Neena, for the most part, did the recruiting. And judging by Neena's unexpected visit and interest in Kiarra, he reckoned that the recently rescued first-born was as good as inducted into their fold. Not that Neena would listen to him in this instance, but Jaxton wasn't sure if Kiarra was the type of recruit they were looking for. At least, not until after she'd had time to heal.

Whatever Neena decided, he just hoped she would hurry the hell up so he could get on with questioning Kiarra. The sooner he had answers, the sooner he could hand her over to a DEFEND trainer. He not only needed to catch up on his own DEFEND workload, but he also needed to focus on his brother's recovery.

He refused to believe Garrett was a lost cause.

For the time being, since his brother was still drugged unconscious, Jaxton decided to check in with Taka about their research on a prominent *Feiru* politician named James Sinclair.

He headed toward the room at the end of the hall, where he'd set up an ad-hoc workspace. Taka sat in front of a monitor split into four boxes, each displaying a view of a room or the house's perimeter. Off to the side of the room was a giant whiteboard with the words "Adams" and "doctoral research" scribbled in blue pen. Stacks of paper and newspapers covered the table in the corner, while black ashes of what used to be paper curled in the cold fireplace.

Kiarra and Neena were in one of the boxes displayed on the monitor. They were standing in the middle of the front room talking. Satisfied that they hadn't tried to sneak out the back door, he turned toward Taka and said, "How're you progressing through the intelligence backlog?"

Taka scribbled a few more words and then looked up. "I'm about a quarter of the way through, but I found something I wanted to show you." He shuffled through his stack of papers and handed a set to Jaxton. "One of DEFEND's sources reported a series of meetings between James Sinclair's deputy chief of staff and several staff members from the Council of Eastern Australia. My guess is that Eastern Australia is Sinclair's next target."

Jaxton nodded while skimming the account. James Sinclair was influential with both the central *Feiru* governing body, called the *Feiru* High Council, and the AMT Oversight Committee. Over the last ten years, Sinclair had worked behind the scenes to influence general worldwide *Feiru* policy. But recently, Sinclair had shifted his focus to the smaller *Feiru* local councils. "Sounds similar to what happened in Wales and Northern Brazil."

"Exactly. And if it follows the same pattern as those two other local councils, then the Council of Eastern Australia will soon be announcing their policy shift toward Article I."

Article I of the *Feiru* Five Laws restricted what the *Feiru* people could and could not do in the human world, especially with regards to human governments and multinational corporations. Many *Feiru* resented the law and what they viewed as second-class citizenship, which was strange considering that first-borns were already being treated as second-class citizens, and nobody seemed to care.

Jaxton looked up from his papers. "That would make it now five *Feiru* local councils who support Sinclair's recent Repeal Article I and Contain First-born Magic campaign. For years, Sinclair pushed solely for stricter AMT enforcement, so his shift in focus must mean it's because he knows something we don't."

Taka gestured toward the monitor. "Have you had any success with questioning the woman? Maybe she knows something about what's happening inside the AMT that could tell us why Sinclair changed his focus."

"I'm working on it. If Neena could just keep her bloody nose out of everything, I could get something done." He glanced at the monitor and saw Neena walking up the stairs, alone. Kiarra was still in the front room, sitting on the sofa and looking a bit shell-shocked. "Speaking of which, it looks like Kiarra is recovering from Hurricane Neena in the front room. I need to go take care of it." Jaxton stood up. "I'll check back afterward and we can divide up the remaining backlog. In the meantime, see if you can find out what other councils Sinclair is targeting."

"No problem." Taka turned back to his stack of papers. "Let me know if you need help questioning the woman."

Jaxton nodded and left the room, but just as he reached the top of the stairs, he heard Neena's voice behind him. "Jaxy, darling, we need to chat. Come, I even have scones to share with you."

Resisting a sigh, Jaxton turned around and followed her to an empty bedroom. Even if he discounted the debt he owed Neena for helping with Garrett's rescue, he knew better than to disobey Neena to her face. The woman was bloody vicious when it came to teaching someone a lesson about obedience.

Inside the room, Neena sat on one of the windowsills and motioned to a plate of scones. "Care for one?"

Jaxton shook his head. He knew the best way to deal with his boss was to cut straight to the point. "What did you want, Neena?"

Neena nibbled on a scone before she said, "You're going to train Kiarra."

He frowned. "Why? Surely someone else could do it. Not only do I need to focus on my brother, but my research on James Sinclair is too important to put off. You more than anyone know the man is up to something."

Neena took another bite and Jaxton gritted his teeth while he waited for her to finish chewing. He knew from experience that his best bet at finding answers was to let Neena answer at her own pace, no matter how frustrating that pace may be.

One second passed, and then another. Finally, she swallowed and said, "You owe me for sharing your brother's location and serial number, and I'm calling in my favor."

He raised his eyebrows. "Why would you waste your favor on this?"

Neena waved her hand in dismissal. "Oh, it's definitely worth it. This favor might even put me in your debt, not that I'll ever acknowledge it."

He grew suspicious about this 'favor.' No one knew what Neena would say—let alone do——from one minute to the next.

Still, he was going to try and rationalize with her. "Wouldn't it be better for Kiarra to go to Amma's place first and rejoin DEFEND later, when she's healed and ready?"

Amma Gyasi ran the most effective rehabilitation center for former AMT prisoners. Jaxton had briefly considered sending his brother there before deciding to take on the job himself.

Neena jumped up from her perch on the windowsill and strutted to the other side of the room, near the door. Her smile disappeared, her features more serious than he'd ever seen before.

The sight made him nervous.

"The Four Talents must be found," she whispered, "and quickly."

He blinked. "Pardon?"

In the old *Feiru* legends, the Four Talents were first-borns with extraordinary power over the elements. Not much was commonly known about them, but if the legends were true, some great oncoming catastrophe would trigger their unusual magical abilities.

Neena's smile reappeared before she peeked her head out the door, into the hall. "Kiarra is only the first of your guests to arrive. You'll soon have a full house." She glanced back at Jaxton with a stern look that failed to scold. "Don't let Marco turn this place into the Animal House of DEFEND safe houses. I like fun as much as the next person, but let's take care of business first."

She was trying to change the topic, and while he had little hope of steering Neena back on course, he was going to try. "Neena, let's go back to the bit about the Four Talents. Are the legends true?"

Neena ignored him and motioned with her hands.

Kiarra stepped into the room.

Neena wrapped an arm around Kiarra's shoulders, and Kiarra tensed before easing into Neena's touch. Either Neena was using her healing elemental wind magic to soothe the other woman or Kiarra was progressing faster than he would've guessed.

Neena squeezed Kiarra's shoulder. "So, Kiarra, have you made your decision?"

What decision? Jaxton was not doing well with finding out information today.

Kiarra eyed Neena's hand on her arm. "Will I be able to stay with you?"

Neena patted Kiarra's shoulder. "I'll take that as a yes. But as lovely as my company is, I'm a bit slammed for time right now." She gestured toward Jaxton. "Buzzkill Jaxy here is going to train you. Let me know right away if he does anything rude or naughty."

Kiarra blinked. "Naughty?"

Neena gave Jaxton a sly glance. "He may not be able to control himself around such a beautiful woman."

"Neena," he growled in warning.

Neena laughed and blew him a kiss. "No worries, Kiarra. I wouldn't leave you with someone dangerous, although I think a *little* danger makes life interesting." Neena moved her gaze to Jaxton. "Of course, others just need a kick in the posterior once in a while to keep them in check."

Ignoring Neena, Jaxton looked Kiarra straight in the eye and motioned forward. He could only imagine what she thought of him now.

She hesitated, but after Neena gave her a gentle push, she came a little closer. The unsure woman now in front of him was the exact opposite of the woman who'd stabbed him. There was strength in there somewhere and he would have to extract it the only way he knew how—by pushing her boundaries.

Jaxton put out his hand. "We'll start training tomorrow morning."

CHAPTER FIVE

The room swayed back and forth as Kiarra struggled to stay upright and focus on what Neena and Jaxton were saying to each other. Between shaking off the aftereffects of the tranquilizer, her lack of food, and an overload of new information, Kiarra was exhausted.

She'd contemplated sitting down on the nearby bed, but then Neena had given her a push. Kiarra stood in front of Jaxton, his hand out, telling her they'd start training tomorrow.

Taking his hand would make things easy. Yet due to her exhaustion—or maybe fueled by her newfound hope, Kiarra didn't know—she ignored his proffered hand and blinked to bring his face back into focus. "I haven't agreed to stay with, let alone work with you yet."

He retracted his hand. "It's not open for discussion. I'll train you, and when you're ready, you'll work for DEFEND. Think of it as the price for rescuing you from the AMT."

So bossy. "I never asked you to rescue me…" She paused as the room spun. Kiarra closed her eyes, hoping the lightheadedness would pass.

Lights danced across the inside of her eyelids. She took a deep breath, smelling a familiar combination of soap and clean male, but the dizziness didn't go away. She knew what was coming. This had happened before, a few months earlier, after a grueling three days of medical tests.

She was going to faint.

Opening her eyes, she ignored Jaxton's outstretched arms and tried to take a step toward the bed. If she could just sit down a minute and put her head between her legs, she could regain her composure and avoid showing any more weakness in front of Jaxton and Neena. For some reason, she wanted to show them she could be strong if she tried hard enough.

She took another step toward the bed, but faltered, her knees buckling. Warm hands grabbed her arms before she blacked out.

$*\sim*\sim*$

"Kiarra, lovey, focus."

The darkness around Kiarra gradually faded as light came over the horizon, highlighting the trees of the surrounding forest. Birds chirped in the distance, their song joined by the bubbling creek somewhere behind her.

Looking around, she realized she was standing in the middle of a forest, with no memory of how she'd gotten there. She heard a whistle and looked up to see Neena perched in a tree, her blue cape swirling in the nonexistent wind.

"Neena?"

Neena smiled. "Do you like my cape? It makes me feel a bit like a superhero."

The woman swung down from the branch and flourished her cape before taking Kiarra's hand in hers. "Yes, my dear, it's me, Neena. You fainted, but a little unconsciousness is nothing to me."

She frowned. She didn't remember fainting. Was she dreaming?

Neena said, "Of course you are, my dear. Few people can converse with the unconscious. Believe me, I've tried." Neena tilted her head. "But let's get serious for a moment. If you ever need to talk to me, you can contact me through your dreams. It will take a little training to learn how to do it properly, but if you think of me whilst dreaming, I will try to get in touch."

"How can you—"

"That explanation is for another time. Just remember, think of me in your dreams and I will try to answer."

Neena snapped her fingers and the forest disappeared.

Kiarra opened her eyes. She was back in the blue bedroom where she'd first woken up, except the room was low-lit with shadows on the walls. She sighed in relief. "It was only a dream."

"Was it one of those good dreams where you wake up all hot and bothered? Those are my favorite."

A light turned on, Kiarra shot up in the bed and her head exploded with pain. Her hands flew to her pounding head, but after a few deep breaths, she was able to focus again. Opening her eyes, she saw a man with light brown skin and short, spiky hair sitting across from her. He seemed vaguely familiar.

Before she could convince herself otherwise, she asked, "Who are you?"

The man picked up a blue covered cup with a straw and walked toward her. He was shorter than Jaxton, but broader through the shoulders. "It figures that the boss forgot to mention me. He doesn't like the competition, especially since women prefer me ten to one." He grinned and winked. "I guarantee a good time."

She frowned. She wasn't sure how to respond to that. His wink and full-on grin made her suspicious.

When she kept quiet, he whistled and shook his head. "Jax wasn't kidding when he said you might be afraid of me, despite my undeniable charm." He held out the covered cup. "I'm Marco, the boss's right-hand man."

She gingerly took the cup, but didn't drink as she eyed the easygoing man. Marco's manner was definitely different from the guards and researchers inside the AMT.

Holding out his hand, Marco wiggled his fingers. "If you're worried the smoothie is poisoned, give it here. I'll drink first to prove it's safe, and then when you take a sip, I'll revel in our indirect kiss."

Blood rushed to Kiarra's cheeks, and unsure of how to respond, she held out the cup to Marco. He winked as he placed his lips around the straw and took a deep pull. He sat back, smacked his lips and said, "Tasty. Try it for yourself."

Kiarra took a few sips; the tart, fruity taste was almost too much for her taste buds.

Since her stomach was no longer rumbling, she eyed Marco and decided a man with laugh lines around his mouth and crinkles at the corners of his eyes probably wouldn't strike her for asking questions.

She cleared her throat. "Where are Jaxton and Neena?"

He waved his hand. "Neena's gone home and Jaxton is busy. I'm here to take care of you and make sure you eat something." He stared pointedly at her cup.

Kiarra took another sip to avoid replying right away.

She needed to continue her earlier conversation with Jaxton, but had a feeling he would call her bluff. While she was trying her hardest to be the woman she was inside her head, things weren't going to plan. No doubt Jaxton would use her fainting and display of weakness to his advantage.

Aware of Marco's gaze, Kiarra pulled the straw from her lips. While waiting for Jaxton, she could work on at least one of her weaknesses and force herself to talk with Marco. "Will Jaxton be stopping by later?"

Marco placed a hand over his heart, an exaggerated look of pain coming across his face. "You wound me, madam. Are you that keen to get rid of me?"

Kiarra nearly spat out her drink at his absurdity.

Marco winked and said, "No worries, boss man should be around later today."

Anxious to know what her immediate future held, Kiarra was about to press further when a man's scream reverberated down the hall, making her jump. "What's that?"

Another scream rent the air and Marco sighed. "If he keeps this up, we're going to have to drug him unconscious again."

Kiarra remembered the man she'd glimpsed during the escape, the one unable to hold himself up. That was where she'd seen Marco before—he'd been the man standing in her doorway, struggling to keep her cell neighbor upright. "Are you talking about the other person you rescued from the AMT?"

Marco shrugged one shoulder. "I see no reason to lie. He's not doing as well as you."

Another scream and a chill traveled down her spine. The sound reminded her of some of the other AMT inmates.

A man clawing his own face, blood running down his cheeks; a pregnant woman throwing her belly against a counter and then the floor; a catatonic child being led down a hallway.

Many of their screams had been identical to the ones echoing down the hallway.

There was a possibility that the screaming man was too far gone to ever fully recover, but there were techniques to help ease his pain and bring him some measure of peace. Jaxton and his men, however, probably didn't know what they were or how to treat him.

Kiarra had always wanted to help the tortured prisoners she'd seen inside the AMT, but had never been allowed the opportunity.

Of course, she was no longer inside the AMT, meaning those restrictions didn't exist. She could finally reach out and ease someone's pain. Most of all, she could be useful.

She didn't care if Jaxton would get angry at her or not—she had to do something to help.

Kiarra jumped up from the bed, faltered a second before finding her balance, and headed for the door. Marco grabbed her wrist and she prevented herself from flinching as he demanded, "Whoa, wait a second. Where do you think you're going?"

Kiarra made a fist and pointedly looked at his grip on her arm. "Let me go." She raised her gaze to meet Marco's eyes, trying her best to look calm despite her racing heart. "I know how to calm him without the use of drugs."

Marco stayed silent, the grins and winks gone. He might like to joke around, but it was obvious he took his duty seriously. Kiarra opened her mouth to try to convince him some more, but he beat her to it.

"Fine, but if this is a trick, just know that I will handle you myself. Are we clear?"

The command in his tone surprised her, but Kiarra nodded and Marco directed her down the hall. She heard another scream, but this time it was louder, coming from the door to her right. Marco made a gesture with his hands, indicating for her to go inside. She took a deep breath and opened the door.

The screams were high-pitched, but she resisted the urge to cover her ears. She took in the scene in front of her and instantly understood the root of the problem.

Jaxton stood next to a bed, trying to hold down a thrashing man, yet every time Jaxton touched the man, he screamed again. The sound went straight to Kiarra's heart and something inside of her clicked into place. She wasn't defenseless any longer. This time she had the power to help.

She gathered her courage before shouting, "Don't touch him!" and charged straight at Jaxton.

~~*

Garrett was screaming again.

Jaxton rushed to his brother's side and tried grabbing his hand, but Garrett screamed louder at the contact.

Garrett bucked and nearly punched him in the face with his free hand, forcing Jaxton to pin both of his brother's sweat-covered arms to the side.

What the fuck happened to Garrett inside the AMT?

At this rate, he was going to have to drug him again. Jaxton racked his brain for some other way to calm his brother and break through his wild haze. Growing up, Jaxton and Garrett had been best mates. Surely, he could think of something.

His brother continued to squirm, but Jaxton refused to pity Garrett's condition. The Ward family was always blunt and honest with each other, and Jaxton hoped that business as usual would bring Garrett back from the edge. Struggling to keep his brother pinned to the bed, he said, "Garrett, mate, you need to calm the fuck down."

Garrett only bucked harder. With his arms restrained, Garrett kicked out with his legs and Jaxton grunted when a kick landed on his thigh.

He maneuvered to pin his brother's legs when he heard a woman yell, "Don't touch him!"

Jaxton turned around and saw Kiarra barreling straight for him.

Stunned at the sight, Garrett managed to kick him in the stomach right before Kiarra's shoulder impacted with Jaxton's chest. Jaxton lost his balance and landed on his arse on the floor.

"Kiarra? What the fuck?"

There was a flicker of fear in her eyes, but it vanished as quickly as it had come. She stood in front of Garrett's bed and raised her arms in protection. "Touching him is the last thing you want to do. It'll only make it worse."

Jaxton slowly stood up, never taking his eyes off Kiarra. "Make what worse?"

"First, tell me who he is to you."

He bit back his first reaction, to call her out on insubordination. Then he realized Kiarra had spent a good chunk of her life inside the AMT and might know something he didn't.

Garrett's screams morphed into a mixture of mumblings and quiet outbursts, but he was still writhing on the bed in obvious pain. Jaxton would do anything to make it stop. Taking a step toward Kiarra, he growled, "He's my older brother. Tell me how to help him."

Kiarra lowered her arms and looked from Jaxton to Garrett and back again. Luckily, they shared the same deep eyes, solid chin, and dark blond hair. Judging by Kiarra's expression, she saw the resemblance. She raised her index finger into the air. "Give me a second."

The woman who had fainted, fucking *fainted*, less than an hour ago was giving him orders in his own house. Jaxton clenched his jaw to prevent himself from saying something stupid.

He watched Kiarra bend over Garrett, hovering close to his ear, but careful never to touch him. She whispered, "Shh, it's okay. No one's going to take you to the experiment wing today, or ever again." She motioned for Jaxton to come closer. "Your brother Jaxton is here. See? He'll protect you."

Garrett's murmuring stopped, but his eyes were still wild, darting around the room. Standing up, she whispered to Jaxton, "Talk to him. Remind him of who he was before the AMT, but just remember not to touch him."

Jaxton motioned for Kiarra to leave, but she shook her head and stood her ground. He didn't want to share such a private moment in front of an audience, but yelling at Kiarra might send Garrett into a relapse, and he wasn't about to risk it.

He crouched down next to Garrett's bed. "You've missed a few pub nights and everyone's been asking after you." At least they had for the first few months after Garrett's capture. "You're their favorite tone-deaf karaoke regular. Without you, hard liquor sales have dropped. Your singing is bloody awful, but good for business."

His brother said nothing, but some of the wildness cleared from his eyes, so Jaxton kept talking. "You know how much I hate singing, but if you pull out of this, Gary, I'll sign up for the first amateur karaoke contest you can find. This is a one-time offer, so you'd better take advantage of it, mate."

For a second, Garrett met his gaze. Jaxton held his breath until Garrett mumbled, "Jax."

Jaxton resisted the urge to grip his brother's shoulder. "I'm here, Gary, and I won't let anyone hurt you again."

Kiarra began to hum a familiar tune he couldn't name. Jaxton maintained eye contact with Garrett, hoping for more, but his brother didn't say anything else. The longer Kiarra hummed,

48

the more his older brother's eyelids drooped. Soon he was out, his face calm and finally free of pain.

There was nothing more Jaxton could do for Garrett until he woke up again. He turned away from his brother's sleeping face and switched his mind back into work mode.

After his brother, his top priority was to address the situation with Kiarra. Jaxton was in charge of her training and it was time she accepted that and gave him the information he needed.

He motioned toward the door with his head, took one last look at Garrett, and headed into the hallway. Marco was nowhere to be found. He'd have to deal with the young man later.

He waited for Kiarra to close the door behind her and gestured down the hall with his arm. She avoided his gaze, but took the hint, and they headed down the hall toward her room.

Noticing the goose bumps on her arms as she passed, he decided he needed to find her some clothes. Not that he cared that she was cold, he told himself, just that she couldn't fight properly wearing her baggy AMT uniform.

While Kiarra had a long way to go before she'd take orders like a soldier, he was more concerned about her mention of an experiment wing inside the Cascade AMT compound.

That was as good a place as any to start finding out about Garrett's altered state. He could only imagine what type of experiments would cause his brother to thrash about at the merest touch.

Clenching his fingers, Jaxton vowed the AMT bastards would pay. However, he first needed some answers from the only person who could give him the information he needed. Jaxton entered Kiarra's room and closed the door.

CHAPTER SIX

Kiarra was huddled in an oversized chair, hugging her arms to her chest, staring at the floor. The bold woman who'd shouldered Jaxton aside a few minutes ago was gone. It was almost as if she were waiting for him to punish her.

Jaxton knew the AMT compounds had strict sets of rule and regulations, recently made stricter by the current members of the AMT Oversight Committee. However, reading about it and seeing a woman ready to submit to punishment for doing the right thing, without putting up any kind of fight, were two different things.

His regular training program, which stressed the importance of following orders and strict discipline, wasn't going to work with Kiarra. Without confidence and the ability to make decisions regardless of consequences, she wouldn't be of any use to him, let alone DEFEND.

He needed Kiarra to become the woman who'd stood up and tried to protect Garrett from a man twice her size. He would have to create a new regimen on the fly, one that would coax out the woman hiding behind the AMT's conditioning.

Kiarra shivered in her chair, but she didn't reach for any of the blankets on the bed next to her. Determined to show he was different from the AMT guards, and to start gaining her trust, he plucked a blanket from the nearby bed and tossed it into her lap.

She blinked a second before reaching out to touch the blue material.

When she didn't move to cover herself, Jaxton decided that the first rule of Kiarra's training would require the Ward family specialty: bluntness.

He gestured toward the blanket. "If you're not going to use the bloody thing, then I'm going to take it back." She looked up, her eyes widened in surprise. "Well, what's it to be?"

She caressed the blanket like it was a long-lost treasure, but made no move to cover herself. Jaxton, never one to back down from a threat, reached out with his hand to snatch it back. That kicked her into action and she pulled the blanket tightly around her body.

Kiarra stopped shivering and a part of him relaxed at the fact, but he didn't think too hard about why her well-being mattered. "Right. Now that you're no longer in danger of catching pneumonia, let's get down to business." He took a step toward Kiarra and she huddled deeper into the blanket before squeezing her eyes closed.

Oh, hell no. He was having none of that. Jaxton crossed the space between them and took her chin in his hand. She flinched and he forced his voice to remain level yet gentle. "Look at me."

The second rule of Kiarra's training: push.

When she didn't react, he squeezed her chin gently and Kiarra finally opened her eyes, but he couldn't read her expression. "What do you think I'm going to do to you, Kiarra?" He raised her chin another inch. Her breathing was fast, tickling his wrist. "And be honest. I can tell if you lie to me."

He held her gaze, glad she didn't look away. She tugged the blanket closer around her body and mumbled something, but he couldn't make it out. "Say it louder."

"Punish me."

He pushed aside his anger at her answer and asked, "And what do you think is a good punishment?" She mumbled again, so he tapped the soft skin under her chin. "Never mumble. Your words are meant to be heard."

She searched his eyes, but said nothing. He tapped her chin again and she finally spoke up. "Whatever you think is best."

Jaxton let go of her chin and crouched down so he was eye level with her. "Take a look around you. Does this look like the AMT?"

She glanced away and back. "No."

"Exactly. No one's going to beat you, starve you, or whatever the hell else they do inside the Cascade F-block." He leaned in closer and the smell of sweet grass filled his nose. Despite his proximity, she didn't flinch. "As long as you don't betray me or my men, no harm will befall you. Do you understand?"

They stared eye to eye, her scent surrounding him. He wondered if her hair smelled just as good.

Where the hell did that come from? This was a mentally scarred first-born, put into his charge. He could not view her as anything other than a recruit.

Luckily, she nodded, interrupting his thoughts. "Yes," she said clearly, without mumbling.

Jaxton stood and took a few steps back to clear his head. "Good. Make sure you don't forget it."

~~*

When Jaxton finally put some distance between them, Kiarra let out the breath she'd been holding. She'd managed not to flinch beyond his first touch, but it took everything she'd had not to fidget under his direct gaze.

She still couldn't wrap her head around his actions. She'd openly stood up to him, at one point even attacking him when she'd rushed to help the other rescued AMT prisoner, but he hadn't issued any punishment. Not even a mild one, such as withholding food for the next twenty-four hours.

No, instead of a punishment, he'd given her a blanket.

Jaxton took another step back, garnering her attention. "Now, why don't you tell me about the experiment wing inside the Cascade F-block?"

Kiarra rested her chin on her knees. It was only natural Jaxton would ask about the experiments, but talking about them might bring back the memories she'd fought so hard to forget.

However, she was willing to try if it meant she could get more information, especially since Neena had been less than helpful.

She looked up at Jaxton. "Only if you tell me about DEFEND first." He kept quiet and she waited for him to strike her for speaking up, but he said nothing, so she added, "Neena mostly talked about what the letters stood for, but not the organization itself."

He stared her down a few more seconds and Kiarra wondered if she'd made a mistake. Luckily, his lilting voice filled her ears before she could panic. "Neena rarely makes sense and only tells you what she wants to tell you, never a word more." He moved to lean against the dresser. "In a show of good faith, I'll give you the overview. But don't fuck with me, Kiarra. If you don't hold up your end this time, don't expect me to ever exchange information again."

His honesty was refreshing, but his tone only reinforced the idea of staying on his good side.

She nodded. "Tell me about DEFEND."

Jaxton uncrossed his arms and placed his hands on either side of his hips. "DEFEND is a first-born activist group, started a little over ten years ago by two escaped first-borns. Its goal is to gain enough public support to dismantle all of the AMT compounds and set the first-borns free."

This might be her only shot at information, so she forced herself to say, "But the AMT compounds still exist. First-borns aren't running around on the street, enjoying their freedom. What has DEFEND accomplished in the last ten years? Anything?"

Jaxton leaned forward. "I think you've forgotten that we agreed to an information exchange. It's your turn, pet."

She wanted to protest and say that two sentences didn't really constitute an overview, but Kiarra didn't want to push her luck.

Still, this wasn't going to be easy. Each first-born was required to keep their experiment-related experiences private or risk being carted away to a secret room, never to be seen again.

She took a deep breath, the smell of clean laundry soap filling her nose and reminding her she was no longer a prisoner. No one was going to cart her away for more tests, or enforce compliance.

Meeting Jaxton's gaze, Kiarra found the strength to say, "Within the first year of entering the AMT, first-borns are put in front of a panel and assigned to one of three types of experiments."

Everyone remembered their sorting day. Even years later, she couldn't block out her memory as a young teen.

She'd stood up in front of a panel of men and women while they'd discussed her as if she wasn't there. While afraid, Kiarra hadn't yet morphed into a compliant inmate. She'd kept her chin up, unafraid of punishment, looking for ways to challenge them.

Eventually, her refusal to answer the panel's questions had cost her. Within the hour, they'd whisked her away to her first compliance session.

After a full day of verbal abuse and conditioning, she'd experienced firsthand that the AMT wasn't a compound created for first-borns' safety; it was a prison, where first-borns had no rights.

She'd only been thirteen years old.

"Earth to Kiarra."

Jaxton's gentle yet firm voice brought her back to the present. She looked up at his face, surprised to find a lack of pity, only interest, and that encouraged her to keep going. "Each experiment track has its own pros and cons. Once assigned, the inmate goes through weekly sessions, unique to each individual."

"But what are the three tracks?"

"They refer to them officially as the psychological, breeding, and gene therapy tracks."

Jaxton clenched the edge of the dresser, his eyes dangerous. A second later, his expression was neutral again. "Which one do you think Garrett went through?"

"Who's Garrett?"

"My brother."

So F-840's name was Garrett.

She opened her mouth to explain, but snapped it shut as she realized this was supposed to be an information exchange and presently, the scales were tipped in Jaxton's favor. She wanted to even it out, but after that flare of danger a minute earlier in

JESSIE DONOVAN

Jaxton's eyes, withholding information about his older brother might set him off.

She heard tapping and looked up. Jaxton's expression was still unreadable. "Don't hold back with me, Kiarra. Always tell me what you're thinking."

She'd better seize that offer before she lost her nerve. She raised her chin a few inches. "I've given you more information than you've given me, and I think I should be able to ask you another question."

His lips twitched, confusing Kiarra. She hadn't said anything funny.

Jaxton stood and took a step toward her. This time, she found it easier to hold her ground compared to twenty minutes earlier.

"Then ask me something," he said.

He'd told her to say what she was thinking, so she jumped in with both feet. "What's going to happen to me once I finish your training?"

"Honestly?" He shrugged. "I don't know. But after we figure out your strengths and weaknesses, Neena, or Aislinn—the other DEFEND co-leader—will probably give you an assignment. Whatever it is, you'll have DEFEND's network at your disposal. Someone will always have your back."

Neena deciding her fate was a scary prospect, but maybe the other person, Aislinn, would be more normal.

From her experience, people only helped others for personal gain. Jaxton's words were probably meant to comfort, but Kiarra wouldn't fall into his trap, hoping and wishing someone would give a damn about her.

Jaxton glanced at his watch and straightened from leaning against the dresser. "I know this is a lot to take in and you're

56

probably tired, but I need you to answer my questions about Garrett. Tell me and you'll have the rest of the night free."

"Do I have to stay inside this room?"

He shook his head. "Just stay inside the house. Don't open doors without knocking, or you might not like what you see."

Why would he...*Oh*. Kiarra's cheeks heated. It had been almost ten years since she'd last seen a naked man.

He cleared his throat, which made her cheeks burn hotter. She hoped he couldn't read her mind.

"So, which type do you think Garrett suffered through?" he asked.

Garrett's condition was a cold slap in the face. Torture, because that was what honestly happened inside the AMT, no matter the nomenclature, would do that. "I could be wrong, but his symptoms of wild fits, aversion to touch, and his response to that particular tune all point toward the psychological experiments."

Jaxton raised an eyebrow. "What do they entail?"

Kiarra gave a sad smile. "I don't know. But the guards often took bets on how long a prisoner would last. Usually, it wasn't long."

She peered at Jaxton, but despite her revelations about his brother, his face remained expressionless. That was a trick Kiarra was going to have to perfect on the outside, too. Inside the AMT, disguising emotion was tantamount to survival, but ever since Jaxton had charged into her cell, she hadn't been able to control her emotions.

Jaxton went to the door and said, "Be downstairs tomorrow at nine a.m. We're going to start your self-defense training right away."

Then he left before she could reply.

CHAPTER SEVEN

The next morning, Jaxton stood at the foot of the stairs, tapping the flat top of the newel post with his hand.

Kiarra was late.

After finding little of import last night in his intelligence backlog, in addition to only nabbing four hours of sleep, his temper was short.

Last night, Taka had urged him to push Kiarra for more information. The man had a hunch about why she had had a knife pressed to her wrist, but declined sharing the information until he was more certain. When Jaxton tried ordering Taka to tell him anyway, Taka said he was keeping quiet on Neena's orders and Jaxton would have to take it up with her.

In their two years of working together, Taka has always been forthright with him. Something had to be going on, and once Jaxton had a moment, he would find out what.

The floor creaked from above and he looked to find Kiarra standing at the top of the stairs. Gone was her gray baggy AMT uniform and in its place were tight, black workout pants and a billowing, purple shirt.

Like any straight, red-blooded male would, Jaxton gave her a once-over. As his gaze lingered on her shapely legs, Kiarra tugged on her shirt as if she could hide her body if she only tried hard enough.

Resisting a frown, he wondered why. Any man would love to have legs like that wrapped around his waist.

Jaxton's hand stilled on the newel post. What the fuck had happened to his ironclad discipline? That was twice he'd slipped in less than twelve hours. It must be his lack of sleep playing with his mind.

Anxious to begin, he motioned for Kiarra to descend the stairs. Self-defense training would help clear his mind and keep the blood in his brain. "Let's get moving, pet. I have other things to do today."

As expected, her mouth pinched at his words. Yet he'd take anger any day over seeing fear in her eyes.

When she was three steps above him, Jaxton decided training was in session. Reaching out, he grabbed her loose shirt and pulled, ripping the fabric. She fell forward with a squeak and crashed into his chest.

Expecting the landing, he caught her with ease, gripping her around the waist with one arm and the back of her neck with his free hand.

Smashed up against him, enveloped by his arm, she appeared tiny and fragile. She needed to gain at least a stone or two before he'd clear her for any kind of field work.

The AMT's blatant disregard for human, or rather *Feiru*, rights was just what he needed to ignore the softness of her breasts pressed against his chest. "The first rule of self-defense: Avoid loose clothing. An enemy will use it to draw you close enough for an attack, a kill, or worse, to capture you. The danger usually outweighs any benefit when it comes to concealing extra weapons or explosives. In your case, don't risk it."

As if his voice was a trigger, Kiarra pressed against his chest and he released her. She eased back, her cheeks flushed. She hid her annoyance quickly, but not quickly enough. He was confident

Kiarra would break her conditioning by the end of the month, if not sooner.

He continued, "While in training, I'm giving you special permission to say whatever comes to mind. Call me a bastard if it helps to channel your anger. Swear like a sailor. The control of your emotions is the only way you'll excel in the training room or out in the field."

She remained silent, her expression unreadable. Most people would be annoyed as hell with her reluctance, but Jaxton knew the basics of a successful rehabilitation for former AMT prisoners. To get her to act and think without hesitation, Jaxton just needed to give her some encouragement.

He saw the seam of her shirt was ripped on one shoulder, the band of a blue sports bra peeking out, and knew what to do. He darted out a hand, fisted her shirt again, and pulled. But as she fell, he spun her around so her back was to his front. Before she had the chance to struggle, he tugged at her shirt until it ripped all the way down the seam and he was able to pull it away from her body.

Then he wrapped his arm around her ribcage, but despite the chill in the air, her skin was almost feverish.

Tossing the rag aside, he murmured, "Come to your lessons prepared, which means no loose clothing. If you come tomorrow with another shirt, I'll just rip that one too. Don't disappoint me, pet."

~~*

For a split second, the familiar feeling of fire danced across Kiarra's skin before fading, leaving only anger. Destroying the first new clothes she'd had in more than a decade, in addition to taking liberties with his touch, was going too far. She wanted to teach Jaxton a lesson.

The thought sobered her enough to think clearly. He had instructed her to channel her anger. She was going to take him up on his offer.

She remembered how some of the guards had taken down, or at least incapacitated, some of the unruly inmates inside the AMT. Maybe mimicking those moves would work.

She forced herself to relax, hoping she could catch Jaxton off guard. His hold loosened and Kiarra threw her weight against his arm, bending down to elbow him hard in the stomach. He grunted and Kiarra was able to push out of his grip and dash halfway up the staircase.

Her heart was racing; she'd managed to break free, and it felt pretty damn good. She couldn't stop smiling.

She turned to let Jaxton know the boundaries he shouldn't cross, but her words dried up in her throat at the man's expression.

Anger was not a strong enough word for it. However, he'd been the one to give permission, and she wasn't going to let him scare her again. Taking a deep breath through her nose, Kiarra lifted her chin an inch and said, "You're the one who wanted me to do whatever it took, and I did. Next time, don't underestimate me just because I'm small."

Without a word, he climbed the stairs. Every muscle in her body screamed to get moving, but she held her ground. Somehow, she knew that if she didn't stand her ground in this moment, she never would.

He stopped three stairs below her, their eyes level, and she noticed the unusual ring of gold around his irises.

Jaxton reached his arm out toward her, but Kiarra didn't move; at least, not until he brushed his fingers across her back and she shivered at the ticklish warmth. His voice was low, almost menacing. "How did you get these scars?"

Shit. In the heat of the moment, Kiarra had forgotten about them. The scars were ten years old and whatever pain she'd endured at the time had helped shape Kiarra to who she had become.

However, judging by the expression on Jaxton's face, he didn't view them as nonchalantly.

Telling him the whole story would not only upset him further, but would bring back memories best forgotten, possibly undoing all the hard work she'd done so far.

Kiarra was smart enough to know Jaxton wouldn't let her walk away without some sort of answer, so she said, "I would think it was obvious. I got them while inside the AMT."

Something flitted over his face, and he drew his fingers away from her back. His green-gold eyes narrowed. "You're under my protection now, but unless I know what we're facing, I won't be able to protect you. I need details, Kiarra."

Hearing that someone wanted to protect her was new, foreign even. But, as much as she wanted to believe it, not even her own parents had fought to keep her. There was no way a man she'd only known for two days would risk his life to save hers.

Besides, information was all she had to offer. If she gave it up easily, she'd have nothing to bargain with later. "Then teach me to defend myself, and you won't have to worry about me." Jaxton looked unconvinced at her demand, which irritated her. "So, will you train me or not?"

62

He looked at her for a long moment before nodding. "I will find out the truth, Kiarra, but right now, I'm more concerned about you being able to defend yourself. Follow me."

Jaxton turned without another glance, and Kiarra struggled to keep up with his long strides.

~~*

As Jaxton led Kiarra to the makeshift basement-turned-training-room, he repeatedly clenched and unclenched his right hand, wanting to punch someone. The AMT bastards had *whipped* her.

He'd only seen a fraction of the scar tissue on her back, peeking out from the straps of her sports bra, but the scars had been raised and thick, which meant someone had deliberately wanted to leave a mark. The pattern suggested more than one session.

Kiarra was providing him a closer look at what was really happening inside the AMT, and while it did nothing to help his blood pressure, the revelations kept giving him ideas of how to get the general *Feiru* public on DEFEND's side. But he needed more information and proof to offer. Kiarra wasn't talking much yet, but he was nothing if not tenacious.

All he could do for the moment was make her a little less vulnerable. While he would slowly get her into shape, it would be months before she could take an opponent in hand-to-hand combat. His best option was to train Kiarra on how to use her elemental magic.

Jaxton wasn't a first-born, and had no latent abilities that he was aware of, but he'd worked for years with three first-borns who were highly skilled in elemental magic. He'd learned enough from them to get a novice's training started.

He stopped on the mat in the middle of the room. Kiarra finally caught up with him, looked at him expectantly, albeit with a scowl, and said, "Well? What's first?"

The stunt on the stairs must have triggered her true colors, allowing them to the forefront. Time would tell if they stayed front and center or retreated as soon as Kiarra was out of his sight.

They stood a few feet apart, giving Jaxton his first real look at Kiarra in nothing but a sports bra and stretchy black pants. He still couldn't believe this tiny woman had knocked the wind out of him not five minutes ago. "Right. Size and muscle aren't everything. You need to play to your strengths. Some people have speed, others quick reflexes. In your case, you need to learn how to control your elemental magic."

She shifted her weight, her newly earned confidence fading. "What if I can't use it?"

He wondered what had caused her sudden unease. "There will be times when you can't, but we'll get to that later. As long as your hands are free, you have a big advantage over others." He glanced at the compass on the far wall to check his bearings. "Now, put one of your hands to the south, like this." Jaxton demonstrated, his palm facing down, slightly outstretched.

He waited, but Kiarra remained silent and shifted her weight again. Clearly something was wrong.

He raised an eyebrow. "You made a huge fuss about me training you and now you won't cooperate? What's going on?"

After a few seconds of silence, she answered, "It's not that I don't want to train, but learning how to control my elemental fire is a waste of time."

He resisted a sigh. "Spit it out already, Kiarra."

Some of the fire returned to her eyes, but her voice wasn't as defiant as before when she stated, "I don't have any elemental magic."

"What are you talking about? You're a first-born, aren't you?"

Her cheeks flushed. "No, I just decided to take an extended holiday somewhere cheap and the AMT was my best option."

He narrowed his eyes. "I don't need your sarcasm, pet. Just answer the bloody question."

Kiarra took a step toward him. "I am not your pet. And, of course, I'm a first-born. But just because I was born with the ability to control elemental fire doesn't mean it can't be taken away."

Jaxton blinked. What the hell was she talking about? Tired of the run around, he took the last step between them and gently gripped her shoulders. "Explain yourself."

She tried to push him away, but he had at least a hundred pounds on her. Giving her a little shake, he growled. "Now."

Her eyes burned with a mixture of emotions that Jaxton couldn't decipher. But there was definitely anger. Fury, even. Yet at the same time, she looked about ready to cry.

As if sensing his thoughts, she snapped her eyelids closed, shutting him out. He gave her a gentle shake. "I let the information about your scars go, but I won't let you out of my sight until you answer my question. What do you mean elemental magic can be taken away?"

A few more heartbeats passed before she opened her eyes, looking far more composed than a minute ago. She unclenched her jaw, never breaking her gaze. "I will tell you if you promise me a favor in the future."

He resisted the urge to pin her up against the wall and intimidate the answer out of her; that would only scare her more.

She continued to stare at him, and he decided to speed up the process. He answered, "Fine, I promise."

Her deep brown eyes searched his. "Swear on your brother's life."

Only years of training kept his temper in check. "I swear on Garrett's life. Now you'd bloody well better tell me what you mean when you say you can't gather elemental magic anymore."

When she finally spoke, her voice was barely audible. "Inside the F-block, they're developing a formula that messes with our DNA and mutates it so that the ability to control elemental magic fades. It doesn't work on everyone, but it worked on me. I haven't been able to gather elemental fire in nearly two years."

~~*

Kiarra waited for Jaxton to call her a liar, but he simply gripped her arms in silence.

Her heartbeat thundered in her ears. Once again, she was waiting for someone to decide her fate. If he handed her back to the AMT, or to another research facility, Kiarra wasn't sure she could survive it.

For a brief time, she'd felt like a person again. Not a test subject, nor a lab rat, but a person with feelings and opinions. She wanted the chance to do many of the things she'd spent her adult life reading about. She hated how the man in front of her would decide whether that future was possible.

Jaxton released her and gently lifted her bandaged left arm. He traced the edge of the bandage, the light touch nearly a tickle.

"That's why you were trying to kill yourself. You didn't want to become patient zero."

"Yes," Kiarra breathed, surprised at how quickly he'd worked that out.

"Right." Jaxton released her arm and took a step back. "When we're done here, Darius will draw some blood." He put a hand up to silence her. "No arguments. We need to know what they're brewing inside the F-block, and quickly."

Kiarra swallowed, afraid she'd start crying. He was going to use her as a lab rat, just like the others.

She turned and started walking toward the door, but Jaxton beat her too it, blocking the exit. *What does he want now?* "Get out of the way."

"Not until we're done with your lesson."

She looked up at that. "You still want to train me?"

Jaxton nodded. "Especially now. You're weak, physically, and if we're to get you in any kind of fighting shape, it's going to take a lot of hard work. Are you up to it, pet?"

She was speechless. It was foolish to hope, but maybe this man was different.

He raised his arm, palm out toward her. "If you're in, give me your hand."

She looked at Jaxton's palm, but didn't reach for it. "Why would you commit to so much effort when I will never be strong enough to fight as well as you or your men?"

Jaxton wiggled his fingers. "The second rule of self-defense: have confidence. If you falter for even a second, your enemy will spot it. So I need to know if you're going to keep doubting yourself or do you believe you could become the best arse-kicking, magic-free first-born in the world?"

CHAPTER EIGHT

James Sinclair sipped his whiskey while he waited for his security guards to finish patting down his latest visitor. Geoffrey Winter wouldn't be the first person who'd tried to sneak in a recording device or a weapon. Not everyone understood Sinclair's vision.

Collins, his chief security officer, gave the all-clear and stepped aside, allowing Winter into the room before closing the door. Sinclair waited for a red light to turn on above the door, signaling the jamming device was engaged.

He gestured toward the paper at the far end of the table. "I need you to set up a meeting with the people on that list, at one of the pre-approved locations, within the week."

Winter scanned the names. "What reason should I give?"

"Tell them I have information that will impress their superiors."

Winter looked up. "Does MI5 know about the information you're going to share?"

"No, and it's going to stay that way." Even from across the table, Sinclair saw Winter clench his jaw. He could tell that the man was close to breaking after all these years, so Sinclair placed his drink down and reminded him who was in charge. "I hear your daughter is doing well in school, Winter."

Winter clenched a fist at his side. "Leave her out of this."

Sinclair ignored him, needing to make his point. "Children grow up so fast, and to think, the little half-*Feiru* will hit magical maturity before you know it."

"My daughter won't have any elemental abilities."

Sinclair raised his brows. "Ah, but her mother is a *Feiru*, and you know the ability passes through her. What would your superiors think if they heard one of their chief *Feiru* liaison agents had slipped and dallied with one of his charges? Even you realized the mistake, tossing away the poor *Feiru* woman to marry a human."

Pain and anger flashed across Winter's face. "Malia understood the circumstances. We did what was best for our daughter."

"Tell yourself that if it makes you feel better. All I care is that you keep this information private and secret from MI5. My eyes and ears will alert me if you slip up. You don't want to waste the few remaining years you have left with your daughter, now, do you?"

Winter remained silent and Sinclair smiled. All it took was a reminder of what Winter had to lose, and the man morphed back into one of his more cooperative contacts. Whenever he threatened his daughter's life, Winter understood he wasn't bluffing—one of Winter's co-workers had tried to outsmart Sinclair; as a result, they were spending a life sentence inside a mental health facility.

Sinclair's methods and staff may be unconventional, but they did their jobs. Unlike the human intelligence agencies around the world, where petty arguments and internal battles for power overshadowed efficiency, Sinclair's people believed in the bigger picture and realized it would take patience to achieve it. Each and every one of his staff had something riding on the success of his

R&C—Repeal Article I and Contain First-born Magic—
campaign.

Winter stood up straight, his face once again emotionless. "Anything else?"

"Do you have any news on the concentration of DEFEND activity in the North of England?"

Winter shook his head. "We know they have a training facility there, but we haven't pinpointed its location. A few agents are undercover, working their way through the pubs in Manchester. There's talk of a subterranean network near the Manchester Arndale shopping center."

Sinclair's reports had said the same thing, but he'd wanted to test Winter's coerced loyalty. He'd passed this time. "Check the underground Manchester and Salford Junction Canal tunnels. If I were to have a 'hidden' facility, I'd put it in those old tunnels."

"Some of my staff had the same idea, but many parts of the former canal are deemed unsafe. It's going to take a few weeks, maybe a month, for the local human government to grant access."

"Fine. Let me know when you receive permission to explore them so I can send my people up north to search alongside the *Feiru* liaison agents." Sinclair waved his hand in dismissal. "You can go now."

Winter nodded. He knocked at the door and Collins escorted him out.

DEFEND was growing stronger and becoming a pain in his arse. Between the meeting Winter was coordinating and locating DEFEND's base in the north, he might finally be able to get rid of them.

There was a knock on the door and Sinclair's assistant, Phuong, entered the room. She handed him a folded note, sealed with wax. An old method of security, but combined with the hidden ink pocket that would release when the wax seal was broken, it had proven an effective one.

He slid his finger under the seal, careful to let the ink absorb into the paper and not his finger, and read the note: *D.K. on board. Tonight, 9 p.m.*

Sinclair smiled and forgot all about DEFEND. At nine p.m., Dean Kelley would make his announcement in support of Sinclair's R&C campaign. With five local councils on his side, he only needed ten more before he could start Phase II of his campaign.

CHAPTER NINE

When Kiarra finally placed her hand in Jaxton's, a jolt of heat shot up his arm, but disappeared as quickly as it had come. He'd learned with Garrett as a teenager that elemental fire left behind a burn, so the heat couldn't have been real.

Her response earlier, to his reasoning as to why she'd tried to commit suicide, had been genuine. At least she believed it to be truth. Her blood would either confirm or deny it, creating even more questions.

He would discuss Kiarra's confession later with Taka. At that moment, he needed to address her weaknesses and vulnerability as best he could. He would start at the beginning and test out her endurance and strength levels.

Kiarra was staring at their clasped hands, a mixture of panic and confusion on her face. He couldn't allow her to retreat back to her AMT-conditioned persona, so Jaxton went into trainer mode and took a better grip on her hand. "No matter how big or strong a person appears, everyone shares the same delicate places on their body that, with the right amount of applied pressure or force, can buy you enough time to get away.

"Hands and wrists are delicate." He adjusted his grip, taking hold of her wrist. "So when someone grabs you like this, you can break their hold in one of three ways…"

After demonstrating the three methods, Jaxton once again took hold of Kiarra's wrist. "Now try it."

She smacked the heel of her palm against his forearm to no effect. "Harder. In this situation, you want to inflict as much damage as possible, which requires greater force." Kiarra hesitated, so he added, "Don't worry, you can't hurt me."

His dismissal had the desired effect. Kiarra narrowed her eyes and swung hard. This time he actually felt a sting on his arm, even if she hadn't managed to break free. "Better. But remember, your best weapon is surprise. Try something else, so I won't brace myself for the same attack."

Jaxton once again took hold of her wrist and noticed the faint sweat on her brow. After a scant fifteen minutes, Kiarra was already getting a workout.

The arm in his hand went slack and Kiarra teetered. Jaxton went to catch her, but Kiarra snapped into action, her free hand moving to his grip and prying his fingers back. He tightened his hand and moved his arm just in time to prevent her from succeeding.

He gave her wrist a gentle squeeze. "That was good, but can you do it under pressure?"

She raised her chin. "I will with practice."

Jaxton smiled. "All right, pet, I'm taking off the kid gloves. Let's try this for real."

He spent the next hour demonstrating and making Kiarra perform escape techniques. Much like her fake fainting move, she surprised him by knowing some of the moves without instruction, claiming she had seen them before inside the AMT.

He added "observant" to her list of strengths.

When fatigue slowed her reaction time, Jaxton tossed her a towel from the side table and said, "That's all for today. Make sure to do the stretches I demonstrated before bed, and meet me again tomorrow, at the same time."

73

Slightly out of breath, Kiarra wiped the sweat off her face and neck. Jaxton followed the movements with his eyes. Without the demands of training to distract him, he noticed Kiarra as a woman again.

The celibacy he'd enforced over the last year as he'd searched for Garrett was taking a toll.

Kiarra caught his eye and tossed the towel away. "I want one more go."

With years of practice under his belt, Jaxton kept his face expressionless, unwilling to show Kiarra how she affected him. "I appreciate your enthusiasm, but one of the most important rules of training is to not overstretch yourself. An injury would only set you back."

A look that Kiarra wouldn't have dared give him a mere two hours ago, one of a face pinched in irritation, was in full force. He started to rethink his no-holds-barred approach.

She raised an eyebrow. "Are you afraid I'll best you?"

"You're kidding, right?"

Kiarra walked toward him, her hips swaying like she meant business. "Come on, grab me."

He coughed to cover his laugh. "Do you know what that sounds like to a bloke? Unless you want me to cop a feel, you'd better think of a different way to phrase that."

Her cheeks flamed and Jaxton tried not to smile. Instead, he focused on her discombobulation. If she wanted one last go, he was going to make it authentic.

Rushing from the side, Jaxton managed to get behind Kiarra. He took her throat in his hands, careful not to hurt her, but gripping her firmly enough so she couldn't pull away easily. She swung her left arm around, straight and firm as he'd taught her, and he was forced to lean back a fraction to avoid a blow to his head. As Kiarra twisted around, she chopped her right hand into the side of his neck, giving her the distraction she needed to run away.

Three steps away from Jaxton, Kiarra whooped as she jumped up and down in place. "I did it!"

Jaxton rubbed the sting on his neck and shook his head at her actions. "Lingering around, celebrating, defeats the purpose of temporarily disabling an opponent."

Kiarra beamed. "Somehow I think I'll walk away from this one unscathed."

A second later, Jaxton had her back pressed against his front, with one arm around her waist and the other around her shoulders. Kiarra was tense, her breathing ragged.

He'd scared her, just as he'd intended.

Jaxton leaned close to her ear and said, "Until you can trust someone with your life, keep your guard up at all times. I'm not joking about this, Kiarra."

She shivered, and he released her. He quickly spun her around and took her chin in his fingers, determined to hammer this lesson home. "Do you understand me?"

Kiarra nodded, still obviously shaken by the encounter. Maybe someone had tried to restrain her in a similar manner sometime in her past. Somewhere in the course of their training session, he'd forgotten that she was a recently rescued first-born.

He released her chin. "Darius will be up shortly to draw your blood. After that, you're free 'til tomorrow morning." As she turned to leave, he said, "Good job today, Kiarra."

She peered over her shoulder and nodded. As she walked off, she straightened her spine and carried herself with more confidence than she'd displayed since arriving. The thought of her confidence being stripped away again if she were captured and tossed back inside the AMT made Jaxton want to protect her all the more.

And that scared him a little.

~~*

Kiarra turned the lock on her door and then headed for the small bathroom suite attached to her room. Her arms and legs were borderline numb from her training, but she managed to shed her clothes and turn on the shower. As she stood under the hot spray of water, she closed her eyes and enjoyed how the warmth relaxed her muscles.

She had enjoyed tackling new self-defense techniques and had a better understanding of what the guards had used against her and the other prisoners inside the AMT. Unfortunately, Jaxton's stunt at the end of her training session, when he'd hauled her up against him, had driven home the point that she still had a lot of work to do.

As she massaged her scalp with shampoo, she remembered the spark of heat she'd felt every time Jaxton had touched her. It wasn't quite the same feeling as when she'd been able to gather elemental fire, but there was something familiar about the process. At least with Jaxton overseeing her training, she could see if the same thing happened again in their next session. It might just be a strange response to touch after so many years without it.

She had also caught Jaxton watching her. Part of her dismissed it as nothing more than a trainer observing his student, but another part of her remembered the last time a man had watched her so closely.

She finished her shower and dried off, but before she dressed, Kiarra reached around and felt the raised surfaces of her scars. There were no mirrors in the AMT, except for the two-ways in the exam rooms, and she'd put off taking a look at her body, afraid of what she'd see.

After taking a deep breath, Kiarra decided she needed to conquer this small fear or she'd never be able to tackle her larger ones. She wiped the steam off the mirror and looked at her reflection.

Her breasts were high, her waist narrow. Even though her hipbones poked out a little more than she liked, her front looked like any other woman, soft and rounded where it mattered. Then Kiarra turned and peeked over her shoulders to look at her back.

The scars were ugly, crisscrossed in a random pattern over the top half of her back. She reached a hand behind and touched the raised surface, her deadened nerves barely registering the movements of her fingers. Jaxton had only seen a fraction of the damage to her back. She wondered how he would react to the full spread; a web of scars was hardly attractive.

Not that his opinion should matter. More importantly, she wouldn't let it matter.

Jaxton might be helping her, and was probably the closest thing she had to an ally, but she needed to keep her distance and learn how to control her emotions. What he'd said at the end, about never letting down your guard until you could trust someone with your life, rang true. The only person Kiarra could trust was herself.

A knock at the door startled her. She threw on some pajama bottoms and an oversized t-shirt before crossing the floor to the door. "Who is it?"

"Darius. I'm here to draw some blood."

Taking a deep breath, Kiarra opened the door to find a tall, smiling man with dark chocolate skin. She liked how he didn't try to push his way into her room. Kiarra stood back and opened the door. "Let's get it over with."

Darius went to the oversized chair in the corner and gestured for Kiarra to take a seat. As she made her way across the room, she decided this was a prime opportunity to work on her uneasiness around strangers. She knew nothing but the man's name and that he worked with Jaxton, but at least his smile had been sincere when she'd opened the door.

After she settled in the chair, Darius held the tourniquet in front of Kiarra and raised an eyebrow. "Ready for the heavy-duty rubber band?"

Kiarra nodded, unused to people asking for her permission.

As she stared at Darius's profile, a memory from her rescue flashed inside her mind. Right before she'd passed out from the tranquilizer, this man and two others had positioned their hands toward various compass directions. There was only one way to find out if the memory was true or from a dream. Kiarra shifted in her seat and asked, "You're a first-born, aren't you?"

Darius's eyes darted up, but quickly focused back on tying the tourniquet tightly and searching for her vein. "Yes." He took the blood-collection needle out of his kit and held it up. "Ready for the pinch?"

Kiarra nodded absently, wanting to know why Darius, despite being a first-born, was outside the AMT. Would he get mad at her personal question?

The needle secure, Darius took out the collection tubes and secured the first one. As her blood filled the tube, she looked away. The sight only reminded her of what had been taken away.

"Shortly after my mother discovered she was pregnant," Darius said, "my parents hightailed it to the mountains of Virginia. They went off the grid to conceal my identity and saved me from having to go into the AMT system."

Kiarra swung her gaze around, watching Darius closely, but he was focused on his task. This time, she would ask what was on her mind. "Then how did you learn to use your elemental magic?"

Darius swapped the full tube for an empty one. "You could search the Appalachian Mountains for the rest of your life, but you might never find the person you're looking for. The rogue *Feiru* Masters knew that. My parents convinced an acquaintance to set up a meeting, and one of the rogue first-born Masters took me on."

Part of her wanted to ask to see his abilities, but another part of her resented the fact Darius still had them. She knew it was silly, but she was jealous of his parents' actions to protect him.

She had no idea who or what was a *Feiru* Master, but before she was able to ask, Darius pressed a cotton ball to the needle's entry point, eased the needle out, and taped the cotton ball to her arm. He looked up and patted her arm. "If there's a way to bring back your elemental fire, rest assured that DEFEND will find it."

"How did you…"

Darius smiled. "There are eyes and ears everywhere in this house. Remember that."

Then he was gone before she could ask another question; that seemed to be a pattern with the men in this house.

Kiarra was skeptical that Darius's words would come true, about bringing back her elemental fire, but secretly she longed for it. Every time she had been allowed to use her fire during supervised observations inside the AMT, the flames had felt like old friends, caressing her skin and comforting her in a way nothing else could.

But she longed for the return of her fire for a much more important reason than simple nostalgia; with elemental fire, she wouldn't have to rely on Jaxton or his men for protection. At the end of her three-month trial, she could leave and defend herself against the AMT enforcers.

CHAPTER TEN

After thirty minutes of searching her room, Kiarra was convinced Jaxton or one of his men had stolen the rules and regulation book Neena had given her. No doubt the book was somewhere else in the house, but to go looking for it meant she'd have to leave her room.

She stood at her door, trying to work up the courage to open it. Having met Marco and Darius, Kiarra wasn't afraid of bumping into one of Jaxton's men. Each time she met them, she was able to strengthen her tolerance of interacting with people again.

So what was keeping her standing like an idiot in front of the door? The clothes Neena had packed into the red duffel bag for her to wear.

The tight jeans, long-sleeved purple t-shirt, and knee-high boots felt like an advertisement that screamed, "Stare at my boobs and ass; you can't miss them." After spending her entire adult life trying not to catch the eye of the AMT guards, drawing attention to herself was counterintuitive.

But as she darted a glance toward the window, Kiarra remembered that she wasn't inside the AMT any longer. Jaxton and his men might stare, but they most likely wouldn't touch her without consent.

This was another step in her training. She could do this.

Kiarra took a deep breath before opening the door and heading down the stairs, toward the front room. She remembered seeing a bookshelf in the room when she'd talked with Neena yesterday. Maybe she'd get lucky and find the DEFEND book there.

She needed to learn the rules. Not only because she wanted to become less reliant on Jaxton, but also in case she decided to stay and work for DEFEND past her three-month trial period.

Careful not to make a sound, Kiarra peeked into the front room and breathed a sigh of relief when she saw it was empty. Late afternoon sunshine streamed through the windows, allowing her to scan the bookshelf without flicking on the lights.

Most of the books were nonfiction. The topics ranged from geology to history to psychology, with a few fiction titles tucked away on the bottom shelf. But she didn't see Neena's book or anything about DEFEND or its rules and regulations. She would have loved to find a book on the history of the AMT compounds or *Feiru* legends, but again, she came up empty-handed.

So much for trying to become less reliant on Jaxton. She'd just have to confront him about it the next time she saw him.

Kiarra bent over and scanned the fiction titles on the bottom shelf. Reading had been one of her sanity-sustaining techniques inside the AMT, but all of the titles had come from a pre-approved list to ensure the inmates wouldn't get any ideas about escape or revolt. The thought of reading something that might not be on the approved AMT reading list made Kiarra a little giddy.

She finally plucked one with "Highlander" in the title and read the back cover when a voice behind her said, "The steamy ones are tucked away in the back."

BLAZE OF SECRETS

~~*

Jaxton had been planning to read more about post-traumatic stress disorder on his tablet when he'd stepped into the front room and seen Kiarra bent over, her lovely, heart-shaped arse on display.

Jaxton leaned against the doorframe and watched her. He knew what Kiarra was looking for, but to give her the book outright would be too easy. Instead, he would use this opportunity to work on the emotional side of Kiarra's training. If she was to be effective in the field, she needed the ability to control all of her emotions, and Jaxton had the perfect plan to test it.

After making a comment about his sister Millie's sexy romance stash on the bottom shelf, Kiarra jumped up and turned around to face him. He waited to see if he'd be dealing with the hesitant AMT inmate or the woman from his training session.

Kiarra's brows drew together. "You shouldn't sneak up on people. It's not very nice."

Excellent, he had the woman from the training session. "I wasn't sneaking, you just weren't paying attention. Another rule for self-defense is—"

"To pay attention. Yes, I get it."

At least she wasn't hesitating at everything he said or did, which was progress. He walked over to the bookcase. "What're you looking for, pet?"

She looked at him askance for a second before she said, "Neena gave me a book to read, but it's not in my room."

He plucked a book from the topmost shelf and held it up. "This one?" Kiarra reached for it, but he held it up out of her reach. "Everyone who works for DEFEND knows the rumors about Neena's personal copy of the rules and regulations book. Supposedly, it gives clues about her overall plan for the organization. My question is why would she give it to you?"

"Does it matter? She gave it to me; therefore, it's mine."

Jaxton raised an eyebrow. "You're turning into a greedy one, aren't you?"

"If wanting to keep the first present I've received in my adult life is greedy, then so be it." She put out her palm and waited.

When she put it like that, it made him feel like a bit of a bastard. "You can have it back if"—he stooped down and fished out Millie's favorite book—"you take this one too."

Kiarra took both books. After reading the title and taking a look at the cover image of the romance book, her cheeks turned red.

Jaxton stood up and tapped the cover of *The Dark Warrior's Secret*. "My sister has read this at least four times, so I reckon it's good smut."

Her cheeks turned a brighter shade of red. "Smut?"

He was enjoying her discomfiture and couldn't seem to stop himself. "A book full of sex and the like. She swears it has a good story, but I bet she only reads it for the sex scenes."

She stared at the cover, unwilling to meet his eye. "Normally, I'd thank you for the book, but I'm not sure you deserve it."

Jaxton snorted. "Spot on, pet."

She looked up. "Spot on," she mimicked in a horrible British accent. "Who talks like that?"

"The people who speak English properly."

"You are less than helpful."

Jaxton fought a smile. "Maybe if you didn't make fun of my accent, I would be more helpful."

She hugged the books to her chest. "I didn't know you were so sensitive."

"I'm not the one who goes red at the sight of two people going at it on a book cover."

She peeked at the cover again, but this time, her expression remained neutral. "See, I can do it."

He leaned in. "That is what you should've done the first time. A second of hesitation when someone attacks and it's game over, pet."

As they stared at each other, Jaxton was overly aware of Kiarra's breath on his cheek, the sweet scent of her skin. She leaned in a fraction, only to take three steps back. "If the lesson is over, Mr.——"

"Ward."

"Mr. Ward, then I have some studying to do."

While she was trying to be distant, her actions were amusing. Jaxton motioned to the couch. "You can read here; I've things to do."

"I prefer to read in my room, really—"

"Enjoy the sunshine. You need it more than I." He turned and left the room, not quite sure if he'd been as successful with Kiarra as he'd planned. Men, women, teenagers, he'd trained them all over the years, but never before had he had the urge to kiss one of them. If he wasn't careful, Kiarra might ruin his reputation.

~~*

With Jaxton gone, Kiarra plopped onto the couch and punched one of the pillows. Why did the man insist on making everything into a training lesson? He purposely antagonized her, only to lecture her about it afterward.

Her three months of training couldn't be over soon enough.

Kiarra stared at the two books in her lap. She needed a distraction, and while the cover with "two people going at it" would be more entertaining, the book about DEFEND was more important for her future. After getting comfortable on the couch, she opened Neena's book.

The title page was covered in random handwritten words, such as *Cantabria*, *Edinburgh*, and *Victoria Falls*. Hearts adorned all the i's on the page, and there were several words written in a language she couldn't understand. Curious to see what made Neena's copy of the book so famous, she flipped to the first page of text and started reading:

DEFEND is a volunteer organization whose aim is to promote equality for all Feiru, *regardless of birth order or unusual abilities. By reading this guide of rules and regulations, you agree to keep this information secret and away from those who would wish to harm our organization. Violation of your silence will result in consequences put forth in Section Three.*

In the side margin, there was a note in the same handwriting as the title page, and it said: *And they'll have to deal with me.*

That comment fit with what she knew of Neena's personality, but it wasn't the least bit helpful in revealing more about DEFEND.

Kiarra flipped a few pages and stopped when she came to one filled with scribbles in the margins. She read the handwritten part first:

A shifter will be needed to set things in motion. Coercion may be necessary.

Unsure of what a shifter was, Kiarra frowned and looked at the title printed at the top of the page: *Latent Roles and Uses.*

Latent what? Maybe if she read from page one, all of this would start to make more sense. Kiarra flipped back to the beginning, determined to find out how DEFEND functioned and figure out why Neena expected her to skirt the rules.

Chapter Eleven

Hours later, when the sun began to set, Kiarra tucked away her books to find something to eat. Neena's handwritten comments were giving her a headache; the woman had no lack of confidence, to the point of being haughty.

The book mostly detailed the hierarchy, departments, and restrictions on outside communication. DEFEND seemed like a good organization on paper, but then most *Feiru* probably thought the AMT compounds sounded good too. In other words, she wasn't ready to make a decision just yet.

Her stomach growled and she took that as her cue to hurry up. She wanted to tuck the books away safely in her room before using the kitchen. She barely remembered how to fry an egg, but all that mattered to her was the fact that she could eat when she wanted, without following a timetable.

After stashing the books in her room, Kiarra paused at the top of the stairs and looked down the dark hallway toward Garrett's room, wondering how he was doing. She didn't want to wake him up and maybe cause another fit, but seeing to his care was the only thing she seemed capable of doing with any skill; it was the only thing she didn't have to rely on Jaxton to teach her.

Besides, she could always hum Garrett back to sleep if she woke him up.

Counting the doors, she arrived at the one that was Garrett's and she put her ear to the door, but there was only silence. She turned the knob, grateful to find it unlocked, and gently pushed the door inward. She let out a silent breath when the door opened without a sound, and Kiarra slipped inside.

The curtains were drawn, the material so thick it cloaked the room in darkness except for the glow of a nightlight near the bed. Her eyes grew accustomed to the dark as she scanned the room. Apart from the bed and a few wooden chairs, the room was empty, devoid of any color or signs of life. If Jaxton was planning on using this room permanently for Garrett's recovery, he'd have to make the decor more homey. Bare walls and sparse furniture would only remind Garrett of his time inside the AMT.

Garrett stirred and she began humming a section of Holst's "Jupiter." The mound of man and blankets on the bed calmed, and that was her cue to sneak back out. She'd have words with Jaxton when he woke about decorating the room and ask if she could help more with his brother's recovery. Ideas floated around inside her head, and she wanted the chance to try them out.

As she turned toward the door, a movement in the corner caught her eye. She peered carefully, but saw only shadows. The light must be playing tricks on her. But she took another step and this time a dense, dark cloud rose out of the shadows. She blinked, but the thick, dark mist kept expanding toward her. While she might have just triggered a security defense system, Kiarra wasn't taking any chances. Looking around, she grabbed one of the chairs and lifted it up just as a woman holding a dagger appeared out of the dark cloud.

The woman lunged at Kiarra, but she smashed the chair as hard as she could at the woman and yelled, "Help!" Garrett's high-pitched scream sounded behind her, but Kiarra kept her eyes on the mysterious woman and watched as she smacked aside the chair, the dagger still in her hand.

Grabbing the other chair in the room, she tried to think of what else she could do. Her self-defense lessons hadn't included how to disarm an attacker.

The woman feinted right then came around Kiarra's left side. Just as the woman's dagger came down, a bluish-white blur smashed through the window, and Kiarra threw up her arms to protect her face from the flying shards of glass.

The lights came on and Kiarra blinked a few times, trying to adjust to the sudden brightness. Jaxton was standing in the doorway, his gun pointed at the ground. Marco and Darius were right behind him.

She looked to where Jaxton's gun was pointing and saw two women on the floor, one straddled on top of the other. The top woman had her gun trained on the captured woman's head.

The gun-wielding woman smashed her prisoner's head against the floor, rendering her unconscious. She adjusted her aim and pointed her gun toward Jaxton before she said, "Don't bother with the elemental ambush. It won't work on me."

Jaxton's gun arm didn't waver. "Who are you?"

The woman turned her head a second and met Kiarra's gaze, but before Jaxton or his men could respond, her head whipped back around.

Something about the woman's dark hair, dark eyes, and long face were familiar to Kiarra.

Jaxton stepped to the side to allow Darius to pass, but the woman added a second gun to her free hand.

Kiarra blinked at the speed. She hadn't even seen the woman's hand move.

The woman with the guns said, "Nice way to thank me for saving your ass, limey."

Jaxton replied, "I don't usually thank people who point guns at me."

The woman shrugged. "These guns are preventing you from doing something stupid." She motioned her head in Kiarra's direction. "Besides, Kiarra can vouch for me."

How does this woman know my name? Before anyone could accuse her of anything, Kiarra managed to sputter, "I don't know who you are."

The woman raised an eyebrow, but kept her gaze on Jaxton and Darius. "Does the name Camilla Louise ring a bell?"

Kiarra's heart stopped. The woman had to be lying.

Jaxton darted a glance at Kiarra. "What's she talking about?"

She took another look, this time noticing the scar on the woman's jaw. For a second, she couldn't breathe. She realized why the face had seemed familiar—she'd last seen the same scar on the chin of a ten-year-old girl, her arms outstretched, calling Kiarra's name.

"Kiarra? Do you know her?" Jaxton said.

She pried her gaze away from Cam's face, looked at Jaxton, and said, "Cam is my younger sister."

~~*

"Sister?" Jaxton took in the woman named Camilla, from her long, lean body to the weapons crisscrossing her chest. A scar on her forehead and jaw only emphasized the woman's rougher appearance; Kiarra had a somewhat rounder, angelic-looking face. It was hard to believe they were related.

Jaxton motioned his free hand toward the unconscious woman on the floor. "And who is that, your unruly cousin?"

Kiarra's sister was not amused. "Try a Shadow-Shifter, limey, sent by a person working with the AMT enforcers."

He glanced at the unconscious woman on the floor. Shadow-shifting was a latent ability, one that certain *Feiru* could use to shift into a shadowy mist once every twenty-four hours. In the past, they had been used as assassins or spies.

The Shadow-Shifter would be out cold for a little while longer, and Jaxton needed to figure out why Kiarra's sister would show up only a few days after Kiarra's escape. He was also curious as to how the hell she'd made it inside his house despite the tight security.

He motioned toward the Shadow-Shifter. "I understand how she made it past security, but how did you break in through the second-story window? Better yet, why are you here?"

"Aislinn and Neena sent me. I heard Kiarra was out and I wanted to talk with her."

That was very much a non-answer. Jaxton glanced at Kiarra to see how she was handling it all, only to find her humming near Garrett's ear. No wonder his brother was quiet despite the commotion.

"Kiarra." She turned and looked at Jaxton, but even from across the room, he could see the insecure expression on her face. *Fucking fantastic.* If her sister's appearance had undone all of Kiarra's progress so far, he'd take care of Cam himself. "It's your call. What do you want to do with her?"

Kiarra straightened from her crouch and clenched her fists at her side. She might be hiding it well, but he could tell she was upset, and a part of him wanted to comfort her.

"I—" She nearly choked and Jaxton growled; how dare someone upset his charge and make her regress.

But before he could do anything, Kiarra swallowed and said, "Tomorrow. I'll talk with Cam tomorrow."

"Not good enough," Cam said before she disappeared from her perch atop the Shadow-Shifter, only to reappear at Kiarra's side. Cam held Kiarra by the shoulders, one gun still out and trained on Jaxton. "I need to talk with Kiarra tonight."

Kiarra tried to shrug off Cam's grip. "Cam, please, let it wait until tomorrow. I'm not sure I——"

Cam never took her gaze from Jaxton and his men as she said, "I'm not fucking around. Verify it with Aislinn or Neena, but I'm not letting Kiarra out of my sight until I get to talk with her."

Kiarra looked about ready to cry. He needed to defuse the situation.

"Marco, confirm it. Darius, get that other woman secured."

Jaxton never took his eyes from Kiarra's face as Darius moved into the room and hefted up the unconscious woman. Kiarra's expression mirrored one he'd seen during their struggle inside her AMT cell—one of vulnerability and despair. Her sister's sudden appearance had probably triggered memories best forgotten. He needed to get Kiarra alone so he could coax her back.

Once the Shadow-Shifter was secured and out of the room, Jaxton spoke again. "The man on the bed behind you is in rough shape. Let Kiarra go and I promise you we'll talk downstairs." In a show of good faith, he lowered his gun.

Cam lowered her gun too, but kept a firm grip on Kiarra's arm. "How do I know it's not a trick? You could have more people waiting downstairs to attack me."

"If your recent display of speed is any indication, you could outrun or outmaneuver any person here before they had a chance to draw a gun or use elemental magic."

Cam looked at him a moment before slightly turning her head to Kiarra, but only far enough to where Cam could keep an eye on him at the same time. "Will your man keep his word?"

Kiarra blinked. "He's not—"

Cam interrupted her. "Just tell me, will he keep his word?"

Kiarra looked him in the eye and asked, "Jaxton, will you?"

He didn't hesitate. "I swear on my brother's life."

Kiarra looked back to her sister. "Yes, I think he will."

Cam waved a hand toward Jaxton's gun arm. "First, slide your gun over to me." He removed the clip and slid the gun across the floor. Cam released Kiarra and said, "Go to him, if that's what you want."

Kiarra looked like she wanted to say something to her sister, but she eventually took one step and then another in Jaxton's direction. When she was close enough, he tucked her close against his side and wrapped his arm around her shoulders. Kiarra relaxed against him.

With Kiarra's now familiar warmth against his side, Jaxton's tension faded, but he kept his head in the game and never took his eyes off Cam.

He gestured for Cam to precede them. "Lead on, my lady."

Cam scowled at the term, but exited the room, her boots pounding down the stairs. He squeezed Kiarra's shoulders and asked, "How're you holding up, pet?"

~~*

After all this time, her sister Cam was alive. Kiarra had no idea why she would come here, scant days after her rescue from the AMT. If her sister had truly cared about her, why hadn't she tried to find her before?

94

But her mind could barely focus on anything else. Calming Garrett down had distracted her for a short while, but then Cam had been there, holding her by the shoulders and demanding to talk with her.

She was afraid of what she'd hear.

After years of trying to forget her old life, Cam had no right to demand anything of her. Kiarra knew her family had been happier after sending her to the AMT, but she wasn't ready to hear about it. She would probably never be ready to hear about it.

No one wanted to hear they were unwanted.

However, Cam wasn't listening to her and was trying to force unpleasant memories on Kiarra before she was ready.

Kiarra's throat closed up, sweat gathered on her palms, and a sense of helplessness took hold. If the past was anything to go on, she was about to have a panic attack.

No, no, NO. She wouldn't let the past ruin her present. She could beat this.

It took a couple of deep breaths before she could focus on what Cam and Jaxton were saying to each other. Somehow she replied on automatic, until Cam told her to go to Jaxton, if that was what she wanted.

And she did. Jaxton was the only one who had helped her to relax and briefly forget about the AMT. He might be annoying, but he was training her for a purpose, a place with DEFEND.

Even if she didn't yet know his reasoning, it had been Jaxton, and not Cam, who had rescued her from the AMT.

She went to him. When she reached his side, he pulled her close and Kiarra leaned on him for support. His touch was steadying and warm, and as his scent surrounded her, her sense of helplessness faded.

After some more words she didn't hear, Cam marched out the door and Jaxton squeezed her shoulder. His voice rumbled in her ear. "How're you holding up, pet?"

The familiarity of his lilting voice, combined with the stupid endearment, helped snap Kiarra out of the fading attack. "I'm not your pet."

He tilted her chin up, forcing her to look at him, and saw his smile. "If you can snap, you must not be doing too poorly."

He'd used the term on purpose. "Talking to Cam tonight is a bad idea."

"You don't have much of a choice, pet."

She growled at the endearment, but didn't let him distract her. "Cam was ten years old the last time I saw her. A lot has happened since then." She hugged her ribcage. "And I'm honest enough with myself to know that I'm just not ready to confront her."

"But aren't you just the least bit curious about why she's here? I reckon she didn't have super-fast reflexes as a child, for one." He tapped her shoulder. "She might not be here for the reason you think."

She turned to get a better look at him. "Do you know something I don't?"

Jaxton shook his head. "I've never seen the woman in my life. I would think that pointing a gun at her would've made that obvious."

It was true that she didn't know the real reason Cam was here. For so many years, Kiarra had expected the worst of people, but maybe things were changing. She didn't know Cam as an adult, but as a child, Cam would've never tried to cause her deliberate harm. Irritate and trick, yes, but not harm.

BLAZE OF SECRETS

Kiarra took a deep breath and decided she would talk with her sister. She moved toward the stairs, but Jaxton kept a firm grip on her shoulder. She looked up at him and said, "Let go of me, Jaxton."

"No."

"I—"

Jaxton shook his head. "At this point, we don't know anything about her and I won't risk it. I said I'd protect you, and I meant it."

The look in his eye and the set of his chin told Kiarra nothing would change his mind. *So this is what it's like to have someone care about your well-being.*

She tensed. Jaxton had said nothing about caring for her; she was a duty, an obligation. It was delusional to think otherwise. He was simply following Neena's orders.

Or curious about Cam's abilities.

Whatever the cause for his apparent concern, she wouldn't fight his orders. Cam was not the ten-year-old girl she remembered. Something had hardened her, made her tough, and it wouldn't hurt to have someone like Jaxton at Kiarra's side.

Of course, she wasn't about to let him know that. "Fine, protect me, whatever. But let's go before I start getting gray hairs."

Jaxton gave a barely audible snort. "As you wish, pet."

~~*

By the time Jaxton and Kiarra reached the living room, Marco was already there. He stood on the opposite side of the room from Cam, silent with a flush on his cheeks. Jaxton wondered what had happened between the two, especially since

Marco was never quiet around women. Given the chance, he could charm the knickers off the Queen.

When Marco noticed them, he put on his customary smile, probably hoping to fool Jaxton. "Aislinn confirmed Camilla's story. Neena sent her here to patrol the area, along with two others."

Jaxton looked to Cam. "Will the other two be joining us?"

Cam narrowed her eyes at Marco before looking at Jaxton. "That depends. We need to talk, and preferably without your horny sidekick."

Marco's face turned even redder and Jaxton cleared his throat to avoid laughing. "Marco, do a scan of the nearby perimeter and see if you can find anybody else hiding nearby. Make sure to update Darius and Taka on the situation."

Marco said, "Right, boss," before muttering something in Spanish and exiting the room.

Cam's frown vanished and she crossed her arms over her chest before raising an eyebrow, the cue for him to start talking. But he ignored her, wanting to take care of Kiarra first.

He guided her to the couch, sat down next to her, and wrapped his arm around her shoulders. He told himself he was only keeping her close in case he needed to push her out of the way of danger, not because it felt right.

Kiarra leaned into his touch as if it were the only thing keeping her grounded, and when she placed a hand on his chest, Jaxton felt a flare of heat beneath her palm, similar to the heat he'd felt when he'd touched her bare skin at the foot of the stairs.

Focus, Jax. He squeezed Kiarra's shoulders and eyed the woman responsible for her unease.

Cam's gaze flitted to his arm around Kiarra's shoulders and then back to her sister's face. The two women stared at each other in silence. Jaxton decided he would have to be the mediator. "How did you get past our security?"

Cam switched her gaze to Jaxton. "That's not what I'm here to talk about. I wanted to warn you that a lot of people connected to the AMT, both official enforcers and hired hands, are heading this way. The Shadow-Shifter was just the first of many coming to try and haul Kiarra back to the AMT."

Shit. They'd been careful, but not careful enough. A thousand ideas formed in his head of how to handle the situation, but before he could ask Cam any more questions, Kiarra's brows drew together and she asked, "Why are so many coming after me? Is that normal for an AMT escapee?"

"No," Jaxton said, "it's not. They probably want you because of what you told me while training."

~~*

Kiarra had known the AMT would come after her, but she had never expected *Feiru* with strange abilities to be part of the retrieval team. It was almost as if the *Feiru* stories she'd heard as a child were coming to life.

She looked at her sister, but Cam's face was blank. It seemed strange that Cam wouldn't ask for the details behind Jaxton's cryptic response. As a child, her sister had always asked a zillion questions; the woman in front of her was a stranger.

Questions raced through Kiarra's brain, but she lacked the nerve to ask them. Instead, she focused on being practical. "How many people were sent after me and how much time do we have?"

"At least a dozen. And my latest intel suggests that the Shadow-Shifter was just a scout and the rest of the retrieval team will be here late tomorrow night." Cam looked at Jaxton and then back to Kiarra. "As much as I hate to admit it, I'm not in charge here. But I'd say we need to move quickly, in shifts. A single exodus will draw too much attention."

Kiarra looked to Jaxton, waiting to see if he would agree with Cam. He paused a moment before saying, "Where are Kiarra's parents?"

Kiarra froze. Jaxton gave her a squeeze, but never took his eyes off Cam. Part of her was grateful he'd asked what she'd been afraid to voice, but another part of her was afraid of the answer.

Cam's face softened a second before returning to her hard expression. "They died fourteen years ago."

Kiarra's heart skipped a beat. All this time, she'd just assumed her parents hadn't wanted her.

Yet a small part of her was afraid her parents had died because of Kiarra anyway, especially if they had tried to see her.

Jaxton rubbed up and down her arm, reminding her of where she was and how far she'd come in only a few days. The warmth of Jaxton's body, as well as the increasingly familiar scent of male and soap, reminded her that if she could stand up to him, she could certainly ask her long-lost sister a question. "How did they die?"

Cam shook her head. "You're not ready for the answer. But just know that they fought to get you back until the day they died."

Could she be telling the truth? Kiarra was afraid to hope.

Cam leaned forward and said, "I don't know what they told you inside the AMT, but Kiarra, our parents never stopped loving you."

Between the sad tone of Cam's voice and the flash of sadness in her eyes, Kiarra believed her.

She'd thought the worst about her family, yet she might have been wrong.

Yes, her parents had given her up, but if Cam was telling the truth, the possibility that they'd realized their mistake and fought to get her back brought tears to her eyes. Tears she didn't want anyone else to see.

Kiarra slipped out from under Jaxton's arm and flew to the doorway. She managed to race down the hall and up the stairs to her room without anyone stopping her. After reaching the safety of her room, she closed the door and let her tears fall.

After all these years, her parents might have wanted her after all.

CHAPTER TWELVE

Jaxton's first impulse was to follow Kiarra and see how she was doing, but he couldn't leave Cam alone without a guard. Marco might have confirmed Cam's story with Neena, but Jaxton hadn't. He wanted to know why Neena would send a team of people to his house, with AMT enforcers on the hunt, and not tell him.

He eyed Cam. At the very least, he needed to make sure Kiarra's sister would still be here when she was ready to talk with her.

Yet instead of making sure Cam would stick around, he said, "Kiarra's only been out of the AMT for a few days. I'm not sure she was ready for that."

Cam raised an eyebrow. "You're the one who brought it up."

"I'm her trainer, and as such, any remarks that would upset her should go through me."

"Do all trainers snuggle with their trainees in front of company?"

Cam's actions were borderline insubordination. "This is my operation. Neena sent you here and now you're under my command. I want to make sure we're clear on that."

Cam shrugged a shoulder. "It's not like you're going to send me away. We both know Kiarra would never forgive you if you did."

Jaxton stood up and stared down at Cam. "You haven't been in Kiarra's life for a very long time. You have no idea what she wants."

"And you do?"

He ignored her and looked directly into the security camera. "Send Marco down." He turned his attention back to Cam. "Marco will show you to your room and get you settled." Cam opened her mouth to protest, but Jaxton beat her to it. "Yes, Marco. He's going to be your guard until I get all of this sorted out."

"I can't promise you'll get him back in one piece."

"Alive is all I ask for. We'll meet back down here tomorrow at eight a.m. I'll give you your instructions then."

Marco walked into the room. "Yes, boss?"

"Show her to one of the extra rooms and stand guard."

"Sure thing." Marco turned toward Cam and put out a hand. "Shall we, my beauty?"

Satisfied that Cam was in safe hands, he ignored their bickering and headed up the stairs. Cam was a problem he could handle later; he wasn't about to let Kiarra relapse into the hesitant and scared woman from earlier, no matter what he had to do to prevent it.

He knocked, and without waiting for a response, opened Kiarra's door. Inside, Kiarra was on the bed curled on her side, facing the wall. The sight made him uncomfortable.

Before he could think of how to approach the situation, Kiarra said, "I didn't give you permission to enter. Get out of my room."

He took a few steps toward the bed. "Technically, this is my house."

She rolled over and glared. "I doubt you barge into Darius or Marco's rooms."

Her eyes were red and puffy from crying. Part of him wanted to comfort her like he'd done earlier and drag her close, but he ignored it. Jaxton was her trainer, and forcing her back into a routine would hopefully erase this backtracking of her progress. "They can take care of themselves. Until you can do the same, think of me as your shadow. I'm going to show up when you least expect it."

Kiarra rolled back toward the wall. "I can't do this right now, Jaxton. Just leave me alone."

"I know I said you could have the evening free, but I've changed my mind." He strode over and yanked the pillow from under her head. "You're eating dinner with me, so get up."

Kiarra made a noise of frustration, turned around, and sat up. "I know you're used to getting your way, but not this time." She reached for the pillow and tugged. "Give me back my pillow."

He tightened his grip. "No."

He tugged hard and pulled Kiarra up off the bed. She crashed into his chest before taking a step back and slapping him on the chest. "You're an asshole."

He pinned her hand against him. "If you're going to swear, you'd better bloody well try harder. My great-aunt could do better."

She curled her fingers into his chest, her nails biting through his shirt. "You're a fucking asshole."

"That's better. Ta for the compliment."

Kiarra stared at him with narrowed eyes. Neither one spoke, and despite the thin layer of material between his skin and hers, her touch seared his chest. She must have felt it too, because she darted a glance to her hand on his chest, her brows briefly drawing together.

He took a step toward her. Their bodies were now only a few inches apart. "You feel it too."

Kiarra looked up. "I don't know what you're talking about."

"Liar, and I'll prove it." He lifted his free hand to cup her cheek, the skin-to-skin contact sending a jolt through his body. She tried to hide her reaction, but her pupils dilated a fraction, betraying her emotions. "You sure your elemental fire is gone?

He rubbed his thumb against her soft cheek, the heat intensifying with each stroke—warm, but not unpleasant. Kiarra's hand relaxed against his chest. Somewhere in the back of his mind, Jaxton knew he should step away, but he convinced himself that this was the only way to solve the mystery of Kiarra's touch.

~~*

Each stroke of Jaxton's thumb left a trail of heat on her skin. She'd dismissed the same feeling during training, blaming her imagination and her yearnings for elemental fire. But the feeling had returned, and she wasn't sure what to make of it.

When she'd had her abilities, her fire had always radiated outward. She'd never heard of heat flaring at another person's touch.

Even now, she moved her hand a fraction to the south, hoping to feel the tingle of elemental fire particles. But nothing happened.

Jaxton's thumb stilled and she looked into his eyes. He continued to cup her cheek as he said, "Reaching to the south didn't work, did it?"

"How did you—"

The corner of his mouth rose in a half-smile. "I'm your shadow, remember? It's my job."

It's my job. Ty had said the same words to her after her flogging when she'd asked why he hadn't done anything to stop it.

The past was a cold slap in the face. She became acutely aware of Jaxton's touch and the scant inches separating their bodies. She'd walked this road before, allowing someone to get close to her before she really knew much about them. After Ty, she'd vowed never again.

She shook her head and tugged her hand. "Let me go."

Seeing something in her expression, Jaxton released her hand and allowed her to take a few steps away. She put a clenched fist over her heart, as if the act could protect it from the memories of betrayal.

"What's wrong, Kiarra?"

She avoided Jaxton's gaze and focused on tamping down the painful memories. After all these years, she'd thought herself past caring. Apparently, she was wrong.

She closed her eyes and breathed in and out, using the same trick that had helped keep her sanity over the years: visualizing her future. She pictured the freedom to travel, read, and interact with others who didn't see her as a freak or a burden. Her heart still racing, she took another inhalation and thought of returning to Mt. Rainier National Park, the possibility of friends, the ability to make her own decisions.

The hurt and panic faded, her good thoughts overcoming the bad. After a little more concentration, she finally pushed away the memories. She wouldn't let Ty's actions take away her new start; the man wasn't worth it.

Kiarra opened her eyes. Jaxton stood on the far side of the room, his arms crossed over his chest. He said nothing, his expression unreadable.

The silence was too much for her. "I'm fine." He raised an eyebrow and she continued, "At least, I will be, if you leave me alone for the rest of the evening."

He uncrossed his arms, the hardness of his face softening. "Are you sure you want to be alone right now?"

No. "Yes." She didn't trust herself around Jaxton.

He put his hands up in defeat. "I'll send a tray up and expect you to eat all of it. I'm also going to have someone periodically knock on your door, just to check on you." He motioned toward the alarm clock on the table next to the bed. "And set your alarm. Meet me in the front room at eight a.m. tomorrow morning."

She nodded, hoping Jaxton would leave before she lost her resolve. Earlier she'd taken comfort from his touch, and oddly, she yearned to feel it again. "You can go now."

He gave her one last long look before leaving her room.

Without his presence, the room felt empty and cold, but it was better this way. If she spent too much more time with Jaxton, her resolve would weaken, and she might do something foolish. One man had already betrayed her in the past.

Kiarra wasn't about to let it happen again.

~~*

Jaxton walked down the hall, his back ramrod straight, and tried to conceal his feelings. Seeing Kiarra nearly attacked had kicked in his protective instincts. Those he could dismiss; he was responsible for her and would do his duty. But the look on

107

Kiarra's face when she'd pushed him away in her room, the mixture of hurt and fear, had affected him in a way he didn't want to think about.

She may act more unaffected than his brother, but Kiarra had also been damaged inside the AMT—not just physically with the scars, but emotionally as well.

The urge to kill the bastard who'd hurt her still lingered. Judging by her reaction to their proximity and his touch, he reckoned it'd been a man who'd caused her so much pain. Since she'd been imprisoned as a child, the man in question must have been AMT staff. If he ever found out who was responsible, he'd teach the bastard a lesson.

Jaxton halted mid-step. That was taking his duty to protect her a little too far. He had his brother's recovery, Sinclair-related intelligence gathering and analysis, and new additions to his team to worry about. Why was he focusing so much on the feelings of one woman?

He shook his head to clear his thoughts. Kiarra was just one small part of his list of duties and responsibilities. He needed to stop neglecting the others.

He entered the room that served as their headquarters. Taka was inside, browsing some reports while monitoring the split-screen CCTV feed. The first box showed Darius and the Shadow-Shifter. The second, Marco sitting in a chair outside the room assigned to Cam with a tablet in his hand. The third showed the hallway containing Kiarra and Garrett's rooms, and the fourth displayed a split-screen view of the outside perimeter, flashing every few seconds to a different view.

Leaning down, Jaxton peered at the portion of the screen showing Darius, determined to distract himself from thoughts of

Kiarra. "Have we learned anything about the Shadow-Shifter yet?"

Taka leaned back in his chair. "She got tired of Darius calling her 'Miss Shadow' and screamed that her name was Vanessa. Other than that, she only said that others are coming and will free her."

"Nothing turned up when you searched her?"

"No. A pat-down found nothing, and Darius refused to strip search her. Marco started a scan through DEFEND's image database, but nothing has shown up so far."

Jaxton trusted Darius and would ask him later why he'd refused a strip search. "Any signs of the 'others' the Shadow-Shifter mentioned?"

"No. But I'll keep a watch on her and the others through the night." Taka turned toward Jaxton. "With the others coming, we'll have to flee. Where are you planning to take Kiarra?"

"Good question. What did Aislinn tell Marco earlier?"

Taka gave a half-shrug. "Just that she sent Cam here and that you needed to catch up on your sleep."

"Catch up on your sleep" was code for contacting Neena via the method she'd dubbed dream-speaking. "I will, but any word on when Kiarra's blood test results will be ready?"

"It'll take at least a few days. The person I talked with didn't quite know how to test for dormant or nullified elemental magic."

He'd suspected as much, but he had hoped to verify Kiarra's story sooner than that. "Right. I'm going to check in with the others and see if Darius can leave with the shifter tonight. This location has been compromised and we need to evacuate, but gradually, to draw away anyone who might be watching the house. That should give me better odds at escaping with Kiarra." He glanced one more time at the portion of the screen showing

Kiarra and Garrett's rooms. "After that, I'll try to get some sleep and see what I can find out. Keep an eye on Kiarra and Garrett until I'm done."

"Will do."

Jaxton left to talk with the others. This was the work he was supposed to be doing—managing a team, threading together information, and carrying out missions. He'd always been content with it in the past, so why did he have the urge to check on Kiarra one last time to make sure she was doing okay?

CHAPTER THIRTEEN

James Sinclair waited for Praveen Kumar, one of the local *Feiru* councilors of Southern India, to answer him.

It was several minutes before nine o'clock in the UK, making it nearly two a.m. in India, but considering Sinclair's leverage, Kumar had agreed to the late night teleconference.

Kumar finally put down the tablet he'd been watching and looked Sinclair dead in the eye. "So the last four years, and my two children, were nothing more than a lie? Why would you tell me about this now?"

"Because I need your unwavering support for my campaign." Sinclair gestured toward Kumar's tablet. "I'm the only one who knows where the files are being stored, so if you cooperate, I won't leak them and jeopardize your seat on the council."

Kumar glanced down at his tablet, which no doubt still showed a frozen video of his wife having sex with her lover. He glanced back to Sinclair. "And what will happen to Lavani?"

Sinclair shrugged. "That's your concern. I heard that she was paid to make you fall in love, marry her, and provide information for as long as it took. She succeeded. The person who hired her cares little what happens to her from now on."

Since Sinclair had been the one to pay Lavani, he knew the rumor to be true. Not that he'd ever implicate himself.

Kumar gripped the armrest of his chair. "Even if I wanted to keep this indiscretion a secret, I won't be able to get the other councilors on my side. Southern India is a powerful jurisdiction. The last thing the others want is to be seen as crazy conspiracy theorists, which is what will happen if we support your move to repeal Article I of the *Feiru* Five Laws."

Sinclair had known that and was prepared. He switched on the radio and said, "That's why I scheduled this meeting. Rhianna Hayes' report tonight should change your mind about the willingness of the other councilors."

The jingle for the nightly news program played and Sinclair motioned for Kumar to keep quiet and listen:

Thank you for joining us for the nine o'clock Nightly News with Rhianna Hayes. Now, to tonight's top story: Taking a Stance in Eastern Australia.

The year was 1953. Queen Elizabeth II's coronation in July had shown, with an estimated twenty million viewers in the UK alone, that televisions were becoming popular the world over. It was a time when many Feiru *lived in fear of a first-born being caught on camera using their elemental magic. With the horrors of World War II still fresh in their minds, many* Feiru *were afraid that the use of elemental abilities might scare the humans into a possible war, genocide, or worse. Something needed to be done before public hysteria destroyed the* Feiru *way of life.*

Enter the Head Council's debate to amend Article III of the Feiru *Five Laws. They finally ruled that first-borns were considered a danger to* Feiru *society, and the formerly experimental AMT system became mandatory. Since the threat of humans discovering elemental magic was no longer an issue—the first-borns were safe and secure inside the AMT compounds— peace and calm returned to our society, and the* Feiru *managed to prosper once again.*

Nearly sixty years after amending Article III, with Feiru *poverty and unemployment rates on the rise, some argue that our society is facing a similar tipping point that requires action. One of the people who shares this opinion is the local head councilor of Eastern Australia, Dean Kelly. Here is what Councilor Kelly said at a press conference earlier today:*

"Over the past two years, our local council has conducted research, interviewed our constituents, and consulted economic and financial experts. We've dedicated a large amount of our time to this effort, not wanting to dismiss any idea, no matter how unconventional, that would help steer us toward the most successful future possible for our people.

"After hours and weeks of debate and discussion, we have arrived at an important conclusion: we can no longer hide our existence from humans if we wish to thrive and be successful. We must be able to help steer global economic and political policy if we are to keep our people out of poverty and the Feiru *identity alive.*

"In order to accomplish this, I'm proud to say that the Local Feiru Council of Eastern Australia supports the repeal of Article I and will do everything in its power to help achieve that goal."

Over the last few months, comments have emerged about the effectiveness of repealing Article I, primarily from fringe and minor economists. The Council of Northern Brazil made a statement similar to Councilor Kelly's last month, but they were quickly dismissed as a one-time anomaly. But with the addition of another large local council——the Council of Eastern Australia, responsible for four hundred thousand Feiru—*the Head Council may be forced to start discussing the merits and pitfalls of repealing Article I. Change in itself is difficult, especially when we have lived our entire lives believing one way. Is now the time to step out of the shadows and confront the human world, like our ancestors before us?*

113

When the broadcast moved on to the latest developments in America, Sinclair switched off the radio and raised an eyebrow. "Well? Eastern Australia is also a powerful jurisdiction. That announcement—in addition to the talking points I provided—should be enough to convince your other council members to follow suit."

Kumar's face was expressionless. "I'll see what I can do."

The screen went blank.

Lavani wasn't the only one keeping tabs on Kumar; Sinclair's other contact would report the councilor's actions over the next few days.

Since that was done, Sinclair focused on another thread in the overall web of his plan, one that could be problematic if his contact didn't follow through on his promise.

After all, Sinclair hadn't had an update from Dr. Ty Adams in nearly a week.

Adams had been working on a formula for years that nullified elemental abilities. The first success story had spurned a larger trial group, and the results were promising. Adams had assured Sinclair that he needed a little more time to test the formula's effectiveness before he could shift into mass production. He'd promised to give a full report within the next few weeks.

However, after previously receiving daily updates, the sudden lack of communication made Sinclair wonder if something had gone wrong. The formula was a pivotal part of a later phase of his R&C campaign. If the formula was failing, Sinclair needed to know so he could adjust his strategy accordingly. He hadn't spent the last ten years working toward this point only to have some scientist ruin everything.

Sinclair opened his email program, but finding nothing from Adams, he took out his cell phone, scrolled through the contacts, and pressed call.

CHAPTER FOURTEEN

Jaxton stood near the edge of a rock formation, its jagged edge pointing toward the valley below. The contrast of the dark rock and the rolling green fields was one of his favorite sights. Twilight gave it an eerie quality, the pinks and purples in the sky making it magical and formidable simultaneously.

He was back in England, standing on Hen Cloud, near his childhood home in the Peak District.

Turning around, Jaxton saw two figures standing farther down the hill with their heads together, talking. Curious, Jaxton walked down the hill. The outlines of the two people took shape and he could just make out two females, one with blonde hair and the other dark.

He approached them, but even when he was no more than ten or fifteen feet away, the women's faces remained blurry. He called out a greeting and the women raised their faces, linked their arms together, and walked toward him. Soon he recognized their faces and froze.

The fair-haired one was Garrett's ex-fiancée Marzina, and the dark-haired one was Kiarra.

Jaxton took a step forward, but the women took a step back. Each time Jaxton tried to reach out and pull Kiarra away from Marzina, they backed just out of his reach.

"Kiarra," he shouted, but his voice was lost to the sudden wind. He tried running down the rock hill, but the women continued to move farther away until they eventually walked off the sheer side of the hill. Jaxton shouted Kiarra's name as he dove for her, but he was too far away to save her. His heart pounded as he reached the edge of the drop-off and looked down. He steeled himself for the worst, but saw nothing unusual. No bodies, no blood, only the wilderness.

Jaxton heard a snap of fingers behind him and the scenery shifted to the inside of a cave. He turned around and saw a woman dressed in rambling gear.

Neena.

His consciousness was trained to notice her, and Jaxton realized none of this was real. He was in a dream.

He remembered why he was here.

Neena took out a plastic sandwich bag, opened it, and offered it to Jaxton. "Trail mix?"

Jaxton shook his head and got straight to the point. "A Shadow-Shifter compromised our safe house. Marco said you needed to speak to me, so I'm waiting for your orders."

Neena tossed a handful of trail mix into her mouth, and with her mouth half-full, said, "Have you asked Cam and Kiarra about their uncle?"

"Their uncle? What does that have to do with relocating my men?"

Neena waved a hand in the air. "You should know by now not to question me. Ask them about their uncle. And while you're at it, work a little harder at stoking Kiarra's fire." Neena winked. "I mean her elemental magic, of course."

"She lost the ability, or at least believes she did. She can't gather fire."

Neena tossed more trail mix into her mouth. "Nonsense. A Fire Talent can most certainly gather fire. It's right there in the title."

Jaxton's heart skipped a beat. "Kiarra's a Fire Talent?"

Neena tilted her head. "Stop shadowing me. That's what I just said, isn't it?" She tucked her trail mix away and adjusted the straps on her pack. "Ask the Melini sisters about their uncle and you'll know where to take Kiarra. Going alone with her is best." Neena moved toward the cave's exit, but stopped and said over her shoulder, "Oh, and get to work on releasing

*Kiarra's magic. You're usually quicker than this with assignments and I
really hate waiting around for something so simple."*

Neena snapped her fingers.

Jaxton shot up in his bed and tried to get his head around
what Neena had just told him.

He was one of the few who knew that Neena possessed
more than one latent ability. One was dream-speaking, but the
other one was more powerful, and if it ever became public
knowledge, Neena would be forced into hiding.

Neena was the first Feiru in nearly a thousand years who
could see visions of the future.

That was why Jaxton took her words seriously. If she said
Kiarra was a Fire Talent, then it was probably because Neena had
seen it in a vision. He didn't try to comprehend why Neena hadn't
told him about this earlier. Neena worked to her own beat;
Aislinn was the only one who could even come close to
controlling her.

He'd talk again with Neena later. All that mattered at the
present was the fact that Kiarra had lied to him about her
elemental fire.

~~*

Kiarra had slept poorly, but rather than toss and turn or
stare at her ceiling all morning, she got out of bed early and
checked on Garrett.

She needed a distraction, and Garrett had been the perfect
excuse. When she looked at him, she felt nothing but concern for
his health and a desire to help him. A huge contrast to how she
felt about his younger brother.

Spending half the night lying awake, she replayed events from the day: Jaxton's touch, the way he needled her to forget about her troubles, the odd flares of heat between them. She tried getting up to read, but after staring at the same page for ten minutes, she gave up and gone back to bed.

Eventually, she fell asleep, but was plagued by images of him nipping at her lower lip before kissing his way down her throat to her breast, where he took her nipple into his mouth and sucked hard.

Even remembering it made her skin tingle and her lower body tighten. It might have been ten years since she'd last had sex, but her body still remembered the feeling.

Garrett moaned, snapping Kiarra out of her sex dream to focus back on his care. Even as Garrett calmed while she hummed, he continued muttering unintelligible nonsense. The only word that she understood was a name: Marzina.

Then, out of the blue, he clutched the blankets and mumbled, "Why did you betray me, love?"

She nearly stopped humming at the heartbreak behind his words.

It seemed that Garrett had also had a rough time of it. First he'd been betrayed by someone he trusted, then broken by experimental trials too horrible to ponder. She hummed louder, and Garrett calmed again.

He was only one out of hundreds, if not thousands, of first-borns who'd been abused and broken under the AMT system.

Kiarra would never forget the first broken person she'd seen inside the AMT.

On the way back from her yearly medical exam, she'd walked by a girl no more than fourteen, with a vacant expression, scratches covering her neck, and scabs on her head where her hair

119

had been torn out. Her hands had even been tied to her sides to prevent her from harming herself further.

As a guard escorted her down the hall, the girl had slipped free for a few precious seconds to ram her head against a steel doorframe. Hard. While Kiarra had been shut back into her cell before the girl had died, the news had traveled fast. F-368 had died within minutes of the event—some said with a smile on her face.

After watching the girl's actions, Kiarra decided to fight for her sanity and find a way out. The dead girl's family, and others like hers, needed to know what was happening inside the Cascade F-block. The High Council might be using fear to "persuade" parents to give up their children, but Kiarra wanted to believe parents would fight the cruelty she'd seen——if they only knew about it.

She'd only changed her mind and attempted to kill herself when staying alive would have caused more harm than good. But since she was out of the AMT, surrounded by people who might even help her, Kiarra was once again determined to expose the AMT's actions. She needed to become stronger, build a network, and find a way to attack the issue.

Once Kiarra was sure Garrett wouldn't wake back up, she eased out of his room and went to hers.

Garrett had reminded her of what was important. She would forget about what had happened with Jaxton and what Cam had told her about their parents. Too many people needed her help, but in order to help them, she needed to focus on training and becoming strong enough to have a chance of success.

She looked through the clothes Neena had given her and was deciding what to wear when someone banged on the door. The handle turned, but the door was locked.

There was another pound on the door before she heard a shout.

"Kiarra, let me in."

~~*

Jaxton needed to calm the fuck down.

But he had every right to be pissed off. The periodic emergence of the Four Talents was always followed by one thing: some sort of catastrophic disaster. And not just any kind of disaster, but one that threatened not only the existence of both humans and Feiru, but also the exposure of elemental magic.

Each of the Four Talents was a master of their element to such a degree they could both heal and destroy; all other first-borns only had the ability to do one or the other.

There was only one Talent for each of the elements, meaning that Kiarra would be the Fire Talent. He had no idea about the identities of the Earth, Water, and Wind Talents, but since Jaxton knew the Talents' abilities were emerging, DEFEND would have to find the remaining three.

Never before had all Four Talents been gathered in time to fully prevent whatever was coming; they could only stop it from worsening. The Black Death in the 14th century had been a case in point.

The increasing appearance of latent abilities—dormant and rare powers that only emerged when the Talents awoke—also made sense. The Four Talents needed the equivalent of a Secret Service to keep them alive. Many Feiru would do anything to have a Talent under their influence, especially in the current politically charged times. This made the Four Talents targets.

121

Maybe the AMT enforcers were after Kiarra because she was a Talent. It would have been easy enough to condition her to believe that her abilities were gone, allowing the AMT to reawaken them when needed.

The lock clicked and Kiarra opened the door a crack, but after one look at his face, she retreated into her room.

The sight of her face once again flared his anger. Jaxton pushed his way into her room and cornered Kiarra against a wall with his arms. "You've been lying to me," he said coolly, proud to sound more civilized than he felt.

Kiarra didn't flinch from his gaze. "Care to tell me what I'm supposed to be lying about?"

He leaned in closer. "Stop playing games with me, Kiarra. I know you can gather fire."

She poked his chest with her finger. "I already told you, I can't."

"And you're still lying to me."

Kiarra stilled and narrowed her eyes. "Not being able to feel the elemental energy in the air is like being forced to breathe through your mouth. You can do it, but it doesn't feel quite right." She raised her chin. "Wait for the test results from my blood. You can apologize to me later."

Either she was a good actress or the AMT had done a good job of making her believe that her fire was truly gone.

Threats and intimidation were going to get him nowhere. Hell, she'd grown used to them as part of her training and reconditioning. If he wanted the truth, he'd have to think of a clever way to trick her when she least expected it. But it wasn't the time.

He needed to get the Melini sisters together and ask about their uncle.

Leaning close, he stated, "You'll tell me the truth eventually." He dropped his arms from the wall, no longer caging Kiarra. "But in the meantime, we're going downstairs to talk with your sister. She's waiting for us now."

If Kiarra was confused about the topic change, she didn't show it. "I'm in desperate need of a shower. And I'm not going anywhere with you until you calm down and start making sense." Kiarra slipped to the side and headed toward the bathroom.

Jaxton's arm shot out and he grabbed her wrist. "This can't wait. The longer we stay here, the more dangerous it becomes. Do you want the AMT to catch you?" Kiarra pulled her arm, but his grip was firm. "This is your last chance to come willingly." He gave a tug, careful not to hurt her. "Either way, you're going downstairs with me."

What Kiarra did next was unexpected—she dropped down and sat cross-legged on the floor. "Somebody needs to teach you some manners. You can't just bully me into doing whatever you want. I will go downstairs after my shower."

~~*

Kiarra knew she was being childish, sitting on the floor like a toddler, but something had stoked Jaxton's temper and he wouldn't listen to anything she said.

Why was he so convinced she was lying?

She raised an eyebrow at Jaxton. "I can do this all day."

"Pet, I only spend the day in a woman's bedroom if she invites me to do more than hold hands, and somehow, I don't think that's the case here."

Kiarra's skin flushed at the implication of his words. But before she could get her voice working again, Jaxton grabbed her other arm and pulled her upright. A second later, he tossed her over his shoulder.

She squealed before the air was knocked out of her. "You've crossed the line from unreasonable to insane."

"I gave you fair warning but you ignored it." Jaxton patted her ass. "I can be immature too. If you want down, use your fire. Otherwise, enjoy the ride."

"I already told you, I don't have any magic. If I did, you'd be toast by now."

"Then this is a missed opportunity because right now, I give you permission to set my arse on fire."

Kiarra made a noise at the back of her throat. "'Fucking asshole' isn't strong enough to describe your behavior."

Jaxton patted her ass again before he started walking. As annoyed as she was, she still felt the searing heat of his hand through her clothes. Kiarra clutched Jaxton's shirt and forced herself to ignore it. She needed to find a way to get down.

With each step Jaxton took, Kiarra felt his shoulder blade jab into her stomach. She snaked an arm behind her and tried to grab Jaxton's throat, but he caught her hand and twisted it behind her. The hand on her ass moved to hold it in place. Shit.

Next, she tried kicking him with her knee, but his torso was like a wall covered in muscle, and Jaxton acted like he didn't feel a thing. He then jostled her like a sack of potatoes.

"If that's all you've got," he said, with another jostle, "you clearly haven't been paying attention to my lessons."

"Just be glad I can't gather elemental fire right now, or you wouldn't be sitting comfortably for weeks."

Jaxton entered the front room, and Kiarra saw Marco sitting in a chair off to the side. Marco grinned and said, "Are we in for some X-rated action?"

Kiarra glared and Marco laughed. She heard Cam's voice say, "The only X you need to be worried about is an x-ray. Leave my sister alone, you skeevy man-child."

"Stop fighting it, Camilla. Your words are your armor, but I know you secretly lust after me."

Cam growled before Jaxton's voice rumbled against Kiarra's belly. "Enough." He tossed Kiarra on the couch next to Cam. "On Neena's orders, we have DEFEND-related things to discuss."

Cam focused back on cleaning her nails with a knife and said, "Jaxton, this is your warning. Treat my sister with more respect in the future or I'll be forced to use my knife on a tender part of your anatomy."

Kiarra smiled and tried not to gloat. Cam was on her side, no questions asked; maybe they would have a sisterly relationship one day.

Crossing his arms over his chest, Jaxton looked down at Kiarra and Cam on the couch. "At Neena's request, you two need to tell me about your uncle."

Kiarra frowned. What did he have to do with anything? She was going to have to contact Neena in order to start making sense of Jaxton's actions, because he sure as hell wasn't going to be forthright with her.

Cam stopped cleaning her nails, looked at Kiarra, and raised an eyebrow in question. Kiarra shook her head. "I don't remember much about either one."

"How many are there?" Jaxton asked.

"Two," Kiarra answered.

Jaxton looked at Cam. "Tell me about them."

Cam focused back on cleaning her nails. "Only if you ask nicely."

Kiarra grinned and Jaxton shot her a look. Kiarra raised an eyebrow, as if saying, See? I'm not the only one who thinks you need some manners.

She swore she heard Jaxton mumble something about Melini women before he said, "Would you please do me the favor of telling me about your uncles, Ms. Melini?"

"I don't like your tone, but I'll forgive it this one time for Neena's sake." Cam laid her knife across her thigh. "We have two uncles. Their names are Alexander and James Sinclair."

Marco sat up in his chair. "The James Sinclair?"

"Yes."

A look passed between Marco and Jaxton that Kiarra didn't understand. "What are you not telling me?"

~~*

Bloody hell. Her uncle was James Sinclair.

All of Jaxton's assigned research on the man seemed too much of a coincidence, which meant Neena had been planning this for years.

He had Sinclair's nieces sitting right in front of him.

Judging from Kiarra's face, she had no idea who Sinclair was or what he was trying to do. Since Cam remained silent, Jaxton explained at least some of it to Kiarra. "James Sinclair works with the Feiru High Council and is influential with Feiru politicians the world over. He is one of the driving forces behind tightening and enforcing first-born policies. We believe he's pushing to have first-borns locked up from the moment of birth to prevent any sort of familial attachment."

Kiarra blinked. "My...uncle...wants to lock away babies?"

Jaxton's earlier irritation and anger eased at the disbelief and horror he saw on Kiarra's face. He almost went to her, but Cam beat him to it.

"Don't call him uncle." Cam patted Kiarra's arm. "Save it for Uncle Alex, who deserves the title."

As Cam comforted her sister, Jaxton tried to make sense of the million thoughts currently racing through his head.

For years, Jaxton had been sorting through intelligence, hoping for more concrete information and evidence he could use against Sinclair. But at the end of the day, he'd had to work with whatever had been brought to him.

But he had Sinclair's niece.

Between what had happened to his brother and Kiarra's scars, Jaxton would never allow the AMT to take another firstborn from him if he could help it. Still, neither Sinclair nor those close to him would know that, meaning Jaxton had some leverage. He just might be able to use Kiarra to get the evidence he needed.

Suddenly Neena's words, about knowing what to do, made sense. "Kiarra and I will leave for Edinburgh in the morning."

"Edinburgh?" Kiarra echoed.

"The High Council's base moved there from Accra a few years ago, and Sinclair goes where the High Council goes. Getting to Sinclair is impossible, but I might be able to find some of his closest followers and get the information Neena and Aislinn have been searching for."

And find a way to use Kiarra to his advantage, although Jaxton didn't say that part.

Cam picked up the knife on her thigh and sheathed it. "Then I'm going with you."

Jaxton shook his head. "No, Neena said Kiarra and I must go alone."

Cam stared at him at length before finally nodding. He was relieved when she didn't argue. They both knew she could easily check with Neena to confirm Jaxton's words.

When Neena gave an order, it was best to follow it. To understand that meant Kiarra's sister had been with DEFEND for some time.

"I don't like it, boss," Marco piped in from the corner. "You'll need backup."

Marco implied Jaxton would be spending all of his energy protecting Kiarra, and Marco was right. But maybe, just maybe, something would spark Kiarra's elemental fire.

Jaxton's knee-jerk reaction earlier may have been an overreaction at the thought of Kiarra lying to him. Messing with her DNA could have caused her abilities to become dormant. Or she'd been tricked into believing they were. However, no matter what Kiarra believed about her abilities, Neena was never wrong.

"Marco's right," Kiarra said. "I'm more of a liability than an asset. No matter how much I dislike you at the moment, I can't protect you if something goes wrong, Jaxton. And I won't have that on my conscience."

Kiarra wants to protect me? "Don't worry, pet, we'll figure something out."

"What will happen to Garrett? He needs special care and attention right now." Kiarra leaned forward. "Who will look after him?"

Jaxton felt a stab of guilt, but knew he'd find a way to make it up to his brother. "We'll meet up with Amma and she'll take care of him." He briefly explained how Amma often treated many AMT escapees and helped them to rehabilitate to life outside the AMT.

Kiarra frowned. "Do you trust her?"

128

"Yes." Although Jaxton didn't know exactly how Garrett would react to Amma's care. "You have the rest of the morning to pack. We'll leave with Garrett after lunch." He switched his gaze to Cam. "If I leave you two alone, can I trust you to stay put?"

"Like I would upset Neena."

Jaxton nodded. "Good. Then take this time to answer some of Kiarra's questions." Before Cam could reply, he motioned for Marco to follow him.

He exited the room, not wanting to dwell on the guilt pricking his conscience. The guilt was two-fold—one part for handing over the care of his brother to Amma, the other part for feeling jealous of Kiarra's concern for Garrett.

He hoped once they reached Scotland, he could delegate most of Kiarra's training to his sister, who was also a member of DEFEND, so he could focus on Sinclair. Kiarra was becoming too much of a distraction.

CHAPTER FIFTEEN

Kiarra's life had become an emotional roller coaster. Inside the AMT, she'd known what to expect from one day to the next and had been able to control her emotions accordingly. Now, decisions were made at the drop of a hat to send her off to a different continent. No one asked for her opinion; they just expected her to go without a word.

Then Jaxton had disappeared before she'd had a chance to protest, leaving her alone with a sister she'd written off years ago. Cam may have defended her with Jaxton, but Kiarra knew next to nothing about the woman sitting next to her. Cam was a stranger.

Still, this might be the only chance she ever had to get answers. Life inside the AMT had taught her to never take things for granted, and this was something she needed to do, no matter how painful the memories.

She turned toward her younger sister and again faced the scars and unreadable face from the night before. She wondered about Cam's past, but Kiarra was afraid of where those questions might lead, so she started with something safer. "When did you start working with DEFEND?"

"Four years ago." Cam placed her sheathed knife inside a pocket. "Uncle Alex thought it'd be the best chance for me to find you."

Kiarra vaguely remembered her uncle, but she'd never pictured him as the type of person to be connected to an organization like DEFEND. "He made you join DEFEND?"

Cam shook her head. "No, but in my early twenties, Uncle Alex suggested it since he had some contacts within DEFEND. I needed a change and he wanted me to go somewhere that would keep me out of trouble. I tried out, passed the preliminary tests, and here I am."

She wondered what kind of "trouble" Cam had gotten into. Cam was keeping something from her, but Kiarra was in no position to push. Just hearing that someone had looked for her made Kiarra's heart swell. Yet one person was blindingly absent from Cam's answers, so she asked, "What about our brother?"

Cam's lips thinned into a line. "That's another reason you need to find James Sinclair."

"What does that have to do with Giovanni?"

"Sinclair has him."

Her heart skipped a beat. "What?"

"We were split up when our parents died. Uncle Alex tried to win Gio's custody, but failed. Sinclair wanted an heir, and Gio was the perfect solution since he wasn't a first-born who could tarnish his reputation."

Kiarra was afraid to ask her next question. "Does Gio share Sinclair's views?"

Cam leaned forward. "I believe there's hope for him yet, but we need to get him away from Sinclair. Do whatever Neena asks of you, but find a way to get Gio out before it's too late, before Sinclair takes away another member of our family."

Kiarra frowned. "What do you mean before he takes away another member of our family?"

Cam sat back and crossed her arms over her chest. Kiarra thought she wasn't going to answer, but finally Cam answered, "James Sinclair murdered our parents."

Kiarra's stomach dropped. "How?"

Cam looked Kiarra straight in the eye. "He staged their deaths to look like a car accident, but a few years ago, I found a witness who knew the truth. Renee and Arturo Melini had become liabilities with their anti-AMT actions, so Sinclair took care of it."

"But our mom was James Sinclair's sister. Why would he want to kill his own sister?"

Cam's face hardened. "If there's one thing you need to remember, it's this: blood doesn't necessary make a family. Ambition and power change people in unpredictable ways."

"But our mother was his younger sister…" Cam's face looked too much like what Kiarra remembered of their mother, forcing her to look away.

"Kiarra." At the command in Cam's voice, Kiarra looked back. "The man does whatever it takes to get what he wants. Even members of the High Council are afraid of him. Our mother was just another obstacle, just like you will become the moment he discovers you escaped from the AMT."

She was now an even bigger burden to Jaxton, Neena, and all of the others trying to protect her. "Cam, I can't go alone with Jaxton. I don't want him or anyone else to get hurt because of me."

Cam put a hand on Kiarra's shoulder and squeezed. "Neena does things for a reason. I trust her, and whether you'll take my word on the matter or not, I'm not going to interfere, just keep an eye on you as best as I can. Jaxton owes Neena a debt for his brother, and he'll see it through."

From what Kiarra had learned of Jaxton over the last few days, he would see his debt through, even if it took his life.

Still, she was tired of being helpless; she wanted her elemental fire back.

She reached out to the south, but felt nothing. Cam looked at her outstretched hand and said, "What happened to your fire, Kiarra?"

Her instinct told her to tell her sister the truth. "The AMT messed with my DNA and took it away." Cam's face hardened so Kiarra changed the topic to avoid upsetting her further. "Everyone keeps saying to trust Neena, but I learned the hard way not to rely on one person when it comes to your own safety. What if it doesn't all work out? I can't protect myself, let alone anyone else."

Cam stood and pulled Kiarra to her feet. "I know trust takes time, so in the meantime, we need to ease your fears and teach you a way to protect yourself." She took out a small handgun and gave it to Kiarra. "We have a few hours, and I'm going to show you how to use this."

~~*

Jaxton had left Kiarra alone with Cam, confident that the two wouldn't try to escape. While the two sisters had their own issues to deal with, leaving Cam with Kiarra had freed up Marco. Darius had found a way to secure the Shadow-Shifter for transport and had left last night, so only Marco and Taka stood in front of him in the CCTV monitoring room.

He'd filled them in on the relationship between Kiarra, Cam, and James Sinclair. It was time for Jaxton to send his remaining men and new charges on assignment. They would have to scatter, but he wasn't about to waste their skills by merely sending them into hiding. "While Kiarra and I head to Edinburgh, I need you two to take care of some business. The Four Talents have appeared and we need to find them."

The room was quiet, each man taking in Jaxton's words. While he knew them well enough to know they wouldn't think he was crazy, even he had needed a moment to digest the news earlier.

Taka crossed his arms over his chest. "Do we know who any of them are yet?"

Relief filled Jaxton at their trust in him. "Neena has confirmed the identity of the Fire Talent, but we need to find the other three."

Taka made the leap. "It's Kiarra, isn't it?"

Jaxton nodded. "I know accompanying her alone to Edinburgh is risky, but I'm not about to defy Neena's orders."

The men murmured their assent before Marco rubbed his hands together. "Does this mean we get to go to Chichen Itza?"

In the legends about the Four Talents, the *Feiru* High Council had a designated meeting place for a Talent to go and leave a mark or message for the other Talents to find. The designated message center had changed over the centuries, but in the most recent legends of the Four Talents, the designated site had been Chichen Itza, the ruins of a once great Mayan city in southern Mexico.

Since the advent of the AMT, the *Feiru* High Council no longer designated sites as message centers. But if any of the other Talents had awoken, there was a chance that one of them would leave a clue at the last known site—Chichen Itza. "Since Marco speaks Spanish, I'll be sending him to Chichen Itza." Marco did a fist-pump in the air, but Jaxton put up a hand to stall his celebration. "Cam and her team will investigate the ruins while you stay out of sight and watch their backs."

Marco's excitement died. "Boss, you can't be serious. We barely know anything about Camilla, and I've never met her team. I doubt they'll listen to orders from me."

"They won't have to because you and Cam will be on separate assignments, with overlapping but different objectives. Basically, Cam won't know you'll be shadowing her." He hadn't discussed it with Cam, but Jaxton had a feeling Kiarra's sister wouldn't mind heading a mission. He'd checked her records and Camilla Melini had a high mission-success rate. "I'll go over more of the details with you before I leave at lunchtime."

Marco looked like he wanted to say more, but merely nodded.

"What about me?" Taka asked.

"Taka, I need you to find someone with access to the experiments inside the F-block and find out what you can from them, especially regarding the suspected lead researcher, Dr. Ty Adams. We need to know if they're aware that Kiarra's a Talent. Also, check to see if they've found any of the others."

Taka nodded and said, "I have a few contacts I can reach out to who might be able to help."

"Use only those you trust, and most of all, swear them to secrecy. I don't want the AMT or any of Adams' lackeys to find out what we're up to." He looked at both of the men in turn. "Report progress to Neena as often as you can. She'll help if she's able, but for the most part, you're on your own this time. If anything goes horribly wrong, contact me or the others, and we'll see what we can do to help. It doesn't matter if we're scattered around the world; we're still a team."

Taka and Marco murmured their agreement and Jaxton realized they'd been heading toward this crossroads for quite some time. Darius and Taka had been more than ready for missions of their own, and while Marco seemed inexperienced, the young man had surprised him once or twice in the past.

Taka, Darius, and Marco were more than merely his team; they were his friends. Yet as much as he wanted to help them, he would have to trust them to take care of themselves. Someone else needed his help more.

~~*

A few hours later, Kiarra stood in the front hallway and faced her sister, trying to find the words to say goodbye.

Cam had spent their short time together teaching Kiarra the basics of handgun operation and safety. The task had given both women something to talk about. In a reverse from their childhood, Kiarra had been the one asking Cam a million questions; her younger sister currently knew more about the world than Kiarra did.

While going to Edinburgh with Jaxton and helping DEFEND was what needed to be done, a small part of her wanted to be selfish. After all this time, she wanted to stay and get to know her sister.

Marco strutted out from the shadows, stopped in front of Kiarra, and took her hand with a flourish before kissing it. She couldn't help but smile at the man's ridiculous actions.

Marco straightened with an exaggerated look of heartbreak on his face. "Our time together has been too short, but rest assured, I will keep an ear out for both you and your sister, just to make sure you're both safe. The world can't afford to lose two smart, sexy beauties such as yourselves."

She glanced over at Cam and tried not to laugh at her sister's bored expression.

She looked back to Marco. "I think Cam can take care of herself. I'm more worried about you."

"Me?"

Kiarra's smile widened. She'd heard Cam and Marco were being sent to the jungles of Latin America on separate missions. "I think that without a challenge like my sister, your ego will inflate to uncontrollable proportions. And smart, sexy women don't like that."

Marco laughed. "I really hope Jaxton doesn't scare you off."

Kiarra heard a grunt behind her before Jaxton said, "Hurry it up. Do you want to waste your time saying goodbye to Marco or to your sister? You have three minutes until we leave."

Kiarra frowned at his grumpy tone, but she was far from intimidated. "We'll leave when I'm done, not before."

Before Jaxton could reply, Cam touched Kiarra's elbow, garnering her attention. "No, he's right. Taka left a few hours ago to try and draw away any nearby AMT enforcers, but the longer you stick around, the greater the chance they'll figure out Taka was a decoy."

"Cam…"

Cam shook her head. "Save it. We'll see each other soon enough. Just remember what I taught you, and try not to get captured. I don't want to wait another fifteen years to see my sister."

Kiarra nodded, afraid if she opened her mouth, she'd start to cry.

She started to turn away, but Cam grabbed her hand and squeezed. She murmured, "Be safe, Kiarra," before letting go and heading up the stairs.

Willing herself not to think about Cam, she focused on putting her belongings into the car and helping Jaxton and Marco load Garrett into the back seat. They'd drugged Garrett unconscious again, and she could tell Jaxton didn't like it—he was being terse and disagreeable with her.

When they finally drove away, she stared out the window, watching the green forest go by in a blur, pointedly ignoring Jaxton.

Yet her thoughts kept drifting to what Cam had told her about their brother. She shouldn't feel guilty about it, but for some reason, she felt awful about withholding the information about Gio from Jaxton.

Cam had said nothing about keeping the information a secret, but Kiarra's gut told her to wait. If she told Jaxton about her brother, he would mostly likely order her to forget about him until they'd finished their mission with James Sinclair. But by then, it might be too late. The longer it took to find Sinclair and get the information Jaxton was looking for, the higher the chance that Gio would be heavily involved with Sinclair's operations, especially since Cam had said that Sinclair treated Gio as his heir.

If there was any chance of Kiarra persuading her brother to change sides, it had to be sooner rather than later.

She felt Jaxton's eyes on her and she looked over to see him staring. "What?" she asked.

He focused his eyes back on the road and said nothing. He checked the rearview mirror again. Kiarra looked over her shoulder at Garrett, slumped in his seat, and felt her heart constrict a little. The sight couldn't be an easy one for Jaxton.

After being reunited with Cam, she had an inkling of what it was like to want to protect a sibling. "It must be killing you to give up your brother so soon after all the time you spent looking for him."

Jaxton's grip on the steering wheel tightened. "I have complete faith in Amma getting him rehabilitated."

"But?"

"But I wish I could help him, especially since it was my fault he was captured."

CHAPTER SIXTEEN

Giovanni Sinclair walked past his adopted father's assistant and knocked on the door. A muffled reply bid him to enter.

His father had requested his presence, and when James Sinclair called, you came. Those who disobeyed him were ruined. Sometimes they even disappeared.

Or so went the rumors.

His classmates had always given him a wide berth because of the rumors about his father, seldom inviting him out to the pub or to play sports, but over the years, Gio had learned to accept it. Few knew the truth of his father's hard work and sacrifice to ensure that all *Feiru* had the same rights and opportunities as humans. Only in the last few years had his father's quest to repeal Article I gained traction.

Gio himself believed in the importance of changing the antiquated *Feiru* law, but despite his best efforts to prove he could be an asset to his father's work, Sinclair had never tapped him to help in his plans. Sinclair rarely visited London, and Gio saw him even less. Not even his undergraduate work at Oxford or his recent acceptance into the law program at University College London had been enough to attract his father's attention.

Which made today's call to meet all the more mysterious.

Stepping inside his father's office, Gio kept his face blank, aware that his father saw emotion as a weakness. "You wanted to see me?"

James Sinclair nodded. "Yes, son, take a seat."

Gio settled into the large cushioned chair in front of his father's desk and Sinclair got right to the point. "Over the last few years, I've allowed you to dabble in university and the law, but you need to put all of that on hiatus. I have other plans for you."

He kept his face impassive, not wanting to get his hopes up. "What kind of plans?"

"We'll get to that in a minute." Sinclair leaned back in his chair. "First, tell me what you know of my work."

Gio suspected that this was some kind of test, but while some would opt to brown-nose, he knew his father appreciated honesty. "You support the repeal of Article I and wish to contain all elemental abilities. I know you're using politics to achieve the first aim, but I'm not entirely certain how you plan to reach the second."

Sinclair nodded. "And how do you feel about those aims?"

After he finished his schooling, Gio wanted to become a Member of Parliament. As things stood now, two things prevented that: Article I and first-born abilities. "I would do anything if I could to repeal Article I. You know I want to be an MP, but that's impossible until the law changes."

Sinclair nodded. "And what about the first-borns? What do you think should be done with them?"

He shrugged. "As long as they're treated well inside the AMT compounds, I care little what else happens to them."

"What if there was a way to erase their elemental abilities? Would you think it ethical to make the treatment mandatory without exception?"

Gio blinked. "Does such a treatment exist?"

"Answer my question."

He didn't like giving an answer without all the facts, but he knew if he refused to answer, his father might dismiss him and he would lose his chance.

Still, if there was one thing he'd learned from his father, it was how to give an answer without committing to anything specific. "If all *Feiru* were free of elemental abilities, then the reasons for keeping Article I would become null and void. Who wouldn't benefit from that, especially in the case of first-borns? Not only could they re-enter society, but the High Council could close most, if not all, of the AMT compounds and save tremendous amounts of money."

His father nodded. "Exactly." Sinclair leaned forward, riffled through some papers until he found the right folder, and slid it across the desk. "Now, what I'm about to tell you can't be discussed outside of these walls, except to a pre-approved circle of people. Do you understand?"

Hope flitted inside Gio's chest. His father was finally going to trust him.

He nodded and his father continued. "There's a formula about to go into production that plays with a *Feiru*'s genetics, and it erases their ability to feel and direct elemental energy."

He couldn't stop from asking his question. "How long has this been available?"

"It was only proved successful very recently. However, the key person we need to finish the replication process, a patient that's been undergoing treatment, has escaped, and I need you to find her."

While he wanted to immediately jump at the chance to include himself, Gio knew there were others more qualified for the job. "Why me?"

Sinclair said nothing, and Gio wondered if he'd made a mistake questioning his father. Then his father smiled and said, "Always question everything, no matter who does the asking. Remember that." Gio nodded, relieved that he'd done something right. His father continued, "But you have an advantage over most, son, and I hope it's enough."

Without knowing the specifics, he couldn't decode his father's words. "Who's the patient? How did she escape? I thought it was impossible to break out of an AMT compound."

Sinclair remained silent, studying him. Gio had passed his father's first test, but maybe he'd just failed the second. Either way, he knew not to speak again until his father did.

Eventually, Sinclair asked, "Do I have your loyalty, Giovanni?"

"Of course. You took me in when nobody else would. You will always have my loyalty, father."

A corner of James Sinclair's mouth lifted. "That's good to hear, because this won't be easy for you."

Gio felt a sense of unease at that statement, although he was careful not to show it. "Why not?"

"Because the patient we need in order to replicate and mass produce the formula is your eldest sister, Kiarra."

Chapter Seventeen

Fuck. Jaxton never slipped, giving out "private" information about himself, but something about Kiarra kept affecting him. First invading his dreams, and then causing jealousy when Marco made her laugh. He was used to being in control and he didn't understand how a tiny woman with a temper was capable of fracturing his previously ironclad authority.

Maybe traveling alone with her to Scotland was a bad idea.

Kiarra finally spoke up. "How were you responsible for his capture? Judging from what Garrett said, he was betrayed by a person named Marzina."

Jaxton froze and glanced at Kiarra. "What do you know about Marzina?"

She shrugged. "Not much, but enough to know that she hurt your brother deeply. He still calls for her in his sleep."

Garrett had never mumbled or said anything on Jaxton's watch, and part of him was jealous that Kiarra knew something about his brother that he hadn't.

Kiarra poked him in the arm and he felt the same awareness from before when he'd stroked her cheek. "Tell me about Marzina."

"She's no one you need to worry about." She pinched him and Jaxton flinched. "Bloody hell, woman, do you want to cause a collision?"

The instant he said it, Jaxton regretted it. Taka had told him about Kiarra's conversation with Cam, and he knew their parents had died in a staged car accident. A quick look told him that Kiarra didn't look distressed on the outside, but he could only imagine what was going on inside her head.

Kiarra cleared her throat. "All right, if you won't tell me about her, then tell me about your brother's capture, because I have a hard time believing you handed Garrett over to the AMT."

He didn't have to answer her. Jaxton could say nothing and keep it all strictly business. Yet he knew they'd be meeting his sister in Edinburgh, and Millie would probably spin some outrageous tale of Garrett's capture. It would be better for Kiarra to hear the truth from him.

Besides, it would distract her from thinking about car accidents and her parents.

Trying not to think of how easily he'd convinced himself to tell her, he said, "I was in charge of my family after my father died. Garrett is the eldest, but since we faked his death at age twelve to keep him out of the AMT, the responsibility to look after everyone fell to me.

"Garrett was going to uni in Manchester when he met a human girl from Poland named Marzina. They fell in love, got engaged, and Garrett shared the secret of his elemental fire abilities. She didn't believe him at first, but after a quick demonstration, Marzina went mental and ran to the human authorities, which was how the AMT enforcement team heard about it."

"And he was captured."

"Yes. I was responsible for him and should've convinced Garrett to wait before telling Marzina about his abilities. But instead, I focused solely on my career and ignored him when he needed me the most."

He'd seen how love blinded people and how easily someone could break your trust. From that day forward, Jaxton had become overcautious, trusting only those who had proven themselves time and again. Kiarra had yet to do so, and he needed to remember that.

Kiarra touched his thigh and he felt a flutter in his lower belly, his body unwilling to listen to his mind. He took a deep breath and focused on the road, the cans and bottles lining the side, part of an old tire near the median divider; anything to distract him from Kiarra's hand on his leg.

Her voice broke through his thoughts. "You should know by now that you can't control people just because you want to. Just look at me. Have you been able to make me do whatever you wanted? No, because, ultimately, I control my own actions."

He gave her a dry look. "I think you just want to raise my blood pressure."

She poked his arm. "Be serious, Jaxton. The AMT tried for years to break me, and while they came close, I managed to remain sane. If a multibillion-dollar enforcement system couldn't succeed in directing me like a puppet, you sure as hell don't have a chance."

She didn't know how he'd acted back then, before Garrett's capture. Jaxton had spent all of his efforts on investing his family's money, thinking more money would mean more happiness. Only after Garrett had been locked inside the AMT had Jaxton realized he'd been a fool and taken the importance of family for granted.

Not even his sister Millie knew about Jaxton's selfish actions before Garrett's capture. Back then, his sister had been young and sheltered.

He'd had enough of talking about his past so he changed the subject. "Where did you learn to swear?"

He stole a glance and saw Kiarra's raised chin. "Why is it such a big deal? You swear."

"Yes, but I wasn't locked away when I was thirteen."

She removed her hand from his leg and crossed her arms over her chest. "Between my guards and my researcher, I could make your ears bleed with what I learned."

Her researcher. Jaxton gripped the steering wheel again at the image of Kiarra being used as a test subject, little different from a rat or mouse.

Kiarra fidgeted in her seat for a good ten seconds before she blurted out, "Why did you rescue me from the AMT?"

Usually, he would just tell her that it had been an order, but for some reason, he wanted to tell her the whole truth. Maybe knowing she'd been part of a bargain would help put distance between them again. That would make his work in Edinburgh easier. "Neena would only tell me the location of my brother if I agreed to rescue one other inmate." He glanced over. "That was you."

Kiarra's brow furrowed. "Why would she want me?"

Because you're a Fire Talent. But they'd gone down that road before. "You'll just have to ask her."

Kiarra crossed her arms over her chest. "Ask Neena this, ask Neena that. The woman needs to learn how to delegate. What if something happens to her?"

The corner of his mouth twitched at the thought. He was about to tell Kiarra to try to suggest that the next time she saw Neena, but as he checked the rearview mirror out of habit, he realized that the rest of this conversation would have to wait.

"Hold on tight. We're being followed. I'm going to try to lose them."

Jaxton swerved onto the motorway exit at the last possible moment, earning a few honks in the process.

A dark blue SUV had been tailing them for the last hour, shadowing every movement, and were either bloody awful or assumed Jaxton wouldn't know how to spot a tail. He hadn't wanted to alarm the SUV too early, so he'd been keeping an eye on it. But not only had he seen the glint of a gun in the rearview mirror, they had just entered Seattle, where he could easily hide in a parking garage and contact Amma. The tricky part would be losing the tail, plus Garrett would not be easy to move.

Seattle was full of one-way streets, which irritated the hell out of Jaxton. It took so damn long to get to another turn, but he soon reached the Seattle Center and turned back around, heading south. He finally turned down the right street and parked in a garage on Spring Street.

Kiarra turned and looked out the back window. "Do you think they'll find us?"

"Possibly." Jaxton took out a brand new prepaid phone and waited for it to turn on. "Amma will have to meet us here, and then we'll hop on the Amtrak to Vancouver, getting off and back on along the way until we reach Squamish Airport in BC."

"How do you know the area so well? Your accent isn't even American."

Jaxton wished the bloody phone would turn on quicker. "My mother is American." The phone had one bar, so he dialed Amma's number. "I've been here before, and even if I hadn't, I always scout the location where I'll be working."

Amma finally answered and he quickly explained the new plan. He pushed the end button on the phone and turned toward the back seat, for once grateful Garrett was still unconscious.

"He'll be all right," Kiarra said and he turned to face her. "I'm sure he'll forgive you later."

Jaxton remained silent and pulled out his Glock. He noticed Kiarra pull out her own small gun. "Where the bloody hell did you get that?"

"Cam gave it to me. She gave me some lessons."

Jaxton shook his head. "Just don't shoot yourself in the foot. Or anyone else for that matter, unless they're trying to kill you." He unlocked the doors. "I'm going to check out the area. Stay in the car and use the gun as a last resort. The on-duty car park staff works with DEFEND, but he can only do so much tinkering with the security feeds."

"You're going to trust me with your brother?"

"I don't have a choice, so don't fuck up."

$*\sim*\sim*$

Adrenaline filled Kiarra with a sense of bravado. For the first time in her adult life, someone was relying on her. She had a task.

Once Jaxton was gone, she eased out of the car, crouched down, and inched her way to the rear of the vehicle. Maybe she was being overly dramatic, but she couldn't stay in the car. She'd be trapped if anyone attacked.

She had to give Jaxton credit—sound traveled well inside the parking garage. When she heard someone sneeze in the distance, she released the safety on her gun, but kept her finger off the trigger, just like Cam had instructed.

The footsteps drew nearer. A middle-aged woman appeared and headed toward the elevator before disappearing behind a wall. Kiarra released the breath she'd been holding, only to feel something solid poke into her back. She shifted her foot ever so slightly, but the solid object pressed harder. She felt someone's breath near her ear.

"I told you to stay in the car."

Jaxton. As she turned, Jaxton moved his gun away from her back. She wanted to yell, but she kept her voice a whisper. "Why, so someone could trap me inside the car? I think not."

He pushed her behind him before whispering, "A man and a woman are snooping around a few rows down. If they come this way, here's what we're going to do."

Kiarra listened and nodded. Jaxton went in front of her and looked both ways before waving her on. She ran across to the other side, squeezed between two cars, and hunkered down, keeping Jaxton's car in view.

Her heart pounded as she waited. She wouldn't screw up. She could do this.

The sound of footsteps came nearer. Kiarra looked at Jaxton and waited for the signal.

When he finally gave it, she removed her clip and slid the gun across the ground. As expected, the pair walked toward Kiarra's direction with their guns raised. She took a deep breath and said in her best terrified voice, "I'm Kiarra Melini. I surrender. Please don't hurt me."

A woman's voice sang. "*Come with us, child. Your pain will ease, you'll be safe. Most of all, you'll go home, back to where you belong.*"

Kiarra wanted to stand up and walk over to the woman. But just as she was about to do it, she caught herself. *What am I doing?*

She crouched back down just as she heard a few grunts, followed by the sounds of objects hitting the ground.

She stayed put until Jaxton came into view and offered her a hand. Taking it, she let him pull her along toward the car. She noticed there weren't any bodies lying on the ground. "Where'd they go?"

He patted the trunk of the car. "Don't worry. They won't be troubling us. When they wake up and start making a fuss, someone will find them."

Part of her was relieved Jaxton hadn't killed them.

Releasing her hand, he reached inside the car to honk the horn twice. Garrett remained unconscious, but a car slowly turned the corner and stopped right behind them. A pretty black woman about her age, wearing jeans and a black t-shirt, stepped out of the car.

Jaxton opened the rear door and maneuvered Garrett out of the back seat. The woman came over to help, took one of Garrett's arms around her neck, and said, "How much longer will he be unconscious?"

"Maybe an hour, possibly two. Hopefully, that's long enough to get him somewhere safe?"

The woman nodded. "I can move him again later. My only other patient right now is nearly recovered and can help me take care of him."

Kiarra watched as they got Garrett inside the other car before the woman buckled him into harness straps in the back seat. She wanted to say something, but hesitated. Garrett wasn't related to her, but in a way, he'd been a patient of hers, if only briefly.

Finally, she took a step forward. "Make sure not to touch him when he's awake or he won't stop screaming. If you hum the tune of Holst's Jupiter, it'll eventually lull him to sleep."

The woman shut the car door and turned with a smile on her face. "I'll make sure to follow your advice. I'm Amma, by the way."

The woman put out her hand and Kiarra forced herself to take it and shake; touching others was becoming easier. "I'm Kiarra. And thank you for taking my advice under consideration."

Amma's smile turned sad. "All that matters to me is getting him well. Too many don't recover, and your advice might be the extra bit of help he needs. Thank you."

Kiarra didn't know what to say. She couldn't remember the last time someone had thanked her for anything. She'd never get used to feeling needed, either.

Jaxton touched her lower back. "We need to go. The two in the boot have probably missed a check-in call, and their associates might try to track their car's location." He put out a hand to Amma to shake. "Thanks, Amma. I'll try to visit him as soon as I can."

"I understand, no worries." Amma opened the driver's door of her car. "Nice to meet you, Kiarra. If you ever need a place to stay, come find me."

Jaxton's hand moved from her back to her waist and he pulled her closer against his side. She should've been alarmed, but for some reason, the heat of his touch, the familiarity of his scent, it just felt…right.

As soon as Amma was gone, Jaxton released his hold and handed Kiarra her gun. Taking her hand, he led her out of the parking garage on foot.

BLAZE OF SECRETS

~~*

Hours later, Kiarra was passed out on Jaxton's shoulder. Not that he could blame her; after all the changes and stops they'd made, it was late. Yet he was confident no one was following them, at least for the moment.

They'd crossed the US-Canada border without incident not that long ago—thankfully, Kiarra's fake passport had worked—— and they'd soon be in Vancouver. From there, they would take a taxi to Squamish Airport and then a private plane to Toronto, change to an international flight to Glasgow, and a bus to Edinburgh. Some might say he was being paranoid, but he wasn't going to risk Kiarra's safety.

He looked at her sleeping face, gently brushed her bangs to the side, and smiled. She'd done well in the parking garage in Seattle, playing her part and not losing her nerve. Every day outside of the AMT allowed Kiarra to find out more of who she was and what she could be. If it weren't for the physical training she still needed, or her continued hesitation with strangers, she would probably challenge Jaxton for his leadership role the first chance she could.

Unable to resist the softness of her skin, he traced the line of her cheek and it hit him that he wanted to see her healed and ready to take on the world.

The thought of letting her go was becoming harder and harder to accept. When Amma had offered Kiarra to stay with her if she ever needed it, something flickered inside of him and he had pulled her close. At that moment, he had wanted Kiarra to stay with him.

He still did.

153

He let out a sigh and took his hand from Kiarra's jaw. As he stared at his reflection in the window, he cataloged all of the more important things to worry about than a growing attachment to his trainee. If he didn't help find the Four Talents and manage to keep them out of Sinclair's radar, there may not be much of a world left to enjoy, regardless of who he had at his side.

CHAPTER EIGHTEEN

Kiarra was in love with Scotland. The old brick and stone buildings had charm and history, a sharp contrast to the box houses and shopping centers back in the US. Her brief view of the scenery outside the cities, between Glasgow and Edinburgh, made her want to see the wildness of the north. But she didn't have the freedom to explore anywhere yet, so for now, she stared out the window of the bus and devoured everything she saw.

The reality of being in a foreign country was still strange to her, but with each new sight, Kiarra was glad she hadn't died the day she'd met Jaxton.

Jaxton's thigh brushed against hers and awareness coursed through her body, reminding her of what had happened on the plane.

She'd been asleep most of the time between Seattle and Glasgow. Jaxton had forced her to eat something every once in a while, but mostly she'd slept; her body was still adjusting to the shock of being free of the AMT.

When the lights had come on during the flight to Glasgow, signaling their proximity to landing, she slowly woke up, feeling all warm and toasty. She snuggled into the delicious warmth, and a hand rubbed her back. She groaned before opening her eyes to find herself asleep on Jaxton's chest.

Her brain had been foggy, not really caring what or who she was lying against; she felt safe and wanted to go back to sleep.

As she pressed against his chest, Jaxton shook her gently and said something about needing to wake up. She tightened the arm thrown across his chest, clutched his shirt, and said no. Eventually, he managed to get her upright, but at the loss of his heat, she felt cold, alone, and not quite right.

When he tried to lower the armrest between them, she must have made a face because he sighed before lifting the armrest back up and tucking her against his side. The instant their bodies had touched again, Kiarra had wanted more—in particular to feel the heat of his skin against her cheek.

Looking over at Jaxton, she realized she still did.

But Jaxton had been quiet since then, only speaking when absolutely necessary, and pretending as if nothing had happened. Was he really that indifferent to her? Granted, she'd been half asleep, but she vaguely remembered him caressing her cheek during their escape from Seattle.

Kiarra, on the other hand, had thought of nothing else but wanting to sleep on his warm chest again. At least until they'd exited Glasgow Airport and she was introduced to Scotland for the first time.

She studied Jaxton's profile and decided he was pretending to sleep. Whether it was because of what had happened on the plane or not, she didn't know, but she was determined to get him talking. She poked his arm. "You don't seem excited about seeing your sister."

He opened one eye. "I saw her a month ago. She knows a lot of the same people I do, and they've looked after her." He shrugged. "Besides, she's pretty good at looking after herself."

He closed his eye, signaling the end of the conversation. He'd been reluctant to share much about Millie on their way here, and Kiarra wondered if that had more to do with his mistrust of her than nonchalance about his sister's safety.

She no longer denied to herself that she was curious about the man who'd rescued her from the AMT. She needed to work hard at getting his sister Millie on her side.

No doubt, Millie could tell her stories that would help her better understand Jaxton's overcautious nature. She had a feeling that his guilt concerning Garrett was only the tip of the iceberg, and if they were going to work together, she needed to know more about him.

The views outside of her window became more and more crowded with houses and shops, meaning they had entered Edinburgh proper. Fifteen minutes later, the bus arrived at Waverley Bridge and they disembarked.

If not for Jaxton's guiding hand, Kiarra would have gone to investigate the clock tower in the distance, Edinburgh Castle up above, or any of the cute little shops across the street. Instead, Jaxton herded her toward a vast expanse of green that, according to the tourist guidebook Jaxton had bought at the airport, could only be Princes Street Gardens.

Ignoring the heat of Jaxton's hand on her back, she tried to inconspicuously scan her surroundings, just like Jaxton had taught her to do during their train ride to Vancouver.

People were either relaxing in the park or shopping across the street. No one suspicious approached or bumped into them. Maybe they had made it to Edinburgh without being followed.

Yet after the attack in Garrett's room and the scuffle inside the parking garage in Seattle, it all seemed a little too easy.

As they approached a dirty structure with a spire, she noticed a young woman standing near it, staring down at her phone. The woman had the same dark blonde hair and deep-set eyes as Jaxton. She'd bet her life that the woman standing under the monument was Millie Ward.

But even when they stopped a short distance away from the woman, she didn't pay them any attention. Jaxton turned toward Kiarra and said, "What's for dinner?"

Kiarra opened her mouth and Jaxton gave a nearly imperceptible shake of his head. A few seconds later, the woman answered, "Shepherd's pie."

"Good," Jaxton said. "Let's head home to make some."

Kiarra grabbed Jaxton's arm and stood on her tiptoes to put her mouth near his ear. "Is that your sister?"

He gave a nod. "Be patient, pet. Let's head home first."

Kiarra's cheeks turned pink, aware that any passerby could interpret that a million different ways. She just wanted to stop with all the nonsense and actually talk to Jaxton's sister. Kiarra turned on her heel and started walking. "Let's go, then."

She got a few feet before Jaxton grabbed her hand and pulled her in a different direction. Once they reached a patch of green, with no person closer than ten feet away, he stopped and she bumped into his back. Kiarra snatched her hand out of his and glared. "Go, stay, go. Make up your damn mind."

A woman laughed and Kiarra noticed Millie standing at her side. Millie put out her hand. "I've been waiting to meet you, and I'm not disappointed. Any woman who stands up to my brother is a friend of mine." Millie flashed a grin at Jaxton. "He can be a bit of an arsehole at times."

Kiarra instantly liked the woman and shook Millie's hand. "I won't disagree with that."

Jaxton made a noise in the back of his throat. "If you're quite done forming a coalition against me, can we get going? I'd rather not stand out in the open."

Millie put out an arm and motioned for Kiarra to link hers through. "We have plenty of time to conspire. Shall we?"

She gingerly put her arm through Millie's and wondered if this was how female friends acted with one another.

She gave one last glance at Jaxton before Millie started moving. As they went along, Millie pointed out the various sights, telling stories like an amateur tour guide. They went down a couple of streets until they reached a section of houses, went up some stairs, and entered a two-story apartment.

Once they were inside, Millie tossed aside her keys and walked into the kitchen. Not knowing what else to do, she followed, and Millie motioned for her to take a seat at the table. "I'll just put the kettle on and we can talk properly."

Jaxton came in and leaned against a counter. "Make something for Kiarra to eat, too."

For some reason, making sure she ate something in private was acceptable, but treating her like someone unable to make decisions for herself in front of Millie was too much. "Most people would ask if I was hungry rather than just ordering something for me to eat."

Jaxton raised an eyebrow. "But I know you're hungry, right? So why bother with the extra step?"

"Because maybe I'm not hungry, maybe I only want something to drink. Is it too much to ask that I want to control my own eating and drinking habits? Fifteen years of having it all decided for me was quite enough."

"You bloody well know this isn't the AMT and I won't see you hungry again."

Part of her realized the importance of that last statement, but she was too irritated to care. "That is not the issue. You need to stop ordering me around like a lackey, or treating me like a child. If I need your help, I'll ask for it."

Jaxton remained silent, but continued to stare at her until someone slid a cup of tea and a plate of cookies in front of her. She'd forgotten that Millie was still in the room.

Millie patted her on the shoulder. "You are bloody brilliant." Millie turned and pointed a finger at her brother. "And you need to calm the hell down and become the clever DEFEND commander my brother used to be."

Jaxton took a cookie from the plate Millie had placed on the table. "Stop meddling, Millicent. This has nothing to do with you."

Millie made a face. "Call me that again and see what happens."

"Millicent."

A blade whizzed through the air and the point embedded into the cabinet to the left of Jaxton's head.

Jaxton acted as if nothing had happened and took a bite of his cookie. "You missed."

Millie turned away from her brother and faced Kiarra. "How would you like a little girl time? If you want, we can get your hair cut, buy some clothes, and have some fun." Millie waved her hand toward Jaxton. "I know you haven't had any fun with him, so it's up to me to show you a good time. Think of it as a 'Welcome Back to the Outside World' celebration. What do you say?"

Jaxton brushed the cookie crumbs off his hands. "You are not taking her out on the town, Millicent."

Millie turned and scowled. "I have three more blades and I won't miss next time."

Jaxton pulled out the blade near his head. "I only need one to stop you."

As the siblings continued to squabble, Kiarra felt a pang of jealousy. Millie and Jaxton knew each other well enough to threaten each other with knives, whereas Kiarra had even lacked the courage to hug her own sister.

For the time being, her tender thoughts about Jaxton on the bus had vanished and she wanted nothing more than to piss him off, and Millie had given her the perfect way to do it. She stood up from her chair and moved toward the door. Millie and Jaxton noticed and stopped bickering.

Jaxton took a step toward her. "You want to see your room?"

Kiarra raised her chin, ignored him, and looked straight at Millie. "I'd love to go out with you."

Millie grinned. "Brilliant!" She gave Jaxton a shove. "You need to go over the recon on the desk in the office, anyway."

Jaxton weaved around his sister, grabbed Kiarra's hand, and pulled her toward the stairs. "If you could defend yourself, I wouldn't have a problem with you going out. But you can't, and I won't risk it."

Kiarra reached to the waistband at her back and started to pull out her gun, but Millie stepped between them. Millie looked at her brother. "Jax, I can take care of her. You know I can. I would think after what happened with Tasanee, you'd believe me."

Kiarra had no idea who or what was Tasanee, but after scrutinizing Millie's face, Jaxton let go of her hand.

"If you screw this up, Millie, I don't care what Mum or even Neena says. I will not work with you again in the future. Ever."

Millie shrugged. "Like I said, I can handle it." She pushed Kiarra toward the door. "Oh, and did I forget to mention the recon is in code? It may take you all afternoon to break it."

"Millie…"

"Meet us at The Last Drop at eight p.m.!"

Millie whisked them out the door before Jaxton could say another word and Kiarra couldn't help but smile. She and Millie were going to get along famously.

CHAPTER NINETEEN

Millie Ward sat in the waiting area of the hair salon and stared at her mobile phone, wishing it would vibrate with a response. While Kiarra was in the other room getting her hair cut, Millie was trying to get some work done. She liked how she was pissing off her brother by simply sitting here and waiting for Kiarra, but Jaxton and Kiarra's arrival couldn't have come at a worse time.

Everyone in DEFEND knew that Millie did private security and intelligence work on the side. Most of the time she worked with DEFEND, but every now and then, she'd take on a job of her own. Not only did the side jobs help to keep her skills fresh and improve them, she constantly worked to expand her network of contacts.

But people would stop seeking her out, or maybe even stop talking to her full stop, if Millie didn't meet and exceed her clients' expectations. The most basic of those, finishing a job, was now in jeopardy.

So even though she honest to goodness wanted to take Kiarra out for a night on the town, Millie was instead using her as an excuse to go and scope out The Last Drop, a pub in Edinburgh's Grassmarket.

The Last Drop was a popular pub with tourists. The constant stream of new faces made it an excellent location to meet her target, especially as it wasn't the kind of place Millie usually frequented. With any luck, no one would recognize her.

The balance of protecting Kiarra while getting what she needed from her target was going to be tricky. But Millie was stubborn and refused to delay her assignment. It'd taken her a week to plan and prepare; she didn't know when this chance would come up again.

Kiarra walked out from the back section of the salon, her cheeks flushed, sporting a new pixie cut that framed her face. Unable to resist, Millie whistled twice and said, "Someone's looking sexy."

Kiarra's cheeks turned pinker. "I don't know when I'll get the chance to pay you back."

Millie stood up and gave Kiarra a walk around, checking the cut from all angles. "Do you like it?"

Kiarra nodded. "More than anything."

Millie grinned. "Then that's good enough for me."

"But—"

She placed a finger over Kiarra's lips, noting how Kiarra froze at the first few seconds of contact. "If it bothers you that much, think of it as a loan. Pay me back once you start drawing a paycheck for your work. Okay?" Kiarra nodded and Millie removed her finger. "Good. Now that's settled, we have a few more stops to make before the fun really begins."

Kiarra looked off to the side, pointedly avoiding eye contact. "Maybe we should just go back to the apartment."

She had been afraid of this. Kiarra was a recently rescued first-born, and after being locked up for so long, the outside world could overwhelm her.

Yet Millie had seen how Kiarra had interacted with her brother, which meant that unlike some former AMT inmates, Kiarra was on the road to recovery. Millie would just have to convince Kiarra she was stronger than she realized. "How about this? We go shopping for a little while, you pick out something you want to buy, and if you still want to go back to the flat after that, we'll go. Does that work for you?"

Kiarra finally met her eyes. "I've never shopped for myself before."

Millie grabbed Kiarra's hand, determined to condition Kiarra to her touch through repetition. "Well, that changes everything." She opened the door and pulled Kiarra out onto the pavement. Once Kiarra was following of her own accord, Millie tucked Kiarra's hand into the crook of her arm and started talking.

She pointed out some of the best shops and told Kiarra what she could find inside each one, but Kiarra remained silent the entire time. From the occasional glances Kiarra threw her way, Millie sensed there was something she wanted to ask. The contrast of how Kiarra was behaving now compared to how she'd behaved with Jaxton back in the flat only reinforced Millie's suspicions that something was going on between her brother and this woman. Jaxton, her levelheaded brother, had all but thrown Kiarra over his shoulder and slapped her arse while shouting, "Mine!"

When Millie finished telling Kiarra about the latest shop, she stopped and pulled Kiarra off to the side. "Ask me anything."

Kiarra blinked. "What?"

She gave Kiarra her most encouraging smile. "You've been glancing toward me, then away, and back again for the last five minutes. I'm sure you've learned from my brother that Ward children don't often beat around the bush. And at the risk of Jax corrupting my image with blatantly unflattering tales, ask me anything you like. I'd rather you hear it from me than from Mr. Grumpy."

"He's not that grumpy."

Millie fought a smile at Kiarra's defense. "With all the scowling and glares he throws, he's not exactly Mr. Charming. I love him, but he and I are two very different people."

Kiarra looked at Millie from the corner of her eye and smiled. "You two have more in common than you think."

She raised an eyebrow. "You care to back up that statement? I am neither male nor grumpy, which already puts quite a gulf between us."

Kiarra laughed and Millie knew she was making progress. "I'm not saying you two don't have your differences. Most of what I think you share is personality-wise. Both of you are rather…"

Kiarra trailed off, most likely afraid she'd offend Millie, but she was having none of that. "Say whatever you like, as long as it doesn't involve the word 'prude.'"

"Well, you both can be a bit bossy," Kiarra gave her a sideways glance, "and stubborn."

Millie's mouth raised in a half-smile. "Anything else?" Kiarra hesitated and Millie patted her on the arm. "Now, now, you can't stop there if you're to convince me that Jax and I have quite a bit in common."

Kiarra's voice was so low, she almost didn't hear it. "You're both kind, and care a lot about your family."

From Taka's reports, Millie knew a little of Kiarra's background, and her heart reached out to her. Jaxton was annoying most of the time, but he would lay down his life for her, without hesitation. He'd proven as much with his single-mindedness about rescuing Garrett.

BLAZE OF SECRETS

Millie once again linked her arm with Kiarra's and started walking. "Hmm, maybe you're on to something. But if you ever tell Jaxton I said that, I will deny it until my dying breath."

Kiarra smiled again. "He would probably just ignore the comment anyway, so I don't see the point."

"Yes, he does have selective hearing, but that's a universal male thing." Millie stopped in front of a shop window. "This is the place I was talking about. See anything you like? And be honest."

Kiarra looked at the dresses in the window, and finally she nodded and pointed to an ankle-length dress in dark red. A bit modest for Millie's tastes, but it would do the job. As she herded Kiarra inside the store, she grinned to herself. Jaxton wouldn't know what hit him.

~~*

Kiarra was pleased that her new dress went to mid-ankle. Despite the handwritten advice Neena had left inside the duffel bag, Kiarra was unskilled at shaving and had more little cuts than she'd like to admit. The AMT had, for good reason, never handed out razors to its inhabitants.

The dark red dress had a high neckline that showed off her collarbones and hugged her upper body, but flared out from the waist into a swaying skirt. The looseness made her feel a little less exposed and naked. When Millie had walked out in a form-fitting, short, dark-blue dress, Kiarra had wondered if she could ever be so bold; she still felt self-conscious about wearing tight-fitting jeans.

She walked out of the dressing room and Millie gave her an infectious grin and a thumbs-up. Despite barely knowing Millie a day, Kiarra already felt like they were becoming friends. She should be more cautious, but if Jaxton trusted Millie, she did too.

Millie paid for the dresses and handed her the shopping bags, filled with their old clothes and some new things for Kiarra, to carry. Millie winked and gestured toward the bags. "You can start paying off your tab with some manual labor."

Kiarra smiled, wondering how much trouble a charming woman like Millie had gotten into as a teenager.

They eventually arrived at The Last Drop and she eyed the sign hanging overhead. "Why does the sign have a noose on it?"

"This is Grassmarket." Millie waved across the street. "They used to hold executions over there. A bit creepy, but at least it's better than another boring pub named after an animal or two." She took Kiarra's free hand. "Now, let's see if we can find a table."

Inside, hanging lights and lanterns of yellow glass dotted the pub's mostly brick and wooden beam interior, giving it a relaxed and calm atmosphere. Benches with tables and chairs lined the walls, with a few tables near the bar. Despite the number of people in the pub, a small table was open near the bar.

Millie guided her over to the open table and motioned for her to sit. "I'm going to get us some drinks. You stay and guard the table."

She was gone before Kiarra could reply, so she sat down and looked around some more until a picture on the far wall caught her attention.

The buildings in the painting looked like the ones she'd just passed on the street, with Edinburgh Castle looming large above, albeit with an old-timey feel. But it was the wooden gallows, complete with a black bird perched inside the noose that made her uneasy. As a child, she'd learned enough *Feiru* history to know that most of their ancestors who'd been caught using their elemental abilities by humans in Europe had died at the gallows. Only after the industrial revolution and the advancement of science had some *Feiru* migrated to big cities and successfully blended in.

Out of habit, Kiarra again tried reaching to the south, but she still felt nothing.

Millie came back with the drinks—one amber colored and one pink and yellowish-orange. Millie sat down and placed the pink and yellowish-orange drink in front of her. "Since you've probably never had a drink before, I decided it was best to start off with something that doesn't really taste like alcohol." Millie waggled her eyebrows. "That drink is called Sex on the Beach." Kiarra blinked and Millie laughed. "If you can hold your alcohol, and I flirt with the bartender, I might be able to convince him to make a Slippery Nipple later." She raised her glass and clinked it with Kiarra's. "Welcome to Scotland. Cheers!"

A few more days in Millie's company and Kiarra would definitely be able to control her reactions to embarrassing comments.

She sniffed her drink, decided it smelled nice, like some kind of fruit mixture, and took a sip. And then another. Millie placed a hand on her free arm. "Whoa, partner, slow down or you'll be flat on the floor before Jax gets here, and I will never hear the end of it."

Kiarra took one last sip and put the glass down. The cozy atmosphere of the pub, combined with the warm and tingly feeling spreading through her body, made her feel relaxed. She'd put off asking Millie personal questions, but if she was going to find out anything, this would be the time to do it, before Jaxton arrived.

Kiarra scooted her chair in and asked, "So, who or what was Tasanee?"

Millie raised an eyebrow, but Kiarra forced herself to maintain eye contact. When Millie smiled, she let out a breath.

"You caught that, huh? Clever girl." Millie took a drink from her glass. "She's the daughter of a politician." Millie looked around and leaned in close. Kiarra did the same. "I saved her from a very bad situation."

Kiarra leaned back and took another sip from her drink before saying "Does anyone in your family not go around rescuing people in distress?"

Millie laughed. "That would be brilliant, having a family of superheroes, but it's just me and Jax. We've been doing it a long time, though, so we make up for the rest of the family."

Millie waved to someone over her shoulder and Kiarra wanted to curse her luck. She'd barely asked Millie anything. Leave it to Jaxton to interrupt her plans.

Anxious to see how Jaxton would react to her new look, Kiarra smoothed her dress and turned around, but it wasn't Jaxton. Two men, one dark haired and the other red haired, were walking toward them.

Kiarra whispered, "Why are they heading this way?"

"Because they're interested in us, of course."

Kiarra froze. "I really don't want to talk with them. Besides, isn't Jaxton supposed to be here soon?"

Millie patted her hand. "You'll do fine. If they try to harm you, they'll have to deal with me. I always carry a few knives, just to be safe."

Kiarra didn't want to think of where Millie had stashed them in such a skimpy dress.

The men reached their table, introduced themselves, and sat down. Millie leaned on the table, giving Kiarra, and by extension the men, an eyeful of her breasts. Millie waved a hand toward Kiarra. "Forgive my friend, she's a little shy."

The red-haired man looked at Kiarra and gave a sly smile. "Shy ones are often the most interesting when alone."

Was he trying to flirt with her? She wasn't interested in him, and the look in his eyes alone gave her a bad feeling.

But if she could keep her cool back in Seattle and help Jaxton capture those two people, she should be able to handle talking with two strangers. She gave a weak smile, hoping she wouldn't have to put up with the man for long. Jaxton should be along any minute, and his growl would probably scare them away in two seconds flat.

As the red-haired man started talking, she looked down at her drink and traced shapes in the condensation on the glass. Maybe he would take the hint and leave her alone.

But then the red-haired man put a hand on her arm and everything went downhill.

~~*

Jaxton tried deciphering the recon Millie had left for him, but his mind kept wandering. Unable to concentrate, he would get up, pace, look out the window, pace some more, and sit back down. The cycle repeated itself for hours, until it was time to leave and meet Millie and Kiarra at the pub.

He was worried about Kiarra. His sister could take care of herself, but she was unused to working with another person. There was a big difference between only looking out for yourself and ensuring the safety of two or more people.

171

This was the first time Jaxton had been truly parted from Kiarra since breaking into the AMT, and he didn't like it.

If only Kiarra had her fire. Neena had said it'd be easy to bring it back, but for the first time since he'd met her five years ago, he doubted her words.

Jaxton arrived at the pub, opened the door, and scowled at the crowd. There were too many people here, especially for a newly freed first-born. He finally spotted Kiarra and Millie sitting in the middle of the room at a table near the bar.

As he walked toward the women, he noticed they weren't alone; two men were sitting with them.

He was going to kill Millie. Kiarra was definitely not ready for men on a pull.

He could only see Kiarra from the back, but she was looking down at the table, uninterested. The realization pumped his ego up a notch, but it was quickly followed by concern. He didn't want the experience to send her back into a relapse.

But before he could reach their table, one of the men touched her arm and Kiarra visibly tensed. She tried to tug her arm away, but the man didn't remove his grip.

Jaxton narrowed his eyes and fought the urge to punch the man in the face.

He took the last few steps toward the table, placed a hand on Kiarra's shoulder, and squeezed. She looked up, and for a split second, relief filled her face.

He barely had time to register her new haircut and clothes before he said, "Is this man bothering you?" Jaxton then glared at the man.

The man raised an eyebrow. "The lady said nothing about having a boyfriend."

Jaxton leaned forward a few inches. "I think you should leave."

As they stared at one another, Kiarra's voice broke the silence. "Please leave."

The red-haired man put his hands up. "Fine. She's not worth the trouble, anyway."

Jaxton growled at the man, but Millie interjected, "It's not worth it. Let them go."

His sister was right. The last thing they needed was to draw unwanted attention, so he let the men leave without proposing a fight.

Jaxton took the vacant seat next to Kiarra and gave Millie one of his best glares. "I trusted you, and you brought her here, dressed like that? She needs rest, food, and training, not men drooling all over her and trying to get into her knickers."

Millie waved a hand in the air. "Not everyone is like you, with a detailed plan for every second of every day. Most of us just like to relax and see what happens. It's life, not a battlefield."

Jaxton motioned around the pub. "She isn't ready for this, and it's made all the worse by you going soft in the head and sitting right in the middle of the room. You should know by now to sit off to the side."

Millie picked up her pint. "Instead of assuming everything Kiarra can or can't handle, maybe you should talk to her. She's sitting right beside you, in case you've forgotten."

Jaxton was more than aware of Kiarra sitting next to him, but he'd been jealous of the man touching her and he was taking it out on his sister. Otherwise, he might do something daft, like tuck Kiarra against his body and growl at any man who came near her.

173

For the first time in his adult life, he was close to losing his cool over a woman in public.

He took a deep breath, looked over at Kiarra, and felt like he'd been punched in the gut. The woman next to him was almost unrecognizable as the woman who'd tried to kill herself inside the AMT. Her haircut flattered her face, and the red dress made her skin look more alive.

She was beautiful.

And all of a sudden, he felt the urge to kiss her.

But then Kiarra shifted in her seat and he forced his gaze away. Jaxton needed to get Kiarra away from the half-drunk men in the pub as soon as possible, before he did something stupid, like act on his attraction or possessiveness.

Standing up, he offered Kiarra his hand. "You've been out long enough. It's time to get you home. Let's go."

~~*

Kiarra was grateful for Jaxton scaring away the men, but even though she'd kept her mouth shut while the siblings bickered, she wasn't about to let Jaxton order her around. Again.

She wondered if it would ever get easier convincing people that she could handle herself and that she wouldn't break at the first sign of trouble. It wasn't like she hadn't experienced her fair share of problems inside the AMT, as Jaxton very well knew.

Besides, she was more unsettled by the heated look he'd given her a minute ago. That look had not only made her heart pound a little too fast, but certain parts of her body that had been quiet for years had come rushing back to life.

Afraid she'd do something rash if she touched him, such as curl up against his warm chest, Kiarra ignored Jaxton's outstretched hand and took a sip of her drink. "No, I want to stay here a little while longer."

Jaxton curled his hand into a fist before plucking the drink from Kiarra's hand and placing it on the far side of the table. "You've had enough to drink. Let's go."

Kiarra reached for the drink, but Jaxton took her hand and pulled her up out of the chair. "I said stop."

As she bumped against his body, Kiarra fought the awareness sizzling against her skin at the contact and focused on the way he was treating her. She tried to lean back, but he kept a grip on her waist. While tempted to knee him in the balls, she restrained herself, not wanting to make the situation any worse. She poked Jaxton's chest. "You stop it. Maybe I want to stay and have a conversation with someone who doesn't order me around."

Jaxton leaned his face down to hers, his breath hot against her cheek. "From where I was standing, it didn't look like that man was interested in talking. Next you'll be dressing like my sister and putting yourself on display."

"Hey!" Millie said, but Kiarra and Jaxton ignored her.

Kiarra narrowed her eyes and tugged her hand. "Now you're just being mean. Let me go. Millie will take me home."

Jaxton said nothing, just turned and yanked Kiarra along with him. She dug in her heels. "Let me go."

People in the pub were starting to gather around them. She knew people from the AMT were looking for her, and she shouldn't be making a scene, but between the buzzing in her head and her anger, Kiarra didn't care.

One of the staff and a few customers walked over, preventing Jaxton from getting any closer to the door. A few patrons asked if Kiarra needed help, but before she could answer, Millie appeared at her side.

A look passed between the siblings and Jaxton gave a slight nod. Millie touched her shoulder. "Maybe you should go home with him, Kiarra."

She blinked. Just a minute ago, Millie had been on her side. "What?"

Millie placed a hand on her back and whispered into her ear, "There's danger here. You need to leave. Now."

She opened her mouth to ask what kind of danger when Millie whispered in her ear again. "I mean it, Kiarra. Let Jax take you home."

She frowned. The urgency in Millie's voice piqued her curiosity. Something was going on, and she wanted to know what. She looked up at Jaxton. "Will you explain everything and answer all of my questions after we get home?"

Jaxton hesitated, and Millie stepped between them, forcing Jaxton to let go of Kiarra before she said, "Of course he will."

That wasn't good enough. "Jaxton?"

"Fine. Will you come with me now?"

Kiarra studied his face. He'd actually made a request. That meant there really was some kind of danger here.

She nodded and Jaxton put out his hand. Putting hers in his, she decided that if Jaxton broke his word this time, about telling her what was happening, Kiarra would try to contact Neena and ask to work with anyone else. She was done being jerked around.

CHAPTER TWENTY

The flat was within walking distance of the pub, but Jaxton had opted to take the bus since he could use all of the human witnesses he could get, and the bus had at least five of them.

Millie's rapid nose twitching had signaled that there had been trouble inside the pub. Their code wasn't sophisticated enough to say exactly what kind of troublemakers she'd spotted, but with the Shadow-Shifter's earlier warning about others coming to retrieve Kiarra, Jaxton wasn't taking any chances.

Besides, it'd given him the perfect excuse to get Kiarra out of there.

Even he was ashamed of the way he'd acted, and Millie's words about Jaxton needing to be the commander he should be still echoed inside his head. It was his duty to protect Kiarra, but not in such a way as to draw attention. If he had approached the situation with a calm head and had treated Kiarra like a normal recruit, respecting her intelligence, he wouldn't be as worried about their safety right now.

Kiarra shifted her leg and accidentally brushed it against his. Looking over, he studied her reflection in the window. He could tell she was irritated from the set of her jaw. Things would probably turn ugly once they reached the flat.

Before he realized what he was doing, his gaze lowered to her lips and he wondered if they would be as soft as her cheek. Every time his skin touched hers, awareness crackled between them. No doubt tasting her lips would push him over the edge.

And that was a problem.

The right thing to do would be to deny the attraction between them. Kiarra was still fresh from the AMT, and something as simple as a kiss could frighten her away.

Yet when he tried to fight it, such as back at the pub, his actions became unpredictable. If he couldn't learn to control them, he might compromise everyone's safety.

The best thing was to give in and see if she wanted him too. If not, he could go back to treating her as a recruit. He'd still do everything he could to protect her, but maybe he could finally put aside his jealousy and focus on getting the necessary information on James Sinclair. After all, Kiarra was just one out of millions of first-borns who needed DEFEND's help.

Kiarra caught his eye in the reflection and raised an eyebrow in question. Luckily, he was a master of keeping secrets. "We'll get off at the next stop."

Neither one of them said a word as they disembarked, and Jaxton guided Kiarra down a maze of streets and alleys; he wasn't going to risk a tail.

Ten minutes later, satisfied no one was following them, he turned up the alley to his flat and went up the stairs. He quickly checked the security, found it untouched, and proceeded to do a quick sweep of the house with Kiarra in tow. For once, she understood the necessity to stay quiet and not ask questions.

Flat secured, Jaxton switched on the light in the living room and turned to face Kiarra. She was waiting with her arms crossed over her chest. He couldn't read her expression, but he knew she wanted the promised explanation, so he gave it to her. "Millie spotted some troublemakers inside the pub. We don't know if they were after you or not, but it was best to play it safe and get you out of there." Until he settled things between them, he was still her trainer, and he needed to reprimand her as one. "It would've been a lot easier to slip away if you hadn't made such a scene."

Kiarra re-crossed her arms under her breasts. Jaxton forced his gaze to stay on her face as she replied, "I made a scene? First, you bark off the men, and then you start dragging me out the door. All you had needed to do was tell me that there was danger and I would've gone quietly, but no; instead, you decided to keep me in the dark. If we're to work together, you need to treat me as a member of your team, not a child to be looked after."

"All I recall doing is protecting you. If that's treating you like a child, then so be it."

Kiarra let out a sound of frustration and crossed the small space between them to stand in front of him. "There is protecting and then there is belittling. Would you ever forcefully pull one of your men out of the pub or take away his drink? Of course not, you would let them make their own decisions, or at least consult with them." Kiarra narrowed her eyes and raised her face closer to his. "I am not twelve years old, Jaxton Ward. I was imprisoned for fifteen years, but I assure you, I can make decisions on my own and face the consequences."

"Can you really, Kiarra? Any more alcohol and that randy ginger bloke could've coaxed you to do anything. What if he'd raped you? Or murdered you?" Jaxton grabbed Kiarra's chin and tilted it upward, forcing her gaze. "The world is different now, and until you learn how it works, I won't stand by and watch you put yourself in harm's way."

She jerked her chin free of his hand. "Sure, until you get what you want; then you'll just pass me along to someone else and forget I even exist. I may be naïve about the world outside, but I won't be your tool. I'm tired of people only using me for their own personal gain and tossing me aside when it's convenient. You're little different than the AMT staff in that respect."

She turned, and Jaxton growled as he grabbed her wrist. "Don't compare me to them." He tugged and turned her to face him again so he could take hold of her shoulders.

Kiarra didn't struggle, but gave him a cool look. "Let go of me, Jaxton."

"Not until you acknowledge that I'm different."

As they stared at each other, Jaxton knew he was being irrational. Kiarra was saying things in anger, and deep down, he knew she probably didn't mean them. But for some reason, he needed to hear her acknowledge that he was different than the AMT guards and researchers.

He didn't want to use and dispose of her; he wanted Kiarra's help, as well as all of the things she could offer in the future.

Most of all, he wanted to tell her that as soon as she'd mentioned passing her off to someone else, a resounding "not bloody likely" had gone through his head. There was no way in hell Jaxton was going to toss her aside.

~~*

She wasn't quite sure how they'd devolved into yet another argument, but Kiarra had hit a nerve, and while she knew Jaxton was nothing like the AMT staff, she was too fired up to back down. Instead, she'd use the opportunity to get some answers. "Since you claim to be different, answer me this: what will you do with me once we find the information you're looking for?"

Jaxton said nothing at first, but just when she was trying to think of how to keep a grip on the situation, the corner of

180

Jaxton's mouth ticked up. "My sister seems to think I should ask you questions rather than just assume answers. So, what would you like to do once we finish with Sinclair?"

She blinked. She hadn't expected that response. "I want to continue working with DEFEND and help the first-borns. I have a lot of information that could be useful."

"If we succeed with Sinclair, finding the leak that we need, then that is quite possible."

She felt a glimmer of hope in her chest, but a question nibbled at the back of her mind. "What if Ty succeeds in capturing me? What will you do then?"

Jaxton's eyes narrowed. "Who is Ty?"

Her calm and collected façade slipped. Jaxton was volatile enough tonight; she didn't need to add fuel to the fire by telling him about Ty. But he tightened his grip on her shoulders and growled. "Kiarra? Answer me. Who is Ty?"

She'd never told anyone about her experiences with Ty, and it weighed heavy on her heart. Yet she was still wary of trusting another person to not use her past against her.

However, Jaxton had told Kiarra about what had happened with Garrett, and if she confided in him as well, she knew something inside of her would shift. She resisted it because of what Ty had done to her, but from everything she'd learned about Jaxton, he was different. The relationship he had with his brother and sister told Kiarra more about him than he would probably ever realize. From the evidence she'd seen so far, Jaxton would've stood up for her whereas Ty's ambitions had taken precedence.

But she wanted to hear the answer to her question before taking such a giant leap of faith. "First, answer my question. What would you do if he captured me?"

"I'm tired of this game, Kiarra."

She raised an eyebrow and forced herself to remain patient. Jaxton was unaware that his answer would dictate how she viewed him from this point forward.

A few seconds later, he relaxed his grip and sighed. "After seeing what they've done to you, both physically with the scars and emotionally, I would never allow you to go back and rot inside the AMT. I can't promise to move Heaven and Earth to get you out, but I would bloody well try as hard as I could."

Jaxton's eyes were sincere, and she liked how he hadn't given her some hyperbolic answer such as never sleeping until he found her or conquering armies to free her. To her, the simplicity spoke of honesty, and she believed he would try to rescue her if she were captured. No matter how difficult it might be for her to talk about it, if Ty did succeed in finding her, Jaxton needed to know about him.

She took a deep breath and explained, "Ty Adams was the researcher assigned to me. He developed a formula that, after he injected me for years with different prototypes, eventually succeeded.

"His formula is the reason I can't gather fire. I was his first success story, and invaluable to both him and his superiors. They see me as central to erasing all elemental magic. If they can replicate the process with other first-borns, it would allow the *Feiru* to fully integrate with the human world."

Jaxton remained silent and studied her face. Kiarra tried to keep her emotions hidden, but he must've seen something, because he asked, "What else did he do to you?"

For most people, ten years would've been more than long enough to get over a former lover. But Ty had done something much more than break her heart. He had broken her spirit.

182

Kiarra felt a brush of fingers on her cheek. Unaware that she'd closed her eyes, she opened them. She was afraid that she would see pity in Jaxton's eyes, but all she saw was concern and kindness.

So many people in the past few days had been kind to her. Between their kindness, memories of Ty, and the effects of the alcohol, she felt overloaded. Her vision began to blur, and she tried to blink away the tears. Crying was the last thing she wanted to do in front of Jaxton.

He stroked her cheek again and asked, "Is he related to the scars on your back?"

~~*

Jaxton hated to see anyone on the verge of tears, but it was so much worse with Kiarra. The woman had been strong for so many years inside the AMT, and to see her start to break down now, well, it did things to his heart that he didn't want to think about.

He continued to rub his thumb up and down Kiarra's soft cheek, the movements calming himself as much as it was starting to calm her. He wanted—no needed—to know the truth of what Ty Adams had done to her.

He cupped her cheek and tilted her head up until she met his eyes. He was gentle, yet firm, when he asked, "Is he?"

Their faces were inches apart, and Jaxton felt Kiarra's warm breath on his chin. Her cheeks were flushed, her breathing fast. When she spoke, it took every bit of his self-control to focus on her words and not to look at her lips.

"Yes. Ty and I were together for about a year. But once the guards found out about our relationship, Ty tossed me aside. I was accused of seducing him, even though he was the one to start it, and I was punished accordingly."

If he ever came across Ty Adams, Jaxton was going to make the man pay.

But right now, with Kiarra on the verge of tears, he needed to distract her. Riling her up was the best way, so he said, "Bollocks."

Her eyes widened. "You don't believe me?"

"I believe that a spineless worm of a man used you for his own selfish purposes. But, pet, there is no way you could've seduced him."

"And why is that?"

He smiled, determined to make her do the same. "Because you'd be bloody awful at it."

Kiarra looked at him a second before she smiled and ran her hand up his chest. He wasn't sure what to make of the determined glint in her eye.

As her warm hand made contact with the skin at his neck, his heart rate ticked up. The heat from her body, combined with her sweet scent filling his nose, went straight to his cock. Some part of him knew it was wrong to lust after Kiarra when she was vulnerable, and he was about to push her away and tell her to go to bed when she leaned her body against his and whispered, "Is that a challenge?"

CHAPTER TWENTY-ONE

The alcohol in Kiarra's blood made her bold. When Jaxton told her she'd be awful at seducing someone, she not only wanted an excuse to block out Ty and her past, but she felt the urge to prove him wrong. He had a problem with assuming he was always the wiser, always right.

Not this time.

Kiarra ran a hand up Jaxton's chest and around his neck, resting her fingers at his nape. She leaned in to the heat of his body and whispered, "Is that a challenge?"

She heard his breath catch, and Kiarra smiled. For once, Jaxton had nothing to say.

This close to his neck, she could smell the uniquely male scent that was Jaxton. On impulse, she stood on her tiptoes and licked his earlobe. She liked the taste of his skin, but before she could do it again, Jaxton took hold of her shoulders and pulled her far enough away that she could see his face.

His eyes were half-lidded and full of heat. She shivered at the look.

His voice was husky when he said, "Pet, if you know what's good for you, you'll walk away and go up to bed right this instant."

She knew under normal circumstances, when she was not fired up from their argument or under the influence of alcohol, she probably would flee to the safety of her room, where she'd only be able to touch Jaxton in her dreams. But she was tired of fighting the responses of her body, tired of resisting him, tired of not making new memories to replace the old.

This was her chance to make an adult decision and take what she wanted.

She leaned into Jaxton's body until her stomach pressed against his erection, and she smiled at the contact. He wanted her too.

Rather than make her feel uneasy, the hardness of his cock sent a rush of wetness between her legs. Her skin was on fire, making her clothes seem stifling. She wanted to feel the warmth of Jaxton's skin on hers as reassurance that this wasn't a dream.

She shifted her hips and tilted her head back, threaded her fingers through Jaxton's hair, and brought his face closer to hers. She stared into his green-gold eyes, his breathing fast and hot on her face, and she wondered what it would take for him to make a move. She dared to wriggle her hips again and he groaned at the friction.

His response empowered her. She wanted to play.

She leaned forward until the tight buds of her nipples grazed his chest. She resisted rubbing against him and taunted, "What, you're not going to order me to go upstairs and go to bed?"

Indecision flashed across his face, and Kiarra decided she wasn't having it. She wanted—no needed—to start making new memories. If he wouldn't act first, then she'd take her own pleasure, inviting him to join in.

She brushed her hard nipples back and forth against his chest, pleasure shooting though her body with each pass, her panties damp with need. When she finally groaned, Jaxton grabbed her waist and pulled her flush up against him, his heat surrounding her like a blanket.

He lowered his head, his lips a hairbreadth away. "You play with fire, pet, you're going to get burned."

She lightly scraped her nails against the back of his neck. "Well, it's a good thing I'm immune to fire, now, isn't it?"

Jaxton ran a hand up her back, up the skin of her neck, and finally cupped the back of her head. "We'll see about that."

And he kissed her.

~~*

He'd tried to send her away, but then the bloody minx had rubbed against his cock, taunting him. Even when he'd offered her a second chance to back out, she'd rubbed her nipples across his chest. When she groaned in pleasure, Jaxton's resolve shattered, and he kissed her.

And Kiarra was kissing him back.

He sucked her bottom lip before darting his tongue out to the seam of her lips, probing for permission. He willed her to open, wanting to taste her. After the longest second of his life, Kiarra opened her mouth and accepted his tongue.

He plunged his tongue inside and stroked it against hers, reveling in the heady mixture of Kiarra and whatever she had drunk at the pub. Tilting her head for better access, Kiarra finally tangled her tongue with his before sucking it deeper into her mouth. He felt the vibrations of her groan, and suddenly kissing her wasn't enough. He grabbed her arse with his free hand, as full and plump as he'd imagined, and kneaded her cheeks. He gave her a slap and took further advantage of her mouth when it opened wider in surprise.

He groaned. The taste and feel of her made his already hard cock even harder. He wanted nothing more than to feel her soft, warm skin against his.

But despite his lust-filled brain, a rational thought warned him to be careful, since anything could trigger a memory from her past.

He moved his hand from her arse, pushed up the skirt of her dress, and slid his hand up the soft skin of her thigh. However, when he reached the outer seam of her knickers, Kiarra tensed and pulled away from their kiss.

Her reaction cleared some of the lust from his brain. Something was wrong. Jaxton found the strength to drop his hand and lean back to look at her face.

Kiarra looked like a deer about to bolt. Something was unsettling her, and no matter if his cock hardened to granite, he would never force her. He rubbed her back and asked, "What's wrong, pet? Talk to me."

~~*

Kiarra's skin was on fire.

Not in the way it'd felt when she used elemental magic in the past, but every nerve was sensitive, to the point where each of Jaxton's touches had been a temporary brand on her skin.

Jaxton's slap had startled her, but the deeper he took their kiss, the more she'd melted against him.

Until he touched her thigh.

The lust-haze of her brain lifted and Kiarra froze. The head warden inside the AMT had often touched her thigh in the same way when she'd refused to strip for him. Whenever she'd put up a fight, he'd pin her against a wall and ripped off her AMT uniform.

She'd always been terrified that he would do more than watch her, so she'd suffered the humiliation of his roaming eyes in silence.

After a few months, living day to day in fear of rape, the head warden had suffered a heart attack, ending the nightmare.

"What's wrong, pet? Talk to me."

Jaxton's voice brought her back to the present, back to the room where she stood with a kindhearted man who had spent years of his life looking for his brother. A man who, despite not knowing everything about his past, she felt confident would never abuse or humiliate her.

She realized he was rubbing her back, and the motion calmed her. Too embarrassed to talk about the humiliation she'd faced inside the AMT, Kiarra laid her cheek against Jaxton's chest and listened to his heartbeat. With each thump, her memories faded, and Kiarra snuggled a little more against his chest, eventually wrapping her arms around his waist.

With his heat and strength surrounding her, for the first time in a long time, she felt safe.

With her passion cooling, the effects of the alcohol made her sleepy. Her eyes drooped and, eventually, she heard Jaxton's voice rumble in his chest. "Pet, I think it's time to get you to bed."

Kiarra tried to speak, but her mumble was incoherent, even to her. Suddenly, her feet were no longer on the ground and Jaxton was carrying her. Too tired to protest, she snuggled against his chest and muttered, "So warm…" before slipping into unconsciousness.

JESSIE DONOVAN

~~*

Jaxton looked down at Kiarra curled up against his chest and realized he was in trouble.

When Kiarra had refused to tell him what had caused her distress, he'd wanted to shake it out of her. She should be able to tell him anything, and it didn't sit well with him that she hadn't.

Couple that with his possessiveness in the pub and the kiss they'd just shared, which had set his blood on fire in a way no kiss had before, and Jaxton couldn't deny it—he not only wanted her, he cared for her.

Jaxton entered his room and laid Kiarra on his bed. After tucking her under the covers, he brushed the hair from her forehead. She looked so young and innocent when she was asleep. The innocence on her face matched her childlike interest in the world. He remembered her eyes from when they'd first arrived in Edinburgh this morning and wished he could look at the world with the same open amazement.

Maybe he needed Kiarra's influence. Jaxton was skeptical of just about everything.

Besides, if she was a Fire Talent, she would need protection until she could control her powers and combine it with the other three Talents. Once word got out about her elemental abilities, others would be drawn to her then, especially those with latent abilities. But he was, and would always be, her first protector. He would be the one to decide who was qualified and loyal enough to make up her personal guard.

Until then, he was going to continue to train her, take care of her, and help her heal.

He pulled up a chair, took off his shoes, and propped his feet on the bed. Tomorrow, after training with Kiarra in the morning, they'd look for Sinclair's hangouts and acquaintances. Kiarra needed to feel more included, and Jaxton needed to learn to trust her.

He adjusted his still semi-hard cock and hoped he could control himself around her. Unlike with most women, one taste of Kiarra wasn't nearly enough. But the last thing he wanted to do was scare her by making a move before she was ready.

Especially since the memories that had made her freeze a short while ago might still haunt her in the morning. No matter what state she was in, he would do everything in his power to coax out the real Kiarra. She was still his trainee, and as much as he wanted to rip off her clothes and pound into her tight, wet heat, he needed to make sure she stayed alive. That meant duty above his own desires.

Of course, if she ever showed that she was ready and willing, he wouldn't back down until she was naked in his arms.

CHAPTER TWENTY-TWO

Not only did Millie have a pounding headache, she could only wiggle her arms and legs a few inches.

She was strapped to a hospital bed.

She'd regained consciousness a few minutes ago and was trying to patch together exactly what had happened. This wasn't the first scrape she'd had, and it wouldn't be her last. The key was to keep a cool head and not fall prey to emotion.

Once Jaxton had escorted Kiarra out of The Last Drop, Millie had stayed behind, socializing with people in the pub while she waited for her target. She'd also tried to find out why Dominik and Petra Brandt had suddenly appeared. The fraternal twins were honest-to-goodness mercenaries and had caused Millie a problem or two in the past.

From what she'd heard, Dominik and Petra focused mostly on "acquisitions," which was just another word for kidnapping. That knowledge had set off warning bells in Millie's head since Kiarra was a runaway first-born. The Brandt twins had never worked for the AMT before, but Millie hadn't been willing to chance Kiarra's safety.

After Jaxton had left with Kiarra, Millie had kept up a cheery, boisterous façade, working the room to find out all she could. At some point, while waiting for her target, she'd ended up at a table with a trio of Americans. The last thing she remembered was having a lager with the Yanks, and since Millie could usually drink people under the table, it meant that someone must've slipped something into her drink when she wasn't looking.

Knowing what she did of Petra Brandt, Millie would bet money that the German had found a way to drug her. She'd underestimated Petra's skills and wouldn't be making that mistake again.

More concerned with learning from her mistakes than dwelling on them, Millie switched gears and looked around the room she was in. It was filled with medical equipment, but the setup was unlike any of the NHS hospital rooms Millie had seen in Britain. Noticing the two-way observation glass, Millie reckoned that it was a research facility.

Or it could be an information extraction room.

She focused on the straps around her arms and legs, moving to see how much give they had. The straps were only cloth, but after moving her legs around some more, Millie could tell they'd confiscated the knife strapped to her inner thigh.

While inconvenient, being weaponless was not the worst thing in the world. She might be able to convince her captors that they needed her help. Or construct a situation that would require them to undo her straps. Either way, she needed to meet said captors before she could come up with a plan.

She heard a door open on the far side of the room before bright light flooded in from the outside, silhouetting a male figure. The man walked inside and shut the door, careful to keep his face obscured by the shadows in the room. When he spoke, his words echoed, telling her that the room wasn't that large.

"You're going to tell your brother that you are alive and well, but nothing else. No details of this location, about me, or anything you found out last night at the pub."

She noted his accent was from the South of England, yet a little off, and tucked that tidbit of information away. "Who are you?"

The man shifted, but she still couldn't see his head. "That doesn't matter. Do you understand the instructions I gave you? And more importantly, will you follow them?"

"I heard you, but…" Millie's voice died in her throat. She wanted to ask why she should follow them, but the compulsion to answer him in the affirmative made her uneasy.

"Good. And no secret messages either. Do you understand?"

Millie tried to protest, but again, she couldn't get her voice to work. Then she tried to think of a way to circumvent the order, but her mind blanked. She tried again, but failed. It took her a second to realize what had happened to her.

Shit. They'd dosed her with rowanberry juice.

Rowanberry juice was illegal amongst the *Feiru*, but that didn't prevent some from using it. The juice would compel a *Feiru* to listen to your every order and instruction for about a day. More than one dose every two weeks would kill you.

The man walked toward her and Millie kept her face as expressionless as possible. This was a major obstacle, but she wasn't giving up yet. Even if Jaxton answered this man's demands and came to rescue her, she'd find a way to get everyone out of this situation alive.

~~*

Kiarra sat atop a metal examination table, dressed in a hospital gown, and swung her legs back and forth, trying not to smile. Ty would walk through the door any minute, and Kiarra could hardly wait for him to shut the door and kiss her. If he had enough time, maybe he'd make love to her again too. Even after a year, just thinking about his naked body over hers made her blush.

He'd made progress on his special formula, which was good news on so many levels. Maybe one day soon she would no longer be a prisoner, and she could spend the rest of her life with Ty. She could always make him laugh, and he'd taught her so much. Ty had also protected her, ensuring she received better treatment than the other AMT prisoners.

Kiarra was only eighteen, but some of the other eighteen-year-olds had already lost their sanity. Some adjusted easily to life inside the AMT compound, while others fell into despair. Kiarra understood how easy it was to do that, especially since she'd been in a dark place herself until Ty had entered her life a year ago.

She wished she could do more to help the other inmates who didn't have someone as wonderful as Ty for their researcher, but at the end of the day, she knew there was nothing she could do to ease their pain. Ty's work would eventually make all of their lives better; without elemental magic, all of the first-borns could go home to their families and start over.

The door opened and Kiarra stopped swinging her legs when she saw two of her least favorite guards standing in the doorway. She knew better than to ask them why they were here and waited to see what they would do. Maybe something had come up and Ty had rescheduled their session. It wouldn't be the first time he'd had to do that.

But as the two guards stepped aside and the head warden walked into the room, Kiarra sat up straight and wondered why the head warden was here. The only reason he came to see an inmate was if they'd broken at least half a dozen rules—or a major one—and he would issue their punishment.

Since Kiarra hadn't caused any real trouble since she was fourteen, when she'd learned that the punishments were harsh and painful, his sudden appearance made her uneasy.

195

The head warden reached her side, gripped her arm, and yanked her to her feet. He looked her in the eye, a sneer on his face, and stated, "You have been charged and found guilty of seducing and seeking to manipulate an AMT employee for personal gain. The guards will carry out your punishment immediately."

Kiarra's heart stopped and she tried not to panic. There had to be some mistake.

She glanced at the door. Ty would come and clear up this misunderstanding. He would tell them the truth and save her from an unwarranted punishment. Ty had never failed her before and she didn't doubt him now.

The head warden noticed her glances toward the door and gave a cruel laugh. "Dr. Adams was not only your accuser, but he provided evidence. He won't be coming to intervene on your behalf."

Fear gripped her belly. "No!" she shouted, and tried to squirm free of the head warden's grip. Ty would never betray her like that. He'd said he loved her. They'd made plans together.

There was no way Ty would abandon her.

They would throw her into solitary confinement for speaking out, but Kiarra couldn't keep quiet. The head warden's accusation was wrong and she had to make him see that. "This is some kind of misunderstanding. Talk to Dr. Adams again and he'll clear it all up."

The head warden said nothing, but dragged her over to the outstretched hands of the two guards waiting at the door. She continued to struggle and hoped Ty would find her in time. A charge of seduction was one of the highest offenses inside the AMT.

If no one intervened, they were going to whip her.

When the two guards took her upper arms in steel-like grips, she panicked and tried her hardest to squirm free. But no matter how much she twisted or bucked, she was no match for the heavily muscled guards. They pulled her along as if she weighed no more than a feather, and as the seconds

196

ticked by and Ty remained absent, tears streamed down her cheeks. Why would he do this? Was there someone else? Had he just been using her all this time?

Didn't the head warden know about her role in developing Ty's precious formula?

The guards finally hauled her into an adjacent room and she let out a sob when she saw the instruments hanging on the wall. She pulled back with all of her weight, but they lifted her with barely a second of hesitation before they yanked her the final few feet to the metal table in the middle of the room. She was no match for the guards' strength as they tossed her face down on the table and forced her hands into metal bands on either end. Even after the bands clicked closed, she wiggled and tried to pull her hands free until her wrists were slick with blood.

She stilled when she heard one of the guards take something from the wall and slap it against his palm. Reality set in as she realized Ty wasn't coming to save her. There was no way out.

They were truly going to whip her.

With her heart pounding in her chest, Kiarra closed her eyes, turned her head, and laid her cheek on the cool surface of the metal table. Maybe this would be it. Maybe the guards would kill her and end the pain in her heart.

First her parents, and now Ty. Everyone tossed her away when it was convenient. No one ever fought to protect her.

She was unwanted.

The guards ripped the back of her hospital gown and made taunting remarks, but she didn't hear them over the frantic beat of her heart. She just hoped they'd end it quickly. She'd already suffered more in five years than most people did in a lifetime.

The first lash hit her back and Kiarra screamed at the burning pain. The guard hit her again, and again, never lashing at a predictable beat, which made the torture worse than anything she'd ever imagined.

Her body finally numbed, but she couldn't stop her tears. As blood trickled down her sides to the table, pooling around her just like her tears, Kiarra wanted nothing more than to die.

Kiarra bolted upright in bed, choking back the remnants of a scream. She looked around the unfamiliar room, but when she saw Jaxton leaning over her, she closed her eyes and took a deep breath.

It'd only been a dream.

She couldn't remember the last time she'd dreamed of her first whipping.

"Bloody hell, Kiarra, what were you screaming about?"

She looked up and saw Jaxton's scowl. If not for the concern in his eyes, she would've thought he'd forgotten about last night.

Last night. No doubt her memories of the head warden had triggered the dreams again.

She mentally cursed the head warden, and by extension, Ty Adams. The two of them had robbed her of a wonderful night spent in Jaxton's arms. His warm body had made her feel safe, and while part of her wanted to curl up against his chest, she wouldn't allow her past to taint and possibly destroy whatever kind of chance she had with Jaxton. The last thing she wanted from him was pity; she would sort out her mind first, and seek comfort later.

"Kiarra?"

Jaxton brushed her bangs to the side and his touch intensified her urge to jump into his arms, but she steeled her resolve. "It was just a dream. Nothing you need to worry about."

"Bollocks. You were tossing and turning before you screamed loud enough to wake the dead." He put a finger under her chin. "You can tell me anything, pet, because if you can't learn to trust somebody, you'll never be a full-fledged member of DEFEND."

She shook her head and dislodged his finger from her skin. Each time he was kind to her, it weakened her resolve. "You don't understand."

~~*

Jaxton sat down on the bed next to Kiarra's hip and put a hand on her cheek. "Talking about your demons helps to chuck them out for good. You need to tell somebody, so tell me." The indecision in Kiarra's eyes tore at his heart. "I won't judge you, if that's what you're worried about."

"Why should I trust you when you don't trust me?"

Kiarra almost sounded like herself again. "Well, that's where you're wrong. I was planning on taking you out to scout information with me this morning. But if I think you're mentally unfit to go out into the field, then I'll have Millie stay with you while I go out alone."

Millie hadn't come back to the flat yet, but Kiarra didn't need to know that.

Kiarra's eyes widened. "You'll take me out and let me help you?"

Jaxton raised an eyebrow. "Why would I say so otherwise?"

She searched his eyes. When she finally spoke, her tone was solemn. "I've never told anyone about what happened."

"I'm not just anyone, you know."

His deliberately arrogant tone worked, making Kiarra smile for a brief second before she took a deep breath and averted her gaze. "I sometimes dream about the day the AMT head warden found me guilty of seduction, and his resulting sentence."

He held back his anger and kept his tone gentle. "Tell me about it, pet."

There was a brief silence, but Jaxton's patience was rewarded. "They restrained me to a table and whipped me." She closed her eyes and Jaxton traced her jaw until she opened her eyes again. "All I remember was being scared, the overwhelming pain, and then the darkness."

"Unconsciousness?"

Kiarra leaned forward and tucked her head against his chest before she shook her head. "For a time, but even when I woke, it was dark. I spent three months in solitary confinement."

When she shivered, he sensed there was something more that she wasn't telling him. Jaxton drew her closer against him and waited until she had settled before he pushed, "What happened during those three months?"

Kiarra started and pulled away so she could look Jaxton in the face. "W-why would you think something happened?"

"Let's just say I'm fairly good at judging whether someone is hiding something from me or not."

She scowled, and Jaxton knew she was once again becoming his version of Kiarra. She asked, "Is there anything you can't do?"

He grinned. "I can't give birth to babies." She swatted his chest and Jaxton captured her hand and squeezed it. "Now, tell me. What happened?"

She stared at their hands as she spoke. "The head warden often came to my cell for inspections, to make sure my injuries were healing."

"Because they whipped you more than once."

She looked up at that and nodded. "Yes." She looked back to their hands on his chest and he squeezed her fingers gently. "But the head warden had his own kind of inspection." She closed her eyes, her voice a whisper. "He would strip me and force me to stand while he looked at me."

Fucking bastard. Jaxton tightened his grip on Kiarra's hand and she flinched. Loosening his fingers, he apologized "Sorry, pet. I didn't mean to hurt you, but just the thought of what he did to you makes me furious." He rubbed the back of her hand with his thumb. "Did he ever…hurt you?"

"Thankfully, no." She traced designs on his chest with her free hand. "The head warden died within a few months of my confinement, before he ever had the chance. They said it was a heart attack." Jaxton harrumphed and Kiarra looked at his face. "What is that supposed to mean?"

Sulking wasn't his usual way, but Jaxton didn't care. "I wanted to kill him for you."

She smiled. "In an odd way, that's sweet." She searched his eyes. "But you really believe me, just like that?"

The note of skepticism in her voice irritated him. "If given the choice between believing a clever, spirited, beautiful, if somewhat naïve young woman, or believing a man who worked for a system that imprisons and tortures children, which would you choose?"

She blinked at his praise. She was unused to it, which meant Jaxton needed to do it more often. Kiarra didn't know how much she had to offer the world. Certainly more than her lack of elemental abilities or her body. Hell, she could call him out on his shit for one thing, which was a task in and of itself.

Kiarra shook her head to herself and he wanted to know what she was thinking. There would come a day when she wouldn't hide anything from him, especially since he wasn't letting her go for the foreseeable future.

But for the moment, she still didn't feel comfortable enough to confide in him without reserve. He was about to ask what was on her mind, but she beat him to it with her own question. "That's oversimplifying things. What if I'm working for them?"

Neena would never let a traitor into their inner fold, but Kiarra didn't know that. He lowered his face close to hers. "Are you?"

Kiarra raised her chin. "No."

"Then don't bring it up." He tucked her short hair behind one ear. "I was trying to compliment you earlier, you know."

"Was that before or after you started growling and scowling at me?"

Jaxton smiled. Kiarra might have some hardships in her past, but she was stronger than the memories. Any woman who stood up to him was not weak in character.

He lowered his head, stopping an inch from her lips. "Well, if growling and scowling is what it takes, I think I can handle that."

Short breaths puffed against his lips. "To do what?"

He trailed the back of his fingers down her throat and up again. Her breath hitched, and Jaxton smiled wider. "To make new memories strong enough to overshadow the old."

Kiarra raised an eyebrow. "You seem pretty confident about being able to do that."

He moved to her ear and whispered, "It's been working so far, but I might need to change tactics." He bit her earlobe and waited to see how she would react. If she froze, he'd back off and merely hold her, but he had a feeling she was stronger than that. When she moved her hand up behind his neck and groaned, he gave a gentle nip and licked her ear. "Well, what do you think, pet? Shall we try a little harder?"

The fingers on his neck hesitated, but after he kissed the soft spot just behind her ear, she kneaded his skin and tilted her head to the side. Jaxton took that as an invitation. He kissed his way down her neck to where her neck met her shoulder and bit gently. He blew against her wet skin and Kiarra shivered, but this time in a good way.

Jaxton lifted his head and cupped Kiarra's cheek. "I think it's working."

She tightened her grip on his neck and pulled his face down to hers. "Stop gloating and kiss me."

Her mouth swallowed his laugh and opened to invite his tongue. As he darted and tangled inside her mouth, he drew Kiarra's body closer, wanting her to know it was him and not a shadow of the past. When the sharp buds of her nipples rubbed against his chest, he groaned and rubbed his cock against her stomach, letting her know he wanted her too.

But it wasn't enough. He grabbed her arse and lifted her onto his lap. Kiarra wrapped her legs around his waist, her core now against his cock, and despite the layers of clothing between them, he thrust. Kiarra groaned and moved her hips, the friction making him want to toss her on the bed and rip off her clothes. But he concentrated, determined to take this slow and make it good for her.

He trailed kisses down her neck until he reached the neckline of the red dress she still wore from last night. He nuzzled the swells of her breasts and said, "I want your hard little nipples in my mouth." He nipped the top of her left breast. "Lift your dress for me, pet."

She stared into his eyes. At first, he couldn't read her expression, but then she lifted her skirt up over her bra, and he felt a thrill. She was ready for this.

Yet as she pulled the material up over her head, her actions were unsure and lacked confidence. Jaxton could help with that. As he surveyed her breasts and pale skin, he whispered, "You're so beautiful."

She flushed down to her neck and he found it adorable.

It was time. He leaned down and slowly licked her nipple through the lace of her bra. Kiarra let out a little moan and he decided she could take more.

He sucked her nipple deep before nipping the tight bud with his teeth. Kiarra threaded her fingers through his hair and she pushed her chest out in invitation. Jaxton bit her again before releasing her nipple and moving to the other. As he sucked and nibbled, all he could think about was wanting to free her breast and trace her taut peak with his tongue. But just as he gripped the top of her bra to pull it down, his mobile phone rang.

He wanted to ignore it, but it was his emergency mobile. The only people who would call him were the people from his team or family, and only if they were in danger. Jaxton cursed and cupped Kiarra's cheek. "I'm sorry, pet, someone might be in trouble and I need to take it."

She nodded and he reluctantly moved her back to the bed, pride welling in his chest when Kiarra struggled to remain upright. *Just wait until later, pet.*

He picked up the phone from the side table and saw it was an unlisted number, but that didn't mean anything. He tapped the receive button. "Hello?"

"Jaxton?"

"Millie?" She'd better have a bloody good reason for calling him. "What's wrong?"

"I…well…the truth is…" A scuffle came over the phone before Jaxton heard a male voice speak into the line. "Jaxton Ward, if you want your sister to stay alive, I need to talk with Kiarra Melini."

CHAPTER TWENTY-THREE

Kiarra leaned against Jaxton, afraid that if she severed physical contact, what had just happened between them would fade into oblivion. She'd been disappointed when he'd gone to answer the phone, but after hearing it was Millie, Kiarra tugged down her dress and strained to hear what was being said. She didn't care if she'd only known her for a few short hours, she thought of Millie as her friend.

Jaxton's pinched brow eased and was replaced by a look of surprise. She wondered what had happened. Jaxton never would have left Millie alone at the pub last night if he hadn't been confident in his sister's abilities.

She couldn't hear the other person on the line, only Jaxton's side of the conversation. Unable to take the suspense, she put a hand on his arm. "Jaxton, what's happening?"

He shook his head, signaling her to be quiet.

A bad feeling gathered in the pit of her stomach.

After a brief pause, Jaxton answered, "She's not here."

His grip tightened on the phone, and she squeezed his bicep. Once he looked at her, she mouthed, *What?* He put up a hand and Kiarra waited.

A minute later, Jaxton finally lowered the phone, his hand covering the bottom speaker, and whispered, "They have Millie. If I don't let them talk to you, they're going to hurt her. I won't force you, but are you up to it? I need you to learn as much as possible about the man on the phone."

"How do I do that? I haven't been trained like you."

"Just probe and ask questions. The information will help me find Millie."

Taking a deep breath, she nodded. Jaxton handed her the phone. With her heart thumping in her chest, she put it to her ear. "Hello?"

"Hello, Kiki."

Her heart skipped a beat. Only one person had ever used that nickname. "Giovanni?"

"Yes."

Kiarra's heart pounded. *Stay calm and focused until you know how Millie is involved.* "What do you want?"

"Do you even need to ask? You, of course."

Kiarra turned away from Jaxton, hoping to keep her remarks semi-private. No matter who Gio had become, he was still her younger brother and her best bet was to treat him as such. "Giovanni Charles Melini, stop with these games and dramatics and just tell me what you want."

Her whispered scolding must've had some effect, because Gio said nothing for a few moments. However, when someone finally spoke, it wasn't Gio, but Millie.

"Kiarra, don't listen to him. I can take care of myself. I—"

A scream echoed on the line and Kiarra couldn't help but yell into the phone, "Stop!"

Jaxton came to her side, and she shared a glance with him. It now made sense—Millie's screams earlier must've caused him to grip the phone. Kiarra was afraid for her newfound friend, but it must be infinitely worse for Jaxton. She leaned against him and reestablished her nerve at the contact. "Gio? Millie? Anybody there?"

Gio's voice came back on the line. "Do I have your attention now? Unless you want to hear more screaming, here's what you're going to do…"

Kiarra listened closely, hoping later she could figure a way to free Millie without hurting anyone else, even if it meant turning herself over. The AMT would at least keep her alive, and there was a higher chance someone could rescue her later. Millie didn't have the same guarantee.

Her brother hung up and Kiarra lowered the phone, staring at it in disbelief. He'd proven that he wasn't an impostor, but something was wrong. The most prevalent memory she had of her brother was him nursing every sick or injured animal that crossed his path, to the point where their parents had constructed a crude shed to house his animals. That version of Giovanni, the one from her childhood, would never threaten, let alone harm, a defenseless person.

What has happened to him? Maybe Gio was more indoctrinated than Cam had thought and was past the point of saving.

Jaxton touched her elbow, interrupting her thoughts. "Well? What's the bugger want?"

Kiarra braced herself for his reaction. "A trade—me for Millie." She took a deep breath and looked him in the eye. "If we don't follow his instructions, then he'll kill her and send her body back to us in pieces."

~~*

Gio stayed long enough for the doctor to administer a sleeping drug to Millie Ward before he left the room, and then walked as quickly as he could to his new office. After locking the door, he closed his eyes and leaned against the wall.

His father's assignment was turning out to be a lot more challenging than he'd imagined. He'd found a way around torture this time, using a recorded scream to scare Kiarra and Jaxton, but what about the next time? He wasn't sure he could harm someone without a reason, simply for his own personal gain. He couldn't even eat animals, for fuck's sake. Killing living things wasn't his forte.

Kiarra was a first-born, and in the best interests of everyone, she should be inside an AMT compound. He had no problem with retrieving her and locking her away again, to keep her from prying human eyes. But Gio didn't like inflicting pain on innocents, especially on those weaker than him.

At this rate, he might have to.

He opened his eyes and went to his computer. Gio always strove to be prepared, and maybe doing some research would help calm his mind, or at least serve as a distraction.

He now had access to the daily logs of all the AMT compounds. Since he was fighting to keep first-borns inside the AMT compounds, he wanted to know more about what happened on a day-to-day basis. From what he'd seen already, things were not quite what the AMT spokespeople had said they were.

Besides, the information might give him ideas on how to help his father later on.

He scrolled through the files on the computer. Guard rosters or patient files didn't interest him, but as he looked through the records, one file marked "important" caught his eye: *Research Logs for Dr. Ty Adams*.

Adams had been Kiarra's researcher, the one previously in charge of her retrieval. Gio wanted to know more about the scientist who'd designed the nullification formula for elemental magic.

He opened the file and spotted Kiarra's serial number of F-839 in the first paragraph. There was a lot of scientific jargon he didn't understand, but eventually he came to the brief recap of Kiarra's charge of seduction and sentence, as well as a stamp of "completed" for the meting out of her punishment. That seemed unlike the big sister he'd known, the one who'd always played by the rules and had badgered him to do the same, but he quickly dismissed that thought. Fifteen years could change a person.

Gio tucked away the information about Kiarra's sentence and punishment in case he needed it, and kept reading. But the incident's postscript caught his attention:

Tests on F-839 confirm the patient's inability to bear children. The patient is dismissed as a breeding candidate, but due to positive interactions with the Null Formula, F-839 will continue to be protected under FB Experimentation Rights.

His brows knitted together in confusion. What the hell was a breeding candidate? Breeding inmates would only create more first-borns, which would tax AMT, and by extension, all *Feiru* resources further. It didn't make any sense.

Opening a new window on his computer, he searched the files for "breeding candidates." He clicked on the most promising return and read the first paragraph:

F-284 delivered twins today. The first-born was marked with ink, but both children will be transported to the pediatrics facility for observation. F-284 underwent five years of gene therapy and her offspring will be studied for genetic shifts or abnormalities.

Gio stopped reading and leaned back in his chair.

The AMT researchers were using inmates as experiment subjects, forcing them to have children so the AMT could study genetic shifts in the next generation. His gut told him the inmates were probably impregnated against their will.

Did his father know about this? The *Feiru* public bloody well didn't, that was for sure.

Gio glanced at the clock. He had about ten minutes before he needed to check in with various contacts. He queried "pediatrics facility" and waited for the results, anxious to know how they treated the children once they arrived there.

~~*

Jaxton clenched his hands

Fuck, a trade. Trades usually ended with at least one party dead, if not both, as well as a bloody mess of a situation that he couldn't handle without back-up from his team. And, of course, his team just happened to be on separate assignments, scattered across the globe.

It also didn't help that the person in charge of the trade was Kiarra's brother, which meant that Jaxton had to plan carefully or risk upsetting Kiarra. She probably wanted to keep him alive.

Of course, if Giovanni killed his sister, then Jaxton hoped Kiarra would understand his actions when he made her bastard brother pay.

Jaxton needed to find a way to keep both women out of Giovanni's hands—but to do that, he needed to take a step back from the situation, push emotion aside, and try to figure out his options. He'd spent years sorting through intelligence, piecing together facts, and coming up with plans on how to use the information. He could do it now too, but he needed all of the pertinent information first. "What were his instructions?" he asked.

Kiarra maintained eye contact, but raised her chin. "I'm not going to tell you just yet."

He narrowed his eyes. *Bloody woman.* "Don't toy with me on this, Kiarra. Millie's my sister and I plan to get her back before"—*that bastard*—"your brother decides to kill her."

"We have two days before the deadline, and I want a chance to think of a plan."

He growled. "I would think it obvious, but I have more experience with this kind of thing. Not to mention resources and favors I can call on."

Kiarra shook her head. "Gio is my brother and I know him better than you. I might be able to use that against him."

Jaxton threw his hand out and gestured. "He's spent the last fourteen years living with your uncle. An uncle, I might add, who murdered your parents. I highly doubt your brother is going to come crawling for your love and forgiveness after a two-minute phone call."

Kiarra's eyes widened. "How do you know about Sinclair murdering my parents?"

He might've fucked up, but at this point, Jaxton didn't care. "I make it my business to know what's going on in my house, especially when it's full of prisoners who might try to kill me."

"You spied on me."

He shrugged. "Anyone with experience would've done the same thing."

Kiarra made a sound of frustration. "If you're so experienced, then why did you leave your sister alone last night?"

"If I didn't have to babysit you, then I could've helped her."

"So it's my fault?"

"Yes."

"You're an asshole."

"Is that supposed to be a problem?"

Kiarra growled and walked to the door. Jaxton should have tried to stop her, but he was angry. After everything he'd done for her, she still didn't trust him enough to ask for help.

She grabbed the door handle and looked over her shoulder. "Do I need to ask my babysitter's permission to leave the room?"

If she was going to be a smart-ass, then he would too. "Just don't leave the flat. I don't have time to go chasing after you."

She walked out and slammed the door behind her. Closing his eyes, he took two deep breaths. The things that woman did to him.

He would let them both cool down before he tried talking with her again. She always seemed to bring out his temper, but without her presence, it was easy to see that blaming Kiarra for Millie's capture was like blaming a bartender for the next morning's hangover; in other words, she had nothing to do with it. Both Millie and Jaxton knew the risks of working with DEFEND, and sometimes those risks included capture, or worse.

While his temper cooled, he needed to act. He reached for his mobile phone, tossed it on the ground, and stomped on it a few times. Now no one could track it or triangulate future signals.

Next, he needed to call in some favors and leave messages for his team members. He only hoped they were in a state to retrieve them.

He walked over to the secured landline phone on the nightstand, sat down on the bed, and picked up the receiver. As he dialed, Jaxton looked at the pillow next to him and an image of Kiarra from last night, curled up on her side fast asleep, flashed inside his mind.

If not for AMT interference, Jaxton would probably be lying naked with Kiarra right now in post-coital bliss, helping to erase the fears of her past, while at the same time strengthening her trust in him. Instead, he would have to focus on merely keeping everyone alive, and after everything she'd already gone through inside the AMT, Kiarra deserved better.

And one day, he would be the one to give it to her. Provided he could find a way to keep his bloody temper under control around her.

He smoothed the cold pillow before grabbing it and tossing it across the room. The AMT kept fucking with everything that was good in Jaxton's life, and he was tired of it. After rescuing Millie, he'd find Neena, tie her up if need be, and find out her plans in detail so he could start protecting those he cared for.

Fuck finding the Four Talents. With the exception of Kiarra, they could become someone else's problem. It was time for the AMT to stop ruining people's lives.

He just needed to find a way to shut them down for good.

Chapter Twenty-Four

In order to try to forget Jaxton's words, Kiarra found an empty room, slammed the door shut behind her, and made a beeline for the closest window. Getting a look at anything outside of the AMT usually improved her mood.

After scoping out the nearby buildings and shops, she focused on the human traffic below and wondered what it would be like to have a normal life, free of persecution and full of family and friends.

Humans had no idea how lucky they were. The majority were oblivious to the politics of elemental magic in the *Feiru* world and had no idea that the Asylums for Magical Threats existed.

If she'd been human, she never would've been separated from her family. Her parents might even still be alive.

But Kiarra wasn't human and she needed to accept that.

As a child, her mother had always told her stories about how first-borns had once been revered, their abilities seen not only as a gift, but vital to everyday human and *Feiru* life. Telling those stories had been tantamount to treason, but Renee Melini hadn't cared, wanting to comfort her first-born daughter and let her know she was special.

Her mother had done that kind of thing throughout her childhood, and Kiarra had never understood how the kind, comforting version of Renee Melini could've turned over her daughter to the AMT system without a fight. After her talk with

Cam, she knew her parents had fought for her and Kiarra had a feeling it had all been part of a bigger plan. Uncle Alex could probably tell her more about her parents, provided she could save Millie and stay out of the AMT's hands.

If her mother had risked charges of treason to help her daughter, then Kiarra could certainly do just as much to save those who were starting to matter. Millie, Jaxton, Neena, and even Marco, Taka, and Darius had all helped her at some point, and she wanted to repay them. That feeling of debt was what kept her from telling Jaxton about Gio's demands. Well, that and the fact she wouldn't give up so easily on her brother.

Gio had heard their mother's stories right alongside her and Cam, laughing and tensing at all the same moments. She still remembered the boy with the innate trait of caring for the weak and couldn't believe that aspect of Gio's personality would completely disappear, no matter what Sinclair had done. The little brother of her memories had to be somewhere inside of Giovanni Melini—she just needed to figure out how to reach him and draw him back out.

She also needed more information on Sinclair. It would be quicker and more reliable to ask Jaxton for the information, but after the way he'd just acted, she might try contacting Neena and hope for the best.

In retrospect, she could see why he'd spied on her and Cam—Jaxton had been protecting his territory and his team. But to say it was her fault that Millie was captured, well, that wasn't something she could forgive so easily.

It wasn't as if Kiarra wanted to be helpless, weak, or a liability. She was getting stronger, putting on weight, and even had a gun. Given enough time, she could honestly see herself becoming more of an asset to DEFEND than a liability.

Yet she still had the need to prove herself to Jaxton, to show him that she didn't need a babysitter. While his protection was welcome most of the time, she didn't want him constantly shadowing her every move. She wanted some modicum of freedom. But unless her ability to gather elemental fire returned, she had a feeling someone would always be watching her.

The tingling she'd felt when Jaxton had kissed her was the closest thing she'd felt to using her elemental abilities in years. The warmth had pulsed around her fingertips and heated her skin, as if a flame had wanted to ignite. If only she could make that happen.

Just remembering Jaxton's touch and kisses from earlier made Kiarra's skin flush and her heart rate speed up. Even angry, she couldn't deny the attraction between them. The blasted man was always in her thoughts.

The tingling sensation returned to her fingers, and she had an idea. Closing her eyes, Kiarra focused on drawing heat toward her fingers. The sensation dulled, so she mentally pictured Jaxton caressing the skin at her waist, then moving up to cup her breasts with his hands, and the heat built up again. Instead of drawing energy toward her fingers, she focused on spreading the tingling sensation outward and felt a spike in pressure.

Kiarra opened her eyes and stopped breathing. There was a small flame dancing across her fingers.

She imagined the flame spreading higher and the small flame grew, now six or seven inches tall.

Her elemental fire had returned. Her abilities didn't work the same as before Ty's formula, but she didn't care. The flames dancing on her skin warmed her from head to toe, relaxing her in a way she hadn't been able to achieve in years.

Smiling, she concentrated on the flame, afraid it would go out. She was so focused on the task that she didn't notice the position of her hands.

She wasn't reaching to the south—the direction of elemental fire.

~~*

After leaving messages with his various contacts, Jaxton threw some water on his face, packed a few things into a bag, and went to find Kiarra. She might still be angry, but the flat was compromised and they needed to leave as soon as possible.

He walked by the study door, noticed it was closed, and turned around. It had been open earlier.

Jaxton twisted the knob, grateful that Kiarra had forgotten to lock it this time, and eased the door open. His eyes swept the room until he spotted Kiarra standing near the window, a six-inch flame dancing across her hand.

She lied to me.

Jaxton tossed the door open and Kiarra jumped as it slammed against the wall. He took two steps before she turned and a flame shot across the room. He ducked the ball of fire and then stalked across the room until he was only a few inches from Kiarra. "Were you ever going to fucking tell me about the return of your fire?"

Kiarra looked down at her hand and a brief flash of regret was quickly replaced with anger. She clenched her fingers and look back up at Jaxton.

She said nothing, and he took her chin in his hand. "When did your elemental magic return?"

Kiarra put her hands on his chest, and he tried to ignore the heat of her touch.

He took her hands in his and leaned close, but a corner of Kiarra's mouth rose in a half-smile before she said, "Thanks for helping me focus."

He blinked. "What the hell are you talking about?"

She stood on her tiptoes and he could feel the heat of her breath on his face. "This."

Her hands became hot coals, and Jaxton released them. He glanced down at his hands and he saw something strange—his hands were unharmed. No blisters, no burns. He looked up and glared. "Fuck, Kiarra, why'd you do that?"

"That's what you get when you let your temper take charge. You're always calm and collected with Marco and the others, but never with me. You need to work on that."

"Says the woman who nearly singed my head with a ball of fire."

She pointed a finger at him. "You deserved that, and more. If you'd taken two seconds to ask, I could've told you that this is the first time I've used my elemental fire since I've met you."

Jaxton was good at telling lies from truth, and his gut said Kiarra was telling the truth.

He wasn't used to asking for what he wanted, but if it was going to work with Kiarra, on any level, he needed to swallow his pride. The return of her abilities changed everything. "I can't guarantee that I'll never slip up, but I'll try to ask first, act later. Now, will you tell me why you can gather fire all of a sudden?"

Kiarra crossed her arms over her chest, signaling this wasn't going to be as easy as he'd hoped. "Not until you admit it wasn't my fault that Millie was captured."

Millie. He could still hear her screams of pain.

His inability to protect his sister still lingered. However, since he was no longer seeing red, he couldn't remember exactly what he'd said to Kiarra. Judging by her reaction, it'd been hurtful.

But he didn't have time to waste and find out what he'd said so he could apologize. They needed to leave soon or they'd be captured too. "Don't worry about Millie. If she doesn't escape on her own, we'll find a way to get her out."

Kiarra threw her arms out, palms up. "What if that doesn't happen? Until they catch me, your family and friends, everyone you hold dear, will be in danger." She took a step closer and wagged a finger in the air. "If you truly want to protect them, you should walk away while you still can."

He growled, strode forward, and grabbed her shoulders. "I'm not fucking leaving, so stop trying to shut me out."

She remained silent. Jaxton knew they needed to leave the flat, but if he didn't crush her doubts now, he never would. "What else do I need to do? Swear on my brother's life again to make you believe I won't feed you to the wolves?" He leaned in close. "I know you've been betrayed in the past, but you need to trust someone, and I'm the best you have. It'll make it easier to trust the others later on."

Kiarra frowned. "What others? You mean Neena and your team?"

Best to get it out in the open. "You're a Fire Talent, Kiarra. And once word gets out, an army will start gathering to protect you."

~~*

Kiarra blinked. "Fire Talent? Like in the legends?"

Some of her mother's stories had been about the Four Talents. While she didn't remember much, she did recall that each Talent's elemental magic was stronger than other first-borns and full of tricky secrets.

Jaxton nodded and she looked away. True, her powers worked differently now than before the experiments, but that didn't automatically make her a Talent. Jaxton must know something she didn't. She looked back up at him. "Why do you think I'm a Talent?"

He waved a hand in dismissal. "You can play with your abilities later, compare them with what you find in the legends, and find all the proof you need. For now, you'll just have to take my word."

She studied his face, knowing he waited to see what she'd do.

It had been so long since she'd trusted anyone that she barely understood the concept anymore. Yet as she eyed the tall Brit in front of her, she remembered how Jaxton had chosen to stay with her despite the out she had offered. No one had ever really stood by her like that, offering support when the path ahead was difficult.

Even when she'd been faced with Cam's sudden appearance, she'd chosen to go to Jaxton, wanting the comfort of his presence. She'd been fighting it tooth and nail, but deep down, she'd started trusting him since that moment.

Still, the feeling was new and she didn't quite know how to handle it, especially as everyone else she'd trusted in the past had let her down. She would trust him, but on her own terms. "I think you believe your words." She put up a hand to stop him from interrupting. "But I want to find out more about the legends and my own abilities before I start thinking of myself as different from other first-borns. I'm sure you'll agree that's reasonable."

"Fair enough." He released her shoulders and put out a hand to shake. "If we're going to work together, then from here on out, we share everything. Agreed?"

Kiarra hesitated before taking his hand. Something had just shifted in their relationship and it terrified her.

Jaxton tightened his grip and she yelped as he pulled her forward. He whispered into her ear, "Look forward to later, pet, because there's another front I'm not giving up on either."

"And what would that be?"

He moved closer, his breath hot against her ear. "The next chance I get, I plan to do much more than kiss you."

Her breath hitched, but before she could say another word, Jaxton guided her out of the room. He was telling her something about their escape plans but it was hard to focus; her body was on fire, but not because of her magic.

CHAPTER TWENTY-FIVE

Kiarra frowned at the map on the table. "So North Berwick Law is the name of a hill?"

"Law is a Scots word for hill," Jaxton answered automatically. "Where in the watch house ruins on North Berwick Law did Giovanni say we can find the clue?"

She raised an eyebrow. "I thought my job was to get the clue while you played lookout."

Jaxton shrugged. "Anything could happen, you know that."

Kiarra pushed off from the table and dropped into a nearby cushy chair. Their new location was nothing more than a studio flat in eastern Edinburgh. Small, yet cozy, with a bed, a fireplace, and a "wee" kitchen.

It'd taken several hours to reach the flat and Jaxton hadn't wasted a second, teaching Kiarra a few more of his survival tricks along the way.

Jaxton's drills of choosing the safest routes to go unnoticed and reciting DEFEND safe house locations had distracted her from earlier revelations. Even now, she focused on their plan for following Gio's instructions rather than on Jaxton's unfulfilled promise or his claim that she was a Talent. She wasn't quite ready to tackle either one.

She adjusted her position in the chair and explained, "The clue will be buried under a rock in the only remaining corner of the watch house ruins before tomorrow afternoon."

Jaxton took out his new phone and pushed some buttons before laying it on the table. "Right. Some people are going to watch that hill for me and let me know if anyone shows up." He walked over to her and held out a hand. "Now that's sorted, it's time to train for a bit."

Ignoring his hand, she gave a pointed look around the small room. "Where, exactly, are we going to do that? On the roof?"

Jaxton wiggled his fingers. "Are you ever going to cooperate easily?"

"No."

He smiled. "Bloody woman." He grabbed her hand and pulled her up before turning her around and placing his hands on her waist. She should scold his manhandling, yet part of her wanted him to move his hands higher, pull her up against his chest, and encircle her with his arms so she could feel safe again.

However, his hands stayed on her hips, but he did move in closer, surrounding her with his male scent mixed with soap. She resisted a shiver at the heat of his body against her back.

Jaxton leaned down and said into her ear, "You need to strengthen your ability to concentrate, so we'll start there. Call up your fire."

She closed her eyes, but Jaxton pinched her hip and ordered, "Keep them open and on your target."

Opening her eyes, she elbowed Jaxton in the ribs. Hard. "All right, teacher, what's my target? The fake plant in the corner?"

"That'll do."

She kept her eyes on the plant and channeled her heat outward as before. Without looking, Kiarra knew there was a flame surrounding each of her hands. The heat tickled against her skin and she realized how much she'd missed the feeling over the years.

"Now," Jaxton said, "make the fire dance in front of you."

The air was full of elemental energy particles, each compass direction holding a higher concentration of a specific element. If she could find a way to draw the elemental fire particles to her flame, she could direct the fire to jump from energy particle to energy particle, appearing as a constant stream of flame to those without the ability to wield elemental magic.

She concentrated and sensed the change in the air as the particles gathered in front of her. The flame jumped from her hands to its new fuel source, creating an arc of fire that extended out six inches from her chest.

Kiarra wanted to celebrate, but she focused everything she had on keeping the flame alive and dancing in front of her. Then Jaxton nuzzled the side of her head at the same time as he stroked the right side of her ribcage. The combined feel of his late-day whiskers on her cheek and his strong fingers on her ribs sent a rush of heat through her body.

And in the next second, her fire extinguished as her hormones battled for control of her brain.

Jaxton stilled his fingers and she felt his smile against her ear. "Is that the best you can do, pet? Try again."

She clenched her jaw. She wouldn't let his little tricks defeat her.

She repeated the process of creating a swath of fire in front of her. When she had another stream of fire dancing in front of her, Jaxton stroked her side, but this time, she was prepared. His touch only prodded her to expand the flame farther away, creating a larger arc of fire.

Jaxton blew into her ear and she narrowed her eyes, just managing to save her flame from dying again. *Take that, Jaxton.* Extending her fire further, it was now only a few inches short of the plant in the corner.

He whispered, "Now, try to surround the plant, but don't destroy it."

Just as she directed the fire a little closer to the plant, Jaxton traced his finger up the side of her neck. As he stroked her sensitive skin with his warm, rough finger, Kiarra gritted her teeth. She would reach the plant if it killed her.

Careful not to melt the plastic, she encircled the outside leaves, moving closer to the stems. Just as she was about to surround the delicate pieces, Jaxton nipped her neck and the fire disappeared, leaving behind a small branch of melted plastic.

She let out a growl and turned around to find the bastard was smiling. "What the hell, Jaxton? Is it a habit of yours to bite trainees?"

"Only the ones who taste as good as you." He swirled his finger in the air, indicating for her to turn around. "Now, try it again. If you can't concentrate with something as small as a nip on your neck, then you bloody well won't be able to block out the people fighting, and possibly dying, around you."

Kiarra was about to protest, but then she had an idea. She turned around as directed, but before he could tell her what to do, she reached back and grabbed his genitals. He drew a sharp breath and she smiled. "If you can't concentrate with someone's hand on your balls, then you might not be able to block out the distractions around you when you're fighting."

She gave a light squeeze and found him hard. A small part of her was glad he was just as affected by her touch as she was with his.

BLAZE OF SECRETS

Then an image flashed into her mind of his erection free of his clothing, open to her touch and her mouth. The old version of Kiarra would've been afraid to think such thoughts, but the new version was intrigued. If anything, the images made her lower belly tighten, wanting more than just a daydream.

If she were honest with herself, Kiarra wanted him more than anything she'd wanted for a long time.

Where had that come from? But before she could think too hard on it, Jaxton whispered into her ear, bringing her back to the present. "You want to play dirty? Well, two can play at that game, pet."

He slowly slid his hand down her belly, but stopped short of cupping her. The heat of his hand burned through her jeans and her core throbbed in anticipation.

His voice was husky when he said, "Nod if you want me to keep going."

Kiarra's heart pounded in her ears. This was it. With one nod, she could finally be able to make a break with her past.

To say she was unafraid was a lie, but the stubborn and bossy man at her back had done more for her than anyone else. She might not yet trust him beyond measure, but he'd earned enough trust for this.

And so she nodded.

Jaxton licked the side of her jaw and whispered, "Good."

He moved his hand between her legs and rocked against her clit. Closing her eyes, Kiarra gasped as pleasure shot through her body.

Jaxton rocked once more, and she cried out. Then he made a male noise of satisfaction and somehow through her lust-haze, she decided he was a little too satisfied with himself. It was time to even the playing field.

Careful not to let her arousal turn her hands into coals, she stroked Jaxton's erection through his pants and he sucked in a breath. However, before she could gloat another second, Jaxton thrust against her hand and bit her earlobe. "Are you wet for me, pet?"

Kiarra should feel embarrassed at the question, but his words shot straight between her legs. She whispered, "Yes."

"Good." Jaxton tilted her head at an angle and kissed her, exploring her mouth with his warm, slick tongue. She hesitated at first, but soon stroked her tongue against his as she threaded her fingers through his hair, loving the feel and taste of him in her mouth.

Jaxton slowly ran his hands up her ribcage until he cupped her breasts and squeezed. Kiarra moaned into his mouth, wondering what he would do next.

Then he did something Ty had never done; he pinched her nipples. The mixture of pleasure and pain shot straight between her legs, making her wetter than she'd ever been before.

He broke the kiss and she nearly whimpered. After finally making her first adult decision, she didn't want him to stop. But then he nuzzled her cheek and she eased into his caress. His voice was husky when he murmured, "If you want me to stop, tell me now, Kiarra."

He's still worried about me. If she had any remaining doubts about surrendering to Jaxton, they disappeared.

In response, she turned her head and kissed him. His kiss was rougher this time as he nibbled and sucked her lower lip, but she wasn't afraid. She loved the fact she could do this to him.

He pinched her nipples again, and her knees nearly buckled. As if he could read her mind, Jaxton broke their kiss just long enough to turn her around, grab her ass, and pull her up against his body.

She reveled in the feel of her body pressed against his, but before she could kiss him again, he lifted her as if she weighted next to nothing. She instinctively wrapped her legs around his waist, signaling how much she wanted him to continue.

He squeezed her tighter and with his hot, hard body between her legs, she couldn't resist rubbing against him. She purred as the seam of her jeans created a wonderful friction.

But she needed more. She knew what she wanted, without reservations. The past would no longer control her.

"Skin," she managed. "I want to feel your skin against mine."

~~*

Jaxton groaned at the pressure of Kiarra rubbing against his cock. If she wanted skin-to-skin, then he was more than happy to oblige.

He kissed her again, exploring the heat of her mouth as he somehow managed to reach the bed. Once they were on the mattress, he broke the kiss and studied Kiarra's face. Her flushed cheeks and kiss-bruised lips filled him with pride. His cock also pulsed in anticipation.

Tracing her cheek with a finger, all he wanted to do was rip off her clothes and fuck her until they both forgot about their troubles.

But this was her first time with him, and after what she'd revealed about her time inside the AMT, he needed to be careful. She hadn't frozen at any of his touches yet, but there was still a chance she would again.

Looking at him with heavy-lidded eyes, Kiarra pulled up her shirt a few inches, revealing the pale skin of her abdomen. "Before this shirt goes any higher, you're going to take yours off."

He managed not to smile at her attempt to seduce him. Her innocence only made him want to claim her all the more.

He took off his shirt and her eyes lingered on his bare chest. The heat in her gaze made his cocker harder.

Kiarra gently placed her hands on his chest and slowly roamed from top to bottom. Each touch burned his skin, but not because of her magic; the softness of her fingers was like no other woman's touch before.

When Kiarra scraped his nipple, his patience evaporated. He leaned down and kissed her deeply, sucking and biting her bottom lip before trailing kisses down her neck. She arched her back, jutting her breasts forward, but Jaxton avoided them on his path downward, instead kissing the exposed skin of her belly. He smiled at her noise of frustration.

He feathered his fingers across the soft skin of her abdomen before pulling her top up over her breasts.

Small yet round, they were fucking perfect. Tracing the taut peak of one nipple through her bra, his mouth watered. He wanted to suck them deep into his mouth, biting and licking until he made her come.

Before he could pull down her bra to do exactly that, Kiarra pushed away his hands, and Jaxton froze. Had something triggered one of her memories?

Then she pulled her top over her head and slid off her bra straps, and his body relaxed. Chucking, he teased, "So impatient."

"And you, sir, are a tease."

He moved up and traced the skin at the top of her breast, just above the cup. "Don't worry, pet, you'll thank me later."

She snorted. "For a self-assured sex god, you're not doing a very good job."

If Kiarra could tease him, she was more than ready. Jaxton pulled her bra down and gazed at her lovely pale breasts, greedy to see them bounce when she rode him.

For now, he leaned down and took her nipple into his mouth, lapping and biting the taut peak before moving and doing the same to her other breast. Each little noise of pleasure Kiarra made because of his attentions shot straight to his cock.

Then she placed her hands on his shoulders. Wanting to ease any lingering doubts she might have, he rubbed her forearms up and down a few times before he moved to kiss the spot between her breasts. When she melted under his lips, Jaxton continued lower.

His lips reached the top of her jeans, and Kiarra's nails dug into his shoulder. Was it a sign she wanted him to continue? Or, was it because she wanted him to stop?

Glancing up, he only saw Kiarra's heated look. She still wanted him.

He licked her belly just about her waistband and blew. "I can't show you the full extent of my sex-god powers unless we take off your jeans."

Kiarra giggled, the sound a tinkle of delight he would never tire of, and her hold relaxed. Looking back up, he raised an eyebrow as he hooked his fingers under the waistband of her jeans. "Just don't burn me into a crisp, okay? I'm quite fond of my cock."

She tapped his arse with her foot, and Jaxton took that as encouragement. He couldn't remember the last time a woman had teased him in bed. He'd kept women at a distance since his brother's capture, focusing solely on his family, but somehow

Kiarra had found her way around his internal barriers. Not surprising, since the woman was as stubborn as an ox.

Smiling at the thought, he unbuttoned and unzipped her jeans, kissing the patch of skin just above her knickers. This was the point of no return, but a quick glance told him Kiarra was still with him and willing. As he slid her jeans down her long legs, exposing her underwear, his mouth watered; all he wanted to do was taste her.

He tossed her jeans aside and traced a finger up the inside of her thigh to the edge of her knickers, tracing one side and then the other, but never dipping beneath them into her dark curls.

Kiarra made an impatient noise in her throat as she raised her hips. Tracing the crease of her thigh, his voice was husky as he spoke. "Tell me what you want with words, pet. Your wish is my command."

She looked down at him, her face flushed and eyes dilated, and Jaxton couldn't remember seeing a more beautiful sight. She licked her lips and he focused on the act, barely restraining himself from crawling back up to kiss her again. His voice was a growl even to his own ears when he said, "Well?"

"Touch me."

He smiled, rubbing her thighs. "But I am touching you."

She narrowed her eyes, her face a bright pink. "Are you really going to make me say it?"

He grinned. "Show me where."

For a second, Kiarra kept her hands clenched in the sheets and he wondered if he'd pushed her too far. But after a few seconds, she moved a hand to her underwear and ran a finger down her swollen core. What he wouldn't give to be able to tease her when she was naked with much more than his fingers.

All in good time. "As you wish, pet." He traced her opening through her panties, proud that she soaked the material—for him. Deciding she'd had enough torture, he plunged a finger into her curls and groaned at her wetness.

He stroked up toward her clit, but drew a path around the sensitive bundle, avoiding direct contact, and traced back to her entrance. Kiarra breathed his name and he lost his restraint, impatient to taste her. He leaned down and kissed her through her knickers. Kiarra raised her hips, and he dragged her underwear down past her knees and pushed her legs wide.

She was pink and glistening.

He growled, but resisted tasting her just yet. Instead, he took a deep inhale of her mixture of woman and musk, the scent shooting straight to his cock.

His balls were aching, but he was determined to make it good for her. He blew a long, hot breath into her pussy. Kiarra wiggled and parted her thighs even more. He took it as a sign she was still with him and still wanted this.

He finally plunged his tongue into her hot, wet core and groaned. Her taste was better than he'd imagined, and he lapped at her wetness as if he was starving. While Kiarra made small sounds of pleasure, she was still far too restrained. He stopped lapping and instead slowly licked up to her clit before swirling the tight bud with his tongue.

Kiarra thrust her hands into his hair and moaned.

That was more like it.

After sucking her clit between his teeth, he thrust a finger into her pussy, barely aware of Kiarra mumbling his name. He continued to thrust his finger while lapping and swirling her clit with his tongue. Soon she was moving in time to his rhythm, so he added a second finger and thrust deeper.

He bit her clit lightly and he felt her tense before her muscles started to spasm around his fingers as she moaned his name; next time, he wanted to make her scream.

Once she came down from her orgasm and her muscles relaxed, he stilled his fingers, removed them, and took one last plunge with his tongue.

The taste of her orgasm nearly made him come in his trousers.

Jaxton kissed Kiarra just above her curls, before rubbing his hands up her body, gently squeezing her breasts and nipping her neck. Her cheeks were flushed and her eyes half-lidded. Jaxton brushed the hair off her forehead. "I told you that you'd thank me later."

She gave a half-hearted glare, but ruined it with a smile. Kiarra reached up and pulled his head down. "Just shut up and kiss me."

~~*

One minute Kiarra lay boneless, recovering from her orgasm, and the next she ordered Jaxton to kiss her.

As his lips touched hers, the combination of his weight settling between her thighs and the taste of herself in his mouth made her core throb. Jaxton's mouth and fingers had been glorious, but she wanted his cock inside her.

She raised her hips against Jaxton's jean-clad erection and moved. He groaned into her mouth and Kiarra broke the kiss. "Why do you still have your pants on?"

He rested his forehead against hers and looked her in the eye. "Because once they come off, I don't think I can stop myself from pounding into your tight, wet pussy"

234

Another jolt went between her legs at his blunt words. Then she realized he was minding her feelings.

Her heart softened, and she reached up to stroke his shoulders. "But that's exactly what I want you to do."

Jaxton growled. "Be very sure about this, Kiarra."

She ran her fingers under his waistband. "Take them off."

He was up and out of his pants and boxers so fast, Kiarra barely registered he was gone before he laid his weight over her again. His skin touched hers, and she reveled in the heat of his body. There was no panic or fear, only desire, comfort, and a sense of safety.

Jaxton moved his hips and his cock rubbed against her. At the contact, she forgot about everything else but the feeling of his strong, long body against hers.

She tried to wrap a leg around his waist, but he pushed it back down. "I need you to help me with something first, pet."

He sat up and she couldn't keep her eyes off his jutting erection, the tip already glistening.

Again, no fear. Her core throbbed, anxious to have him inside her.

Jaxton growled. "If you keep looking at my cock like that, wetting your lips, I'm going to come right now." Kiarra looked up before he continued, "Now, sit up."

A small thrill coursed through her body. Maybe she could drive Jaxton crazy later. The thought of man desiring her that much was still new to her.

Jaxton put out his hands and she took them, loving the roughness of his skin against her fingers.

Once she was upright, her gaze drifted back down to his cock again. As she reached out to touch it, a bead formed on the tip. Without thinking, she put her finger there, rubbing the liquid around the head. Jaxton inhaled deeply and grabbed her wrist.

"Later, pet. You can touch as much as you want later, but not right now."

She must have looked disappointed, because Jaxton leaned in and kissed her gently. "Pouting doesn't become you. But the choice is yours: I can either fuck you hard or you can take my cock into your mouth. Which will it be?"

She was getting used to his blunt talk in bed. "I like it when you talk like that." His words encouraged her to be bold, and she moved to straddle him. She rubbed her core over his hard cock. "And I don't like waiting."

The next second, she was on her back again, and she heard Jaxton mutter, "Plan B," before taking out a condom and rolling it down his cock.

Then he took her wrists. Pinning them above her head, his free hand went between her legs. All thoughts of reality faded as he stroked first her entrance and then her clit.

He removed his fingers and she made a sound of protest. But as he brushed the tip of his cock against her, she arched her hips up in invitation.

With one swift thrust, he was completely inside her and she gasped at the fullness.

Jaxton leaned down and kissed her, alternating between nibbling her lips and suck her tongue. As he began to strum her at the apex of her thighs, the uncomfortable feeling of fullness passed and she moved her hips in encouragement.

Jaxton pulled almost entirely out before slamming into her again. A combination of pleasure and pain coursed through her, but she wanted more—to touch him, to move with him. She pulled her arms, and surprisingly, Jaxton let go.

He licked her ear and asked, "You ready, pet? I can't hold back much longer."

In reply, she ran her hands down his back, grabbed his ass, and dug in her nails. Jaxton bit her earlobe and murmured, "So demanding. Just the way I like it."

He bent one of her legs and started moving. He thrust deep, her breasts jiggling from the force. Surprising even herself, Kiarra pulled Jaxton's head down and bit his lower lip before raking her other hand down his back. Despite her recent orgasm, the pressure was building again.

Jaxton squeezed one of her breasts, and his other hand flicked her clit again. She moaned and he thrust his tongue into her mouth and pounded harder, the sound of his flesh against hers filling the room.

He moved even harder, reaching a place deep inside of her, and pinpricks of light danced before her eyes. When Jaxton pressed her clit with his thumb, pleasure shot through her, quickly followed by internal spasms.

Jaxton thrust a few more times before he stilled and groaned.

He settled on top of her and kissed the side of her neck. As her heart pounded in her chest, the reality of having sex with Jaxton set in. For better or for worse, the relationship between them had just changed forever.

Tracing patterns on his damp back with her finger, Kiarra didn't panic. Interacting with the man on top of her had changed her from day one, and she liked who she'd become. She only hoped Jaxton wouldn't hurt her.

He nuzzled the side of her neck with his lips. "You're too quiet, pet. What're you thinking about?"

Grateful for the distraction, Kiarra decided to dodge the question. She was far too content to ruin the moment with doubts. "I'm trying to decide if you were good enough to qualify as a 'sex god' or not."

Jaxton raised his head. "Well, then I think you need some more convincing to put aside all doubts."

Kiarra bit back a smile. "Best out of three?"

Jaxton smiled smugly. "I'd say best out of five, except you need to be able to walk tomorrow."

The erotic image of them having hours of sex, in various positions, went straight between her thighs, where Jaxton was still inside her. Jaxton's male smile became smugger when he took in her expression. He leaned down and stopped a hair's breadth from her lips. "Such a greedy thing. Let's see if I can sate your appetite."

He kissed her and tried to do exactly that.

CHAPTER TWENTY-SIX

Gio received orders that a specialist would interrogate Millie Ward. The rowanberry juice was starting to wear off, and her interrogation would require a finer technique without it. While relieved he wouldn't have to torture the woman, part of him wanted to prevent it. Especially after what he'd read about the pediatrics facilities.

There were at least five facilities worldwide, and their main purpose was to monitor DNA mutations caused by their parents' gene therapy trials. All of the children born inside the AMT compounds were sent to the pediatrics facilities, not just the first-borns. Some of the children were the second generation to be born inside the AMT, meaning that the program had been going on for a long time without oversight or *Feiru* High Council jurisdiction.

At least publicly.

Gio clenched his fist. He'd always been a man of the law, and imprisoning *Feiru* without legal basis irked him. Part of the reason he wanted to be a Member of Parliament was so he could draft or change laws for a better future and show that democracy still worked.

His father had always reinforced that everyone should know their place in society. Even imprisoning first-borns had served a purpose—to protect the rest of *Feiru* kind from human hysteria and discrimination. But Gio wondered if his father was more concerned with acquiring power for his own goals than for the good of the *Feiru* public. Holding children without elemental abilities inside the pediatrics facilities did nothing to help repeal Article I, or to develop an elemental-magic-subduing formula.

A beep sounded behind him, signaling the return of Kiarra's tracking beacon on his computer screen. All of the most valuable first-borns had a tracking chip implanted under their skin. While his sister's chip was faulty and blinked on and off at random intervals, it was a type of insurance that had proved useful in tracking his sister's movements. This was the first time the signal had returned since the incident in the pub.

He gave the coordinates to one of his retrieval squads, along with explicit instructions to bring Kiarra, and any others with her, back alive. The more information he gathered, the more likely it was his father would give him another task. Gio wanted to find out more about what was happening inside the AMT compounds, and to do that, he needed access.

He also needed to find out more about his father's motives.

Taking a deep breath, Gio headed down the hall toward the interrogation room. It was time to see if he could stomach an interrogation conducted by a specialist.

~~*

Kiarra woke at the sudden rush of cold air to her back. Opening her eyes, she saw Jaxton sitting upright, a gun in his hand. "What's going on?"

Jaxton squeezed her hip. "The fire escape rattled. Whatever made it was too heavy to be a stray animal."

She sat up, pulling the blanket up with her to cover her breasts, and listened. After a few seconds, she said, "I don't hear anything."

Jaxton rose, unashamed of his nakedness. She watched him walk across the room to the window and forced herself to focus on the possible threat instead of his well-shaped backside. "Well?"

He remained still, probably scanning the surroundings, when he cursed. "There's a small group of people standing near a van down there, and they're gesturing this way. I can't tell if they're armed or not." He threw a glance over his shoulder. "Get dressed, Kiarra. It may be nothing, but I'm not taking any chances."

Great, more trouble. That was just what they needed.

Ignoring the soreness between her legs, Kiarra threw on some clothes and joined Jaxton by the window. He was now fully dressed and craning his head at an odd angle near the top of the window. She wondered what he was looking for, but she simply said, "I'm ready."

"Do you have your gun?" She took the gun from her waistband at her back and he nodded. "Right. I'm going to check the front entrance. Stay away from the window, but keep your safety off." He placed a hand on her lower back and leaned in close. "If worse comes to worst, then use your fire."

He gave her a gentle kiss before he went to the door on the far side of the room. Kiarra kept an eye on the window and wondered who might be outside. Jaxton was experienced when it came to evading people and he had been overly cautious yesterday, so whoever it was, they were good.

Even if they'd interrogated Millie with the hope of finding out their location, Millie hadn't known where they were.

Millie. If they were caught, no one could help Jaxton's sister. That thought kicked her mind into gear. She checked to see if she could still call up her fire on a whim. A flame flickered to life on her hand and then extinguished. She was ready.

Jaxton rushed to her side. "The bloody thing's rigged, which means the fire escape is our only option. We might even be able to go to the roof and jump to a neighbor's house."

"I sense a 'but.'"

"There's a device above the window, most likely set to go off when it opens. Breaking the window might avoid the trigger mechanism, but the noise would surely alert the people down by the van."

So they needed a way to break the window without making any noise. Kiarra put the safety back on her gun and tucked it into her waistband. "I can melt the glass and the device. The people below will probably notice the bright light, but even if they only mistake it for an explosion at first, those precious few seconds might give us enough time to scramble down the fire escape. Once we reach the bottom, I can try to create some sort of fire barrier to give us time to get away."

Jaxton shook his head. "That's going to take a lot of energy, not to mention a phenomenal amount of control. You might burn out."

She poked his arm. "Do you have any other ideas?" When he said nothing, she smiled. "I thought so. Let me help for once, Jaxton. I can do this."

He searched her eyes before cupping her cheek. "You sure?" She nodded. "I'll make sure we survive the climb down. But you need to promise me one thing, Kiarra."

"Yes?"

He leaned down. "If something happens to me, you run. Go to one of the safe houses and find a way to contact Neena or call the phone number I made you memorize. The person on the other side will help you." She didn't want to make a promise she couldn't keep, but then he threaded his fingers through her hair and pulled her head forward. "Promise me."

"Fine. I promise." He rewarded her with a brief kiss before tugging her to the side of the window. When he motioned for her to start doing her thing, Kiarra kept her eyes on the window and concentrated on her fire. If she could pull this off, she would no longer be useless. She could protect not only herself, but those she cared about.

~~*

After double-checking all of his weapons were accessible, Jaxton watched Kiarra and frowned. She should still be in bed, tucked against him, not melting glass and creating fire barriers to help them escape capture.

The people downstairs were most likely here to collect Kiarra and take her back to the AMT. But he wasn't going to let that happen. Kiarra was no longer just his charge.

Sure, the sex last night had been fantastic—Kiarra had proved to be an unashamed and curious bugger in bed—but it was all of the small things she'd done that still made him smile. Her teasing tone and half-hearted glares. The way she held him after and traced designs on his back. Or even the way she slept with her mouth open, drooling a little.

After what had happened with his brother and Marzina, Jaxton had never slept over with a woman because that would signal a tentative commitment, which could lead to an attachment. And when people became attached, they tended to forget their priorities and become blinded to the truth, or so he'd believed.

Now he wasn't so sure. Kiarra was not only determined to help him, but she didn't try to shift his focus or demand all of his attention. Between his contacts and her inside knowledge, they had a real chance to make a difference in the lives of first-borns, especially if they could bring down the AMT system.

He wanted to keep her. Or rather, he wanted to convince her to stay. He could just imagine what she'd do if he mentioned a plan to "keep" her.

A bright flash at the window caught his attention. A second later, it was gone. The glass had melted, but the wooden frame and highly flammable curtains were untouched. Judging by how quickly Kiarra was mastering her abilities, he was starting to believe the legends about Fire Talents.

"Nice work." Jaxton went to the window and crawled out. "Now follow my lead."

Kiarra crawled out behind him, but he focused on the five people down below. Two were making a beeline for the bottom of the fire escape. He tugged Kiarra behind him and made it down one flight of stairs before he saw small lights flashing from the direction of the van. He pushed Kiarra down and fired off a few shots of his own, causing the three people near the van to duck for cover.

Taking advantage of the opening, he looked over the rail and saw a man climbing up the ladder. He whispered, "Close your eyes and plug your ears," to Kiarra before taking out a flash grenade. After releasing the pin, he crouched down with Kiarra, covered his ears, and closed his eyes.

Light and noise filtered through his eyes and ears, but not enough to affect him.

When it was quiet again, he grabbed Kiarra's hand and pulled her along after him. But they had only gone down one flight before people started shooting at them from the van again. Jaxton ducked his head and ordered, "Keep your head down."

A bullet hit the railing next to him, so Jaxton picked up his pace; somehow, they managed to reach the bottom flight without getting hurt.

Since the ladder was already extended, Jaxton motioned for Kiarra to keep down and close to the wall before he turned and checked out his two opponents on the ground below.

The man previously climbing the ladder was now on his arse, and a woman stood in front of him as a shield. She had her oddly shaped gun raised in his general direction, but since she was still disoriented from the flash grenade, she was aiming not at him, but about five feet to Jaxton's right.

He'd seen that type of gun before when he'd rescued Kiarra and his brother from the AMT—it shot tranquilizer darts.

Before he could jump down to the ground, a small arrow of flame shot from behind him and hit the tranquilizer gun below. As the woman dropped her gun, Jaxton jumped down and twisted the woman's arm behind her back. He took the spare tranquilizer gun from the woman's holster and shot both the woman and the man. The drug was quick acting, and it knocked them out within seconds.

Jaxton looked up, but Kiarra wasn't there. A quick scan revealed her location to the side, behind a trash skip with a small flame dancing on one of her palms. He fired his gun toward the van to keep them ducking for cover and went to Kiarra's side.

He waited, not wanting to break her concentration, but after five seconds passed, he whispered, "Is it impossible, pet?"

"I can do it, but I need you to help me focus."

"Tell me what you need me to do."

"I need physical contact. Pull me close."

Despite the odd request, he didn't hesitate. Jaxton placed his hands on Kiarra's hips and pulled her back against his chest. "Like this?"

A heartbeat passed before she answered. "Yes."

He kept an eye out for anyone else, but was soon distracted by a tingling sensation on the back of his neck. A quick sweep confirmed no one was behind them or on the fire escape, but then the tingle spread. Soon there were flames dancing along his arms, moving down in a continuous stream until they collected in Kiarra's palms; the more the flames moved down his arms, the stronger her flame grew.

Bloody hell. This wasn't normal. The fire didn't hurt him, and while Kiarra had successfully surrounded the fake plant last night without damaging it, at least until he'd distracted her, he didn't think she was consciously covering him with fire.

So this was the power of a Fire Talent.

Something slammed against his back right before fire shot out from Kiarra, igniting an eight-foot dancing wall of flame. Kiarra leaned against him for a second before standing on her own without help. Adrenaline was probably the only thing keeping her conscious.

He raised his gun and stepped around the skip to look for enemies. The way was clear. Jaxton took hold of Kiarra's elbow, guided her toward the left and said, "Head down that street and turn left. If we get separated, I'll meet you at the second safe house." The wall of fire began to flicker. He gave Kiarra a push. "Now go."

She hesitated a second, but for once didn't argue. The wall of fire died down, and was now only a foot or two high. One of the men near the van was staring straight at him.

246

Fuck. Now he needed to distract them long enough to allow Kiarra time to get away. He knew Edinburgh well enough that he could find an alternative route to the safe house.

He headed right, in the opposite direction of Kiarra, and fired off a shot to ensure that the people in the van would follow him. Careful to choose the path with the most obstacles to act as cover, he picked his way to the street on the far side. A quick check over his shoulder and he saw that the three people from the van were following him with their guns drawn.

CHAPTER TWENTY-SEVEN

Gio studied Millie's face, relaxed in unconsciousness, and noted the bruise on her cheek and the cut on her swollen bottom lip. By the time he had arrived, the interrogation had been over. The specialist, Ramirez, had extracted little from the woman, but had assured Gio that the first session was usually the least productive. He'd be back in a day to try again.

Something had to be done. He couldn't stomach the thought of Ramirez hurting the young woman again. Her records showed nothing illegal, or even dangerous, about her. She just happened to be related to the wrong person. There was nothing to justify this kind of treatment.

That put Gio in a conundrum, because he couldn't give his father cause to dismiss him, yet he wanted to help this innocent woman. In order to do that, he was going to have to find a way to fool everyone.

He turned, headed out into the hallway, and stopped in front of the nearest com unit. He pushed the button and a male voice answered, "*Yes?*"

Gio leaned in to the speaker and said, "No one is to enter Room 5 without my permission."

"*Yes, sir.*"

"Get word to Ramirez that I plan to take over the next round of interrogation with the prisoner. I'll give him the details later. Relay all communications to my office."

"*Is that all, sir?*"

"Yes." Gio released the com unit's button and walked to his office. Not only did he have to think of how to appear like he was interrogating the woman without hurting her, but he also needed a plan to get her out of the building and stash her somewhere until it was safe to let her go free. If he could clear those hurdles, he had someone he'd met at university who owed him a favor and would keep watch over Millie Ward until she understood the necessity of living under a new identity. Even if it took some convincing, a few verbal threats were better than torture any day of the week.

Then there was the problem of Kiarra. If he wanted to continue his research on the pediatrics facilities and the experiments being conducted inside the AMT compounds, as well as keep his access to the AMT database, he needed to please his father. James Sinclair wouldn't tolerate failure.

It was a good thing Gio enjoyed a challenge, because scheming all of that wasn't going to be easy.

~~*

Something was wrong.

Kiarra paced the room and resisted looking out the window for the fifteenth time. She'd made it to the safe house nearly an hour ago, but Jaxton had yet to arrive.

Leaving him behind had been one of the hardest things she'd ever had to do. She knew her fire had dissipated the instant she'd run, leaving Jaxton with nothing but the weapons strapped over his chest to defend himself. She'd seen Jaxton in action before and knew he wouldn't give up easily, but he'd still been outnumbered. That may not have been a problem, but Kiarra had a feeling that the three people near the van had also been carrying tranquilizer guns. All they needed to do was injure or stun Jaxton and fill him full of drugs, and he'd be done for.

But even if she knew where to find him, she could barely stand on her own two feet. The adrenaline that had kept her going was slowly fading and exhaustion was setting in. She and Jaxton hadn't spent much time sleeping before the visitors had arrived, and creating a wall of fire had sapped the last of her energy. In her current state, anyone could attack, and she wouldn't be able to defend herself.

So much for finally being useful.

She eyed the phone again and wondered if it was safe to use. She trusted Jaxton, but she had no idea what waited for her on the other side of the phone number he'd made her memorize. Would they make her leave him behind? As the minutes ticked by, she was running out of options. The longer she waited, the more she might be putting Jaxton in danger. Maybe the person on the other end could help. Leery as she was, it was worth a try.

After dialing the number, the phone rang twice in quick succession between pauses. She was just wondering if that was a British thing when a woman answered, "Hello."

The voice was unfamiliar, but she trusted Jaxton enough to answer, "Um, hi. I was told to call this number if I needed help."

"A strange American female calling me for help. You must be Kiarra," the woman said in barely understandable English. "Whatever has happened, someone is already on the way to help you."

"H-how did you know I needed help?"

Amusement tinged the woman's voice. "I have my sources."

Kiarra didn't like how vague the woman was being. Jaxton's safety was too important to her not to know what was going on.

She wanted to know the details, because if it didn't include helping Jaxton, she would find a way to help him on her own.

This was another test for Kiarra, another way to sever ties with her past inside the AMT, another chance to prove how strong she could be. She took a deep breath, imagined she was talking to Jaxton, and demanded, "What do you know and what do you plan to do about it?"

The line went silent and Kiarra feared she'd gone too far. If she'd just cost Jaxton the help he needed, she'd never forgive herself. But then the woman chuckled and answered, "After all this time, I should've known better than to doubt Neena's words."

"You know Neena?"

"Aye, better than most."

She wasn't sure if that was a good or bad thing. "So, what's the plan?"

Kiarra swore she heard a buzzing sound on the other end of the line before the woman stated, "Someone should knock on your door in a few minutes and that person will give you the details."

"But—"

"Sorry, darlin', that's all I can tell you for now. Gotta jet."

The line went dead and she stared at the phone. She was starting to hate the word "wait" with a passion.

To stay awake, Kiarra started pacing again. If no one showed up at the door, the only option she had left was to contact Neena, which could end up being no help at all. The next time this happened, she'd make sure she was better prepared.

The next time. Kiarra stilled. Yes, she wanted there to be a next time. The thought of leaving Jaxton in a few months was no longer an option. She needed to keep his stubborn ass in check.

251

Someone knocked on the door and she mustered up what energy she had left. As much as she wanted to hope, she wasn't stupid, so she walked to the door and looked out the peephole. It wasn't Jaxton, but she knew the face.

Stunned, she opened the door and murmured, "Neena."

Neena walked in, dressed in black except for a dark blue scarf tied over her hair. Kiarra closed the door, and Neena placed a hand on her back, steering her toward the bed. Kiarra frowned. "Why didn't the woman on the phone just tell me it was you?"

Neena grinned. "Because Aislinn spoils me and knows how I like to surprise people."

She vaguely remembered the name. "Aislinn, as in the other DEFEND co-leader?"

"That's the one." Neena sat down on the bed, patting the space next to her. "Now, do you want to hear my plan or not?"

"We don't have time for niceties. Just tell me what we're going to do to help Jaxton."

"My, my, someone's starting to sound just like their trainer." Neena tilted her head to the side, studying her. "But by now, I think he's more than a trainer to you. Am I right?"

Kiarra kept her face impassive. She finally understood Jaxton's impatience with this woman. "Either help me or get out. I don't have time for this."

Neena winked at her. "There's the Fire Talent leader I've been waiting for." She patted the bed beside her again. "If you truly want to help Jaxton, then you need to take a nap."

Kiarra blinked. She hadn't seen that coming. "Talent or not, I don't have super dream powers like you, so how is that supposed to help him?"

Neena raised an eyebrow. "Questioning me again, Kiarra? Tsk, tsk. You should know by now not to do that."

"Someone has to."

Neena laughed. "I like you more and more Kiarra Melini." She reached into one of her pants pockets and pulled out something wrapped in a cloth. "But if you aren't going to obey me willingly, there are other ways to make it happen."

Kiarra stepped back, unsettled by the gleam in Neena's eye. Wasn't the DEFEND co-leader supposed to be on her side? Whatever was going on, bluffing was all she had left. She straightened her shoulders and stated, "My elemental fire is back. Don't make me use it against you."

Neena rose and took a step toward her. "Fairly convincing threat, my dear, but we both know that you'll burn out if you call on your elemental fire right now, especially without your Conduit."

What the hell is a conduit? Kiarra eased toward the small desk and chair behind her, ready to use them as weapons if it came down to it. Neena was right about her being close to burnout. But even though her gun was tucked into the end table by the bed, she would still fight with whatever she could find. Jaxton would expect it of her.

Neena sighed and lifted the cloth-covered bundle, still concealing whatever lay beneath. "Let's hope you learn your lesson after this. I really do abhor punishing my own people, especially the clever ones."

Neena's words confused her, but without any other options, Kiarra grabbed the chair behind her and swung it around. But before she could make contact, Neena tackled her to the floor until Kiarra was facedown with her hands wrenched behind her back. She bucked, trying to get free, but then she felt a prick on her hip before Neena said, "You'll thank me later, my dear. Have a nice sleep."

You'll thank me later. Those were the same words Jaxton had said earlier.

Her consciousness slipped as whatever had been in that syringe took effect. Her last thoughts were that Neena had betrayed her and that the man she'd finally learned to trust might die because of it.

~~*

James Sinclair walked into the meeting room and went to the head of the large rectangular table. His bodyguards were right behind him, and once he sat down, they took protective positions on either side of his chair.

A quick glance at the people sitting at the table confirmed that Geoffrey Winter had kept up his end of the bargain. The heads of the *Feiru* Liaison offices from France, Greece, and Spain sat in front of him.

He remained silent, curious to see who would speak up first. As he'd predicted, it was Etienne Mercier, the liaison from France. "Why are we here, Sinclair? A high-alert meeting request from the UK *Feiru* liaison office asked me to come to this location, but unless things have changed in the last few days, you don't work for them."

"You're right. I don't work for them. But I think you want to hear what I have to say."

Gisella Cruz, the liaison from Spain, interrupted, "Just tell us why we're here, Sinclair. I have things I need to do back in Spain."

It was time for some meddling. "You three represent countries with the highest number of *Feiru* rebels in Europe, and the biggest rebel group of them all, DEFEND, is gaining power."

Cruz waved a hand and said, "Yes, yes, this is nothing new. They try to find ways to free the first-borns, but they are harmless and without much power. We're keeping a close watch on them."

Mercier added, "But Sinclair wouldn't bring up DEFEND unless he knew something."

Sinclair smiled. "Gold star for the frog." He leaned back in his chair. "Now, let's cut through the bullshit. There are two reasons DEFEND needs to be stopped. Not only are they developing some illegal weaponry, they're also using elemental magic as part of their operations."

Hector Mitsotakis, the Greek liaison, jumped in. "Impossible. I have someone deep undercover, and this is the first I've heard of any of that."

Sinclair eyed the Greek. "And what if your undercover agent is wrong? If an elemental fire user working with DEFEND decides to use their power in central Athens in front of a group of humans, what do you think would happen next? Is that a chance you want to take?"

When Mitsotakis shook his head, Sinclair continued, "The *Feiru* High Council—and by extension the *Feiru* Liaison offices—can't designate DEFEND as a terrorist group without concrete proof. That is a long way from happening, and as you're all familiar with the glacial pace of bureaucracy, I'm taking initiative, working outside the red tape, and giving you three a heads-up. You're in a better position to direct your own liaison offices to find the evidence we need to convince the others of the threat. DEFEND needs to be stopped."

Mercier jumped in, "Let's pretend all of this is true. You wouldn't give this information to us out of the kindness of your heart, so what's in it for you?"

Having the head of the *Feiru* Liaison office from France here was a gamble; unlike his Greek and Spaniard counterparts, Mercier was intelligent. But Sinclair couldn't leak information to Greece and Spain without including France, which was the European country with the greatest number of anti-AMT rebels outside the UK and Ireland.

Sinclair focused on Mercier. "If elemental magic is exposed to humans, it affects us all. They'll come up with a test to weed out the *Feiru* from the humans and probably lock us all away. I have no wish to spend the rest of my life at their mercy."

Mercier stated, "Which means you'll lose all of your power and influence." Sinclair nodded and Mercier continued, "Fine. I'll take the information if there are no strings attached. Otherwise, I'll rely on my own resources."

Clever lad. "I'm not trying to trade favors."

Mercier raised an eyebrow. "That's a first."

Sinclair ignored the needling. "But if you do find information that could be helpful to other *Feiru* Liaison offices, I only hope that you'll pass it on to both me and them."

Mercier continued to stare at him, but Sinclair didn't fret. He knew when to speak and when to keep quiet.

The Frenchman finally nodded. "Deliver the information to my office and I'll see what I can find out. If I can verify any of it, I'll share it with the other liaison offices and yours, too."

The other two murmured similar sentiments before Sinclair stood to leave. "You'll have it within the day, and I'll make sure to update you with new information as it comes across my desk. If you have any questions, you can contact the person who sends you the report."

With that, he left the room, his two bodyguards walking on either side of him. He noted the frown on Mercier's face and the determined looks of the other two. No doubt Cruz and Mitsotakis both wanted to be the one who could prove DEFEND was a terrorist group. They would do it because they wanted the recognition. While trying to find the necessary evidence, they would leak the information about DEFEND to other countries in the EU, maybe even to America.

Which was exactly what Sinclair wanted them to do. Cruz might have dismissed DEFEND as weak and powerless, but Sinclair knew the truth—DEFEND was the only organization that had a chance of ruining his carefully laid plans. Over the course of the last year, they had shown up and derailed his plans more than once. He needed them gone if he wanted to continue putting things in motion to eradicate elemental magic and change *Feiru* law.

Until he could dismantle DEFEND, a rumor about them not only being terrorists but also using elemental magic for their missions might slow down their recruitment efforts. Or, if he was lucky, it might force them to pull back on some of their operations.

Either way, it should give Sinclair some more time to convince other local councils to support his R&C campaign.

CHAPTER TWENTY-EIGHT

Go to the address printed below by eight p.m. A woman dressed in Feiru traditional garb will greet you at the door.

Kiarra looked up from the slip of paper to make sure she hadn't missed her stop. It was already a little after seven twenty p.m. and she couldn't afford to backtrack if she got lost.

The alarm clock had gone off around three p.m., blaring heavy metal and scaring Kiarra out of her mind. A quick check around the room revealed she was alone, but when she saw Neena's dark blue scarf thrown across the chair at the desk, Neena's betrayal came rushing back.

Then she remembered about the clue on North Berwick Law and would have bolted out the door if not for the large sign taped over the peephole that read: The clue is on the table, under my scarf.

Sure enough, the slip of paper had been tucked inside an envelope, along with a few other sheets of paper.

Kiarra looked out the window of the double-decker bus one more time, but the slow crawl of traffic told her she had a while to go before she reached her destination. She pulled out the papers Neena had left her and reread part of what had convinced her to go through with this wild goose chase:

If I hadn't drugged you, both Jaxton and his sister would be dead right now. Neither one of us wants that, not that I expect you to believe me. I've included the clue from North Berwick Law with this note. Follow my instructions if you wish to save all three of them. If you try to rebel and ignore my instructions, then not only will they all die, but your greatest fear about the first-borns will come true. Is that a chance you're willing to take?

Ultimately, no, it wasn't.

Neena's note also mentioned saving three, not two, people. While she was learning never to presume anything about Neena, Kiarra liked to believe the third person she referred to was her brother Giovanni.

She still had reservations about what she was doing, but after Darius had mysteriously called the safe house at three fifteen p.m., Kiarra found herself with no other choice but to follow Neena's instructions. The call had been short and to the point, but Darius had wanted her to trust Neena, assuring Kiarra that he would be in Edinburgh soon to help get Jaxton back.

It'll make it easier to trust the others later on. Jaxton had been right; without her trust in him, she never would have gone out on a limb with anyone else. While she didn't trust Neena, Darius had been nothing but kind to her and would never wish Jaxton harm. So, through a strange web of logic, she was now tentatively trusting a woman who'd drugged her unconscious, hoping it would be enough to save the man who now mattered most to her.

Still, if Neena's actions caused Jaxton's death, Kiarra would not cooperate with DEFEND, supposed Talent or not. Revenge was not her style, but she refused to work with a person so careless with other people's lives.

At the thought of never seeing Jaxton again, there was a tightness in her chest that she couldn't define. She'd only known him a little less than two weeks, but apart from her parents, no one had understood Kiarra's need to be pushed. Yet Jaxton had. Without him, she never would have had the nerve to try and save someone else's life.

Dead or alive, she would find him. She owed Jaxton that much.

Kiarra tested her abilities and confirmed they were nearly at full strength. At least as full as they could be without Jaxton's touch. She still didn't understand how or why he amplified her powers.

Her thoughts were heading down that path again, but she couldn't afford to think about the way he'd made her feel, either emotionally or physically. She needed a clear head for this meeting.

She unfolded the second sheet of paper that Neena had put inside the envelope with the clue. It was a photocopied page of a journal, which had seemed irrelevant at the time, but it might be the distraction she needed to clear her head. Neena had penned a sentence in the same purple ink as she'd used in her letter. At the top of the page it read: Thoughts and doubts from one fire user to another.

Kiarra continued on to the handwritten journal entry:

March 29, 1918 – Yucatan, Mexico

Another day has passed, but the others have yet to arrive. I know we are isolated from the world here, but I wonder if something has happened to them. Even making allowances for war on the Continent, they should have arrived here two weeks ago.

I have made the best use of my time by practicing and honing my technique to the best of my ability, or at least as much as I can without my Conduit. I sometimes envy Safiye. Not only does she have her Conduit to enhance her powers, there is a love and trust between them that I fear I will never possess.

But in truth, I am happy for them. Our mission isn't easy, and moments of joy can be few and far between. We must overcome the difficulties, however, as the task ahead of us is our only chance to prove the usefulness of first-borns, Talents in particular. Science has become the new magic of our age, one people find easier to control. Possessing the power to both heal and destroy is terrifying to the general F. population, elemental fire more so than the others. But if something isn't done, the spreading sickness will kill most of the world's population and I cannot allow that to happen.

Despite reaching the end of the journal page, Kiarra continued to stare at it in disbelief.

If the photocopied page was authentic, then she'd just read a former Talent's journal.

Could the legends be true after all?

In the bottom margin, Neena had scrawled Thomas Anthony Gladstone. Kiarra touched the name, wishing she could verify its contents. All clues signaled that Thomas Anthony Gladstone had been a Fire Talent. And if what Jaxton had said was true, and she was also a Fire Talent, then there was a lot she could learn from Gladstone if she could get her hands on the rest of his journal.

All texts and letters related to first-born training or elemental magic had been destroyed in the 1950s, with the implementation of the AMT compounds. To possess anything written by a pre-1950s adult first-born was rare, but to possess the writings of a Talent was unthinkable.

She reread the page and stopped at the part where Thomas mentioned a Conduit, the same word Neena had used last night. From context, Kiarra guessed a Conduit helped focus a Talent's abilities, just like Jaxton had helped focus hers.

Maybe Jaxton was her Conduit.

The thought made her pause. Jaxton's effect on her could be a result of attraction, not necessarily some legendary power amplifier.

Continuing her second read-through, Kiarra shivered as she read: *Possessing the power to both heal and destroy is terrifying to the general F. population.*

If such power existed, it would be dangerous in the wrong hands. Jaxton's words about an army gathering to protect a Talent made more sense.

As the person in front of her on the bus stood up, Kiarra forced her gaze from the journal entry and checked her location. She'd asked earlier for instructions, and the bus driver had told her which landmarks to watch for. She spotted the small row of brightly colored shops and Kiarra pushed the button, requesting the next stop.

She would let Gladstone's words stew and ask Neena about it later. For the moment, Jaxton and Millie were her top priorities.

She only hoped she had the strength to carry out the plan and let herself be captured.

~~*

The sound of screeching voices jolted Millie awake.

She tried to focus, but whatever the hell they'd drugged her with earlier had left her groggy. The booming music was not helping matters.

Once her eyes and brain started working properly again, Millie did a quick sweep of the room, on the lookout for the bastard who had interrogated her with his fists.

But she was alone. For now.

Cataloging the aches and twinges, nothing felt broken, and a small wiggle told her the straps were looser. If she could just get the straps removed, she might have a chance.

The last time she'd been conscious, Millie had noted two flaws in the room's design. First, nothing was bolted to the floor. Second, various chemicals lined the far wall.

An experienced interrogator always assumed a person was trying to find a way to escape. An unbolted table or shelf could be thrown or toppled, distracting or even injuring the interrogator. Chemicals only made an escape more likely.

Between the flaws and the medical equipment in the room, Millie deduced that she was inside a research facility acting as an ad-hoc interrogation room.

The music ceased and the door on the far side of the room opened, revealing not the big bastard interrogator from earlier, but the well-dressed young man who had made the phone call to Jaxton and Kiarra.

Unlike before, he didn't keep to the shadows, and she caught her first real glimpse of him—medium height, olive skin tone, black hair, and dark brown eyes. She had suspected he knew Kiarra, but now that she could see his face, there was no doubt that he was her brother. The shape of his eyes, combined with his coloring, gave it away.

He stood beside her and only because she was watching him closely did she notice a brief flash of regret in his eyes. But it was gone between one heartbeat and the next. Curious.

Millie needed to see what the man was made of. "Did they send the posh lad to do the dirty work?"

The man leaned close enough that she could see the gold flecks in his eyes. Did Kiarra have them too? She'd never noticed.

"Fists only accomplish so much." He straightened and walked to the table of chemicals. "I have other ways to make you talk."

He reached for a syringe and Millie thought about her options.

They had administered rowanberry juice just a few days ago, so unless they wanted to kill her, it was unlikely they'd dose her again. If they had some other type of concoction to weaken her defenses, she'd been trained to resist interrogation and knew to lie as close to the truth as possible. She worked investigation for private clients, nothing more. Spinning DEFEND into a human rights activist group was easy enough. Amnesty International would suffice.

And she honestly didn't know Kiarra or Jaxton's location.

Prep review done, she focused on the broad back of Kiarra's brother. Despite his posh clothing and restrained manner, he had a quiet aura of power. Much like people misunderstood Millie's bubbly behavior for daftness, she reckoned people mistook his appearance and behavior for weakness.

The contrast of power and reserve intrigued her.

The man—she still didn't know his name—turned around with a cloth-wrapped syringe in his hand. Clever move, hiding the contents to inspire fear; too bad it wouldn't work on her.

She held his gaze and raised an eyebrow. "Is that a present for me? And to think, I didn't get you anything."

"Antagonizing people will only cause more pain," he said quietly. "You should have learned that yesterday."

Millie shrugged as much as the straps around her body allowed. "You're going to hurt me anyway, so I might as well have fun with it."

The man tapped the side of the syringe and pushed the plunger, and a few red drops squirted into the air. It was the same color as rowanberry juice, but it could just be a red-dyed liquid. She wasn't going to fret, at least not yet.

It was time to try tactic number one. "You seem a bit out of place here, mate. Shouldn't you be in a barrister's office? Or perhaps graduate school?"

Those gold-flecked eyes looked her up and down. "Judging by appearances, you should be a footballer's wife."

To be a footballer's wife meant to be beautiful yet shallow and superficial, or so went the stereotype. "Glad to know you think I'm fit. Or should I use the Yank term of 'hot,' since I've met your sister and know that underneath your posh façade, you're a red, white, and blue American."

Her remarks had no effect, not even her comment about the man and Kiarra being siblings. Clearly, he didn't care about Kiarra, so what had caused his flash of regret earlier? If she could pinpoint the weakness, she could extrapolate it.

He lowered the syringe and stopped a few inches above her arm. If she was going to find his weakness, she was going to have to work fast and keep him talking. "Taunts don't faze you, but I have a feeling that this is the first time you've tortured someone for information." His gaze shifted slightly. Bingo. "You're doing a shoddy job, so here's my advice: stop stalling. Do what you need to do, so I can figure a way around it."

His face was once again a mask of stone. "You've made some fairly big assumptions, but just this once, I will follow your advice." He removed the cloth and revealed a red liquid inside the syringe. "Rowanberry juice. I suggest you tell me everything you know about Kiarra, or we'll find out if you're one of the few who can survive an overdose."

She was debating what convincing-yet-false information she could provide when Kiarra's brother turned the syringe in his hand and revealed a small piece of masking tape with words written on it. If anyone was watching from behind the two-way glass, they wouldn't be able to see it.

She read: Diluted. Pretend it's real.

Right. So now he was helping her? Un-bloody-likely.

Diluting rowanberry juice was a skill she doubted the man possessed. If done correctly and administered soon after a full dose, a diluted shot would render a Feiru unconscious and slow down their heart rate, making a person appear dead to the untrained eye.

Which meant this man didn't want her dead, but to appear so. The biggest question was: why? He'd done nothing to stop the interrogation yesterday. Nor ensure Kiarra's safety. While unlikely, maybe this man was developing a conscience.

The more contradictions she discovered about this man, the more she wanted to find out why they existed. Too bad she'd never get the chance.

Millie met his eyes. "I don't think you have the bollocks to go through with it."

He shifted the syringe and she saw another piece of tape and read: Your freedom.

After she met his eyes again, the man lowered the syringe against the crook of her elbow, just shy of breaking the skin. "I'll ask again: what do you know about Kiarra Melini?"

Millie was torn. If she called the man's bluff, she would probably face Mr. Fist Bastard, who would keep at her until she died. However, if she went along with this man's ruse, she might still die. A few words scribbled on two pieces of tape weren't exactly a guarantee. She'd be unconscious and at his mercy.

But if she could evoke another reaction to reveal more about his character, maybe it would be enough for her to believe he would follow through on his suggestions. It was worth a try. "I know that Kiarra was abused inside the AMT, with no one to stand up for her or protect her. Instead, cowards like you just ignore the realities of the AMT for your own benefit, with no qualms about punishing the innocent."

The needle pricked inside her skin, but Millie kept her eyes on the man's face as he replied, "Everyone has their place. If she broke the rules, then she deserved the consequences."

Millie raised an eyebrow. "If a twist of fate had made you first-born, I doubt you'd think a prison is where you belong. But then again, if you torture innocents on the outside, I bet you'd be one of the guards abusing the inmates on the inside. Do you get your jollies from hurting those weaker than you?"

He pulled her up by her arm and brought her face close to his. "I do not hurt innocents, only those who deserve it."

Millie searched his eyes. "And why do I deserve it?"

This time his regret was scant inches from her face. "Enough. I can see now that you won't talk."

Millie felt the pressure from the injection. The man's reactions had given off mixed signals, but she had no choice but to hope the man would help her escape.

As dizziness overcame her, Millie looked into those gold-flecked eyes and murmured, "Keep lying to yourself."

The man stepped away from her side and the world went black.

CHAPTER TWENTY-NINE

Kiarra approached the four-story brick building covered in advertisements and a big "TO LET" sign attached to the corner. She double-checked the address, but this was the right place.

Taking a deep breath to calm her nerves, she walked up to the building.

The door opened before she could even knock and a woman, sporting upper-arm tattoos and wearing an empire-waist dress that cascaded down in flowing strips of color, greeted her. The style seemed vaguely familiar, but she couldn't place it. This must be the "woman dressed in traditional *Feiru* garb".

The woman remained silent and motioned her inside. Either a security camera was hidden somewhere near the door or the woman knew what she looked like. Kiarra did a sweep with her eyes as she entered, but didn't see anyone waiting to attack her.

She remained alert as they walked down a hall and stopped in front of a door guarded by a large man dressed in black. From the few stolen glances she'd had, the style was similar to the people from last night, which confirmed her suspicions about who had been behind the attack and responsible for Jaxton's capture.

The man guarding the door ordered, "Spread your arms," before he frisked her for weapons. It took every bit of restraint she had to remain still, reminding herself of the bigger picture. Kiarra had left her gun back at the apartment, wanting to make her capture as smooth as possible. To make her plan work, it was vital for them to underestimate her.

The man finished with a nod, and the woman opened the door and motioned her inside. Kiarra held her breath, wondering if she'd finally see Giovanni, but she released it when she saw Ty Adams, her former lover and researcher, standing to the side.

The sight of him brought back memories of her time inside the AMT—the experiments, the helplessness, the isolation. At one time, those memories would have made her freeze, and maybe cower, but now, they only strengthened her resolve. Kiarra was no longer a prisoner. She had her freedom and her fire. And she wanted to help her friends.

It would damn well take more than Ty Adams' presence to stop her.

She stood taller, careful not to let her anger show through. "Ty."

Ty dismissed the other woman and gave Kiarra a wry smile. "I didn't think I'd ever get to see you again, Kiarra."

She ignored his attempt to distract. "I came here to bargain for Millie's life."

Even from halfway across the room, she could see the surprise in Ty's eyes. A second later, he replied, "Something is different about you. But even so, you have nothing to bargain with. The only reason I'm here is because I called in a few favors." He took a step toward her. "You probably won't believe me, but I wanted to make sure you were brought in unharmed."

She raised an eyebrow. "Bullshit and we both know it. You watched from behind the mirror as they carted me off for a whipping. A whipping, I might add, for an offense I never committed." Ty took a step toward her, but Kiarra took a step back to maintain her distance. "You lost the right to care about my welfare the instant you said nothing and let them accuse me of seducing you."

For years, she had been angry and hurt by Ty's actions, but now all she felt was anger at his selfish cowardice.

Since her teenage years, Kiarra had assumed no one cared about anything but themselves. From the perceived abandonment by her parents to Ty's callous behavior, her whole world had seemed self-serving. But thanks to the strange man who'd blazed into her cell, she now knew there was good and bad inside every person. Just as there were people who only cared about themselves, there were also people who put others first.

Kiarra wanted to be the latter.

Any doubts she'd had about seeing her plan through dissolved.

Ty stopped trying to close the distance between them. "Everything I did was for your welfare. I wish you could see it."

She snorted. "Yeah, right. You tell yourself that." She made sure to reach her free hand to the south for show and raised a palm. "Meanwhile, you should know something." Kiarra summoned a flame to her hand and realized how much easier the process was becoming, even without Jaxton nearby. "Your experiment was a failure."

Ty blinked, and satisfaction warmed her heart at his surprise.

"How can you summon fire?" Ty asked. "I nullified the ability."

Kiarra gave a slow smile. "That's why I'm safe without your protection." She flipped her hand, palm downward, and the flame danced to remain on the top of her hand. "The AMT won't kill me because they like to study anomalies."

Her next move was risky, but she had gone into this meeting knowing that this was her only chance to find her friends. If Gio was willing to torture an innocent woman, he wasn't just going to hand over Millie without a fight. And she highly doubted Ty would be willing to negotiate Millie's release.

A first-born who could gather fire despite years of receiving their precious Null Formula, however, would be carted away to the nearest research facility and studied. Since AMT research facilities were few and far between, Kiarra was betting that they'd bring her to the same one as Jaxton and Millie. The AMT staff might try to neutralize her abilities, but if she could direct fire without reaching to a particular compass point, then she might be able to use elemental fire in a neutralization chamber.

The plan was full of a lot of "what ifs," but she hoped her gamble would pay off.

Kiarra gathered energy toward her and created an eight-inch-tall flame before she directed it toward Ty's head. As expected, he reached for a tranquilizer gun as he rolled out of the way and shot a dart straight at her. Kiarra didn't try to dodge it, and once it sank into her arm, she instantly felt the effects.

She slumped to the floor and the world went black.

~~*

And why do I deserve it?

The words echoed inside Gio's mind, much like they had all afternoon. Even though Millie Ward was falsely pronounced dead and being transported to a secure location, her accusations lingered.

Gio shook his head to clear away the thoughts. The woman was gone and under someone else's care. Once his acquaintance informed him that Millie had agreed to live under a false identity, and let her go, he would never have to deal with her again.

The panel on his desk buzzed, signaling that someone was outside his door and wanted to talk to him. He pressed a button. "Yes?"

"Sir, it's Ramirez, with a progress report."

His retrieval team had captured Jaxton Ward earlier this morning, and Ramirez was in charge of getting information out of him. Sources said that Ward was a first-born activist, suspected of working with DEFEND.

Gio pressed a button to unlock his door. "Enter."

Ramirez walked in and quickly closed the door. "The prisoner is still being uncooperative, but now that the escaped first-born has been secured, I have a new strategy I wanted to run by you."

Kiarra's successful capture was news to him, but Gio was careful not to betray that fact. He'd deal with the information lapse later. "What do you have in mind?"

"The prisoner is protecting the woman. From all accounts, he drew the retrieval team away from her so that they would follow him. I think he cares for her." Gio waved for the man to continue. "If I can show she's being abused, her life on the line, he will probably do anything to guarantee her safety."

"Even though the first-born's life is protected by the AMT Oversight Committee, but he won't know that."

"Exactly."

While Kiarra had broken the law and first-borns could be sentenced without trial, there were limits to what he would allow. "Tell me what you have in mind."

"A few bruises and maybe some ripped clothing, but nothing more."

Millie's voice filled his mind: *Why does she deserve it?*

No, this was different. He could justify Ramirez's request because Kiarra had broken the law. "Fine, but have someone else rough her up so you can establish a 'good cop, bad cop' scenario. That way she might be more cooperative with you later on."

Nodding, Ramirez left to carry out his plan.

Gio refused to feel guilty for following the law. Kiarra had escaped and resisted capture. Without making an example out of her, others would try to follow suit. The AMT Oversight Committee and, most importantly, his father would make Gio the scapegoat if he didn't follow through. And any opportunity to learn more about the pediatrics facilities and the AMT-conducted experiments would disappear.

He stilled. When had learning more about the inner workings of the AMT become more important than repealing Article I?

Keep lying to yourself.

The woman. She was partly to blame for this. Without her mistreatment, he probably never would have gone sniffing around the AMT records, nor discovered information about the breeding program. Still, he couldn't be too angry at her; her pain had opened his eyes. He still struggled with the newfound image he was forming of his father, but Gio hesitated to deem him guilty without all the facts.

All he knew was that in order to continue to have access to privileged information, he needed to find out about Kiarra's capture and analyze the report. He needed something to tell his father.

Checking his email, he scanned the report on Kiarra's capture. The basics were there, but at the end, the man who'd taken point hinted at something important, something too risky to be shared over email. Gio sent a text message to arrange a meeting; the man replied right away to confirm the time and place.

With any luck, he could ship Kiarra back to the Cascade F-block within the next few days and have a new assignment from his father soon after that. The longer it took to get Kiarra out of the same facility he stood in right now, the greater the chance of Gio meeting Kiarra. As he'd learned with Millie, reading or hearing about a beating was one thing, but confronting it face to face was another. He couldn't afford to think of Kiarra as anything more than an escaped first-born.

CHAPTER THIRTY

Jaxton grunted as a fist connected with his stomach, and then again, before the interrogator backed off and waited. Despite the pinpricks of light hovering at the edges of his vision, Jaxton forced himself to appear nonchalant, as if he hadn't been beaten to a bloody pulp the day before. He'd learned quickly that the AMT interrogators took advantage of the slightest sign of weakness.

And he needed to stay strong if he wanted to help either Kiarra or his sister.

Kiarra. He hoped she'd arrived at the safe house without incident. No doubt the AMT interrogators would have used Kiarra against him if they'd caught her. But since their questions had mainly focused on first-born activist groups, and not her whereabouts, he was going to assume she was safe until he found out otherwise. Kiarra was resourceful; no doubt, she'd contacted Aislinn and was already planning a rescue mission.

Or so he hoped.

Whatever might have happened, Jaxton needed to focus on finding a way to escape. He wasn't much good to anyone whilst he was tied to a chair.

His wrists were tied behind his back with a nylon rope that also stretched to his ankles. The position was not just uncomfortable; it made escape nearly impossible without a weapon. Anytime he'd been left alone, Jaxton had tested his bonds, but they weren't loose enough yet to slip his hands out.

He needed to think of another way to get free.

Unfortunately, there wasn't much he could use inside this room. Apart from his chair and a few cabinets, the room was pure steel. The drains in the floor only confirmed his suspicions about the purpose of this room—he bet he wasn't the first person to be interrogated here.

As he'd done with the man who'd visited him earlier, Jaxton eyed his interrogator for anything he could use. But the man was clever enough to be dressed in simple attire, without weapons.

His current interrogator noticed his scrutiny, walked over, and smashed his fist into Jaxton's cheek.

Jaxton forced himself not to react to the pain and calmly spat out the blood from his mouth before testing his newly loose tooth with his tongue. The interrogator watched him, and Jaxton could tell the man was sizing up his current state to see how much more he could take.

A few seconds later, the interrogator finally spoke up. "Which first-born group do you work for? Or did the first-born slut simply offer her body in exchange for your protection?"

So this one is going to bring Kiarra into it. Jaxton knew the man was trying to get a rise out of him. But he prevented himself from doing something daft, like telling the man to go fuck himself, and decided to shift the focus by using his own game of provocation.

He lifted the corner of his mouth in a half-smile. "Sorry to disappoint, mate, but women aren't my thing." He gave the interrogator a deliberate look. "But you and I, now there's something I can see."

The interrogator's face crinkled in disdain. "Enough. As much as I enjoy beating the shit out of you, I have something that'll break your silence." The man walked over to one of the cabinets in the room and pulled out a laptop. After fiddling with some keys, he walked back to Jaxton's side. "I think you're protecting the girl, and I can prove it."

Turning the laptop around, the interrogator showed him a picture of Kiarra lying on top of a table, unconscious. Her hair was in the new cut, and her cheeks were fuller than when he'd taken her from the Cascade F-block two weeks ago, meaning this picture was recent.

Had they really captured her? The first feelings of unease gripped his belly, but Jaxton kept outwardly calm. He needed to bluff and determine if Kiarra really was in danger. "Are surveillance photos of a sleeping woman supposed to mean something to me?"

The man said nothing, but clicked to the next photo, which showed Kiarra with a split lip and a dark bruise across her cheek.

Jaxton bit the inside of his mouth to keep his temper in check. While it was possible they'd captured Kiarra, he wasn't about to believe them just yet; these days, any bloody idiot with a computer could mess with a picture and make it look realistic.

Even if the image was doctored, just seeing a beat-up version of Kiarra didn't sit well. Only because of years of training did he manage to keep his voice calm. "I barely know her. Maybe she had it coming."

The interrogator continued to watch Jaxton's face for any signs of emotion, but Jaxton kept his mask in place. *Think of Kiarra. You can't help her if you're dead.* Once he was free, he could teach this bastard a lesson, but not before.

Another click, and this time the photo showed Kiarra unconscious with her top ripped down the front. The torn material barely concealed her breasts. Jaxton bit the inside of his mouth hard enough to draw blood, and clenched his fists behind his back. If he found out these pictures were real, he was going to kill whoever had abused her.

The interrogator gave the picture an appreciative look. "She's a hot little thing, isn't she? Once I'm done with you, maybe I'll tie her up and tease her to frustration." The interrogator leaned down and looked him dead in the eye. "It won't be long before I'll have that bitch begging for my cock."

Jaxton was perilously close to losing his cool. If anyone had molested her, so help him, everyone in this facility was going to fucking pay, one way or another.

The interrogator kept his eyes trained on Jaxton's face as he clicked again, this time showing Kiarra still unconscious, but naked from the waist up. Jaxton couldn't tamp down his growl.

Those were Kiarra's breasts, and they were meant for him and only him.

He tugged at his hands, but the rope held firm. He looked around the room again. The interrogator had forgotten to shut the cabinet door when he'd retrieved the laptop, and inside were trays of medical instruments. If he could find a way to stun his interrogator and get to the open cabinet, Jaxton might have a chance of getting out of here and finding Kiarra.

He focused back on his interrogator and the man gave a cool smile. "So you do care for her." He leaned in a little closer. "Then I'm going to make this perfectly clear. For each session you refuse to answer my questions, I will bring the little first-born bitch to this room and have fun with her, right in front of you. Piss me off enough and I'm going to fuck her 'til she can't walk, then bring in some of the other guards and pass her around." The man grabbed Jaxton's hair and yanked his head back. "Should I get her right now and prove my point?"

No fucking way in hell. Jaxton growled louder this time, his control gone as he strained against his bonds. He didn't notice the lights flicker or the laptop spark and go dark. "You touch her and I will fucking tear you apart." He pulled at his bonds again, but this time they stretched. "I will fucking kill you."

The man eyed the lights, but focused back on Jaxton. "Empty threats, Ward." The man stepped away and headed for the door. "I'm going to get her right now and prove to you that I don't bluff. I bet the first-born whore will spread her legs for me if I threaten your life."

"No!" Jaxton shouted, causing more lights to flicker and sparks to fly. The bastard didn't deserve to be in the same room as Kiarra, let alone touch her. Jaxton gave a final tug and the ties around his arms gave way.

His feet were still bound, but Jaxton lunged for the bastard and shouted, "You will not lay a fucking hand on her."

Sparks flew again as he shouted, and the man covered his ears right before Jaxton slugged the man's jaw. They both went down, but Jaxton kept his position on top and took hold of the man's shoulders. He banged the man's head against the ground. "Where is she?"

The man stared at him wide-eyed. Jaxton barely noticed the blood running from the inside of the man's ears before he slammed him against the floor again. "Where?"

"Wh-what are you?"

Jaxton growled and the man winced at the sound. The lights continued to flicker. His initial haze of fury was fading, allowing reason back into his brain.

If the electrical shorts were limited to this room, someone would probably come to investigate. Jaxton had a few minutes at best, so he pulled the man up to his face and stated, "Tell me where she is and I might not kill you."

"I-I don't know."

Disgusted at how quickly the man's nerve had vanished, Jaxton slammed the man's head against the floor, knocking him unconscious. He didn't have time to waste with a blathering idiot afraid of a few growls and some flickering lights.

He needed to get out of this room, and quickly.

Jaxton frisked the guard and took his access card and gun before freeing his own legs and heading for the door. The room in Kiarra's photos had looked similar to this one, so he only hoped that she—and Millie, for that matter——was being held in the same facility.

He slid the security card through the panel next to the door. The light turned green, and he went into the hallway. As much as he wanted to singlehandedly rescue Kiarra and Millie on his own, he wouldn't risk their safety. His first priority was to find a room with a phone and call for backup.

~~*

Gio stood at the foot of Calton Hill in Edinburgh. While he waited for his contact to arrive, he stared up at the purplish-blue sky of twilight and tried to forget what he'd just seen. But not even the beautiful canvas of the sky could block out the picture Ramirez had sent to his phone, the one showing Kiarra with a bruised face and split lip.

He wondered why, despite explicit instructions to the contrary, Ramirez had shared his handiwork. Did he suspect what Gio had done with Millie Ward? The picture might be a veiled threat, telling him that Ramirez would continue to reject his authority until some condition was met.

Whatever the reason, seeing his sister's battered face after all these years wasn't sitting well with Gio's conscience. Once this meeting was over, he'd contact his father and seek out his next assignment. The sooner he finished his investigation concerning the experiments inside the AMT, the sooner he could decide what to do about it. If the abuse of first-borns was widespread, he couldn't ignore it and do nothing.

A tall figure dressed in jeans approached and stopped a few feet from his location. Gio kept his face neutral despite the surprise; it wasn't his man Huang, but he recognized the blond man from the personnel files.

When Dr. Ty Adams spoke, it was in a gravelly American accent. "It was the season of light."

He'd find out later how Adams had learned the correct pass phrase.

Gio gave the required response. "It was the season of darkness."

How apropos.

He started climbing the steps of the hill and Adams followed. Only when they were far enough up the hill, where the wind would cover their voices, did Gio speak up. "Care to tell me why you're here and what this is about?"

Adams shoved his hands into the pockets of his jeans. "Only if you promise to turn F-839 over into my care later tonight."

Gio stopped and turned, wondering what Adams wanted with Kiarra. Using every trick of arrogance he'd learned during his five years at Harrow, he replied, "You're hardly in the position to negotiate, doctor."

Adams raised his left eyebrow, the one divided in two by a scar. "I can play this game too, son. I have information your father would love to hear."

Gio kept his face impassive. He was determined to keep the upper hand. "He wouldn't be pleased to hear you've been keeping something from us."

"But everyone knows that I'm the only scientist in the world who can do what I'm doing, and Sinclair won't touch me. So, can we stop fucking around and get on with it?"

Gio appreciated Adams' direct manner—a stark contrast to most Brits he knew—and nodded. "If your information is valuable, and you can provide proof, then we may have a deal. What do you know that is worth all this finagling?"

Adams took out his phone, tapped the screen a few times, and turned it toward Gio. "Take a look for yourself."

CHAPTER THIRTY-ONE

As Kiarra stared at the man standing in the doorway, all she could think about was how the resemblance was uncanny.

From the rough features to the slightly too long, blond hair, the man looked just like Ty. Only on closer inspection, when she noticed the lack of a scar through his eyebrow and the straighter nose, did she realize it was someone else.

Despite what they'd done to her earlier, hitting her when she'd refused to answer a question, she couldn't resist asking, "Who are you?"

The man stared down at her ripped shirt and Kiarra forced herself to remain calm. Partitioning her emotions had been the only way she'd survived so many years of being a guinea pig inside the AMT. As long as she acted detached, male staff members had usually left her alone when they'd realized she wasn't the slut her reputation suggested.

It was strange to think she'd learned something useful from her stint as a lab rat.

She focused back on Ty's double. The man who'd tended her face and bruises a few hours ago had murmured something important about using her split lip and ripped shirt as leverage. True, people seemed to be able to take pictures and instantly send them anywhere in this day and age, but she had a gut feeling that Jaxton was in the same facility, in a room not that far from her own. If she could get Ty's double to leave within the next ten minutes, the start of the evening meal would give her a small window of time to escape this room and go searching.

The lookalike finally met her gaze. "I can see why my brother risked his career to fuck you. You might be on the thin side, but your tits more than make up for it."

She just caught herself from frowning. "Ty doesn't have a brother."

The double smirked. "That he knows of."

What the hell? While a small part of her wanted to know more, Kiarra noted the time and decided it wasn't worth it. She needed to get this man to leave.

She forced a bored expression on her face. "Well, as you can see, Ty isn't here."

"He isn't the one I came to see." The man strode forward and took Kiarra's chin in his hand. "You are."

The look in his eyes was unsettling, made creepier by the fact that they were the same shade and shape as her former researcher's. He leaned closer, and when he ran his hand up her arm, the first flutters of panic formed in the pit of her stomach. Only the experiences of the last few weeks, and thoughts of reaching Jaxton, gave her the strength to maintain her bored composure.

Ty's supposed brother moved his head to the side of her face, and she felt his breath on her ear. "As much as I would love to piss off my brother, I can't kill you." The man brushed her cheek and it took every fiber of her being not to call forth her fire and toss him against the wall. "But, before I do the job I was hired to do, I plan to use you to make Ty lose his shit."

She was about to ask what job he'd been hired to do, but then his hand moved to cover her breast, and Kiarra clenched her jaw. The situation was deteriorating fast. She had wanted to avoid drawing attention to herself, but if she wanted to go looking for Jaxton, she had no choice but to make a scene.

Despite being in a neutralization chamber, she'd earlier confirmed that her fire was still active. The guards had been careful, tying her hands behind her back to face north and not south, but those rules no longer applied to Kiarra. She sure as hell didn't know if she were a Talent or not, but her unique abilities were going to allow her to stop waiting for someone else to rescue her.

It was time for Kiarra to take care of herself.

$*\sim*\sim*$

On the fourth attempt, Jaxton finally located a room with a phone. He didn't know how closely security was monitoring the compound, and while security cameras might have already picked up his escape in the halls, there was also the danger that making an outbound call could trigger an alarm.

Still, he didn't have time to try to contact Neena via his dreams, so he was left with the next best thing—hoping Aislinn would answer his call.

He took out the gun he'd swiped from the guard and released the safety before positioning his body to monitor both of the doors in the room. If the guards came through one door, he might be able to fight his way out and escape through the other.

He dialed the number, each ring seeming more like an eternity than mere seconds. On the third ring, a familiar Irish voice answered, "Jax, Darius is right outside the facility and I'm going to patch him through."

Not wasting time on frivolities and getting straight to the point was Aislinn's way. Jaxton followed the same philosophy and would worry about the "how" of the situation later.

Darius came on the line. "Nessa's with me and knows the layout of the place. Just tell me what room you're in and we'll be there."

Jaxton trusted Darius, but it wasn't only his life on the line. He wouldn't risk Kiarra or Millie's, so he asked, "Nessa, as in Vanessa, the woman who tried to kill Kiarra?"

"Yes, I'll explain it all later. Just know that she'll help us and won't betray us."

Aislinn chimed in, "I second that."

Two trusted comrades outweighed his doubts about the Shadow-Shifter. "Fine. The plaque outside the room said 'Research Manager' on it. But to get Kiarra out, I need to talk with Vanessa. Put her on the phone."

A shuffle before a condescending voice said, "Yes?"

"Are all of the exam rooms in the same wing?"

"As of last month they were."

He pushed aside his curiosity at that statement, aware that he had been on this call too long already. "Right. Tell Darius I'll be in the research wing looking for the others. I can't stay here."

With that, he hung up the phone and strained his ears. No, he'd been right. There were definitely noises coming from behind the door he'd entered a few minutes before.

Heading to the door on the opposite side of the room, he swiped the stolen keycard. But the light flashed red, denying him access. *Fuck.*

Normally, he would take a stand, but without knowing how many people could burst through that door, Jaxton couldn't chance it if he wanted to save Kiarra or his sister. He pried open the plastic cover of the security panel and hoped like hell he remembered enough from Marco's lessons to get the blasted door open.

The noises from the hall grew louder as he fiddled with the wires. Finally, he cut the juice and pushed the door, and was relieved when it slid open.

He stepped through the door into in a small observation room, complete with monitors, a desk, and a few chairs. His eyes went to the two-way mirror, and he froze. On the other side of the glass was a man leaning over Kiarra, his hand on her breast.

Jaxton growled and everything vibrated. Somewhere in the back of his mind he knew the vibrations syncing in time with his growl was significant, but he pushed the feeling aside. He needed to find a way to break the two-way mirror before the bastard laid another fucking hand on his woman.

~~*

Kiarra was nearly ready. Another thirty seconds and she should have enough energy to fuel her fire and knock the mysterious asshole fondling her breast across the room.

But then Ty's double ripped away the shirt from her body and exposed her torso. When he tugged at the pants at her waist, fury ran through her, turning her cheeks pink. The asshole mistook it for desire and murmured, "That's right, little slut, you like it."

Enough. Kiarra focused her flame outward, directing it from behind her to the particles floating between her and the man. She barely had time to note his surprise before a massive ball of flame slammed him against the wall on the other side of the room. A split second later, the window behind her shattered.

Her fire had burned away her bonds, and Kiarra turned around, ready to attack. She froze as Jaxton barreled toward her.

As soon as he was close enough, he cupped her face with his hands. "Are you all right?"

She blinked, but brushed aside the shock. All she wanted to do was curl up against Jaxton's chest to make sure he was real and not a dream, but that would have to wait. They didn't have much time. "I'll live. But we need to get out of here."

He shucked off his shirt and threw it over her head. She'd momentarily forgotten that she was half naked.

Jaxton nodded and removed the gun tucked into his waistband, and then they both went over to the asshole on the floor. The man was groaning, yet despite the fact her fire had definitely made contact, he was unscorched. Strange. She tucked that piece of information away for later.

Jaxton hefted the man up by the throat and slammed him against the wall. Judging by the look in Jaxton's eyes, he'd kill the man before they had a chance to question him.

She went over and placed a hand on Jaxton's arm. "Stop. He's our best bet for finding Millie."

Jaxton's grip tightened on the man's throat as he glanced at her, his eyes deadly. "But he deserves to die for what he did to you."

Kiarra's breath hitched at the look in his eyes. He was being sincere. If she wanted Ty's double dead, Jaxton would do it without hesitation. For some reason, she found that oddly sweet, and it meant more to her than she would like to admit. Still, the rational side of her brain knew better. "Surviving his failure will probably be a far worse punishment. Ask him about Millie so we can get the hell out of here."

Jaxton gave a male grunt and returned his gaze to the man pinned up against the wall. He eased his grip on the man's throat a fraction and growled, "They picked up a young woman named Millie Ward from a pub the other night and brought her here. Where is she?"

"Don't...know."

Jaxton leaned closer to the man. "Last chance, where is she?"

The man shook his head and Jaxton slammed the man's head against the wall hard enough to knock him unconscious.

Kiarra squeezed Jaxton's arm. "We'll find her."

"Once Darius—" Jaxton stopped mid-sentence and pushed Kiarra behind him. "People are coming."

She'd been so distracted by Jaxton's interrogation that she hadn't heard the shouts coming from the hall. Kiarra tested her fire, put a hand on Jaxton's arm, and felt her power increase tenfold. "As long as I can draw power from you, I can take care of them."

Sounds filtered in through the broken two-way mirror, and Jaxton turned so they were each facing a door. "You're going to have to explain that to me once we're out of here, pet. For now, we'll take them out together."

She squeezed his arm again. "Thank you."

"For what?"

"Believing in me."

"Between your wall of fire and the force you used to throw that bastard over there against the wall," he motioned to the unconscious man on the floor, "I'd be a bloody fool not to."

Unused to praise, Kiarra bit her lip and avoided Jaxton's eyes by focusing on the door. "I'm just glad you're okay." This time she chanced a look at Jaxton and wished she knew what he was thinking. But before either one of them could say another word, men simultaneously crashed into the room from behind both the broken mirror and the door exiting into the hall.

With guards on both sides, they were trapped. Without hesitation, Kiarra called forth her fire and pushed outward, slamming into the first slew of guards entering the room from the hall. Shots fired behind her, but before she could turn and tackle the guards entering through the broken two-way mirror, Jaxton hooked his arm around her waist and dove down beneath the steel table, taking her with him.

Something ricocheted off the table, but the flimsy barrier wouldn't last for long. Rather than question Jaxton's actions, Kiarra peeked out and saw more guards entering the room. Surprisingly, their position on the floor offered better access. She was less vulnerable and could take out more guards in one go.

While she took a second to decide which pathway would be the most effective for an attack, a strong gust of wind danced around the room and knocked all of the guards up against the ceiling before dropping them back to the ground. Darius entered first, followed by the Shadow-Shifter and a few other people she didn't know.

While Darius and his team checked the guards on the ground to see if any of them were still conscious, Kiarra turned her head to see Jaxton on the floor. He was pale and breathing heavily as he gripped the side of his neck with one hand. Her stomach did a little flip. "Jaxton, what's wrong?"

His eyes had trouble focusing, and Kiarra placed a hand on his cheek. She looked down at his neck and saw that his hand was covered in blood.

CHAPTER THIRTY-TWO

There was so much blood.

Jaxton's injury was beyond Kiarra's basic knowledge of first aid. She needed help.

Her momentary shock passed and she yelled, "Darius," before turning back to Jaxton. She stroked his cheek, hoping the touch would calm him, when Darius knelt next to her and drew in a sharp breath.

"Jax, keep pressure on it. We'll get you out of here." Darius motioned to some of the other people in the room and they lifted away the table. Darius turned back toward Jaxton. "Trying to get a battle scar to impress your lady, eh?"

Jaxton gave a weak smile, but didn't say anything. The sight of Jaxton weak and pale, lacking his usual humor, heightened her fear. She needed to tamp it down and be strong for Jaxton's sake. If Darius could see humor in the situation, then so could she.

She made a stern face and tapped Jaxton on the nose a few times. "Don't you dare die on me. We have an unfinished argument that I plan to win."

His eyes focused on her and he gave a half-smile. "What did I do this time?"

His voice was weak, making his accent thicker, but she forced herself to keep up appearances. "Went and tried to get yourself killed, you idiot."

Jaxton started to laugh, but groaned instead.

The fear gripping her heart tightened a little more.

She brushed the hair from his forehead. "Besides, I know how to kick your ass in sparring now and I'm not about to let you chicken out on me."

Jaxton said nothing, his eyes struggling to stay open. A woman's voice on Kiarra's right said, "Sorry to break up your little soap opera, but we need to get the hell out of here. The facility's been compromised, which means they'll be evacuating now and will 'clean up' after that."

Kiarra looked over at the woman standing behind Darius; it was the Shadow-Shifter.

Darius looked up at the Shadow-Shifter and asked, "What's the cleanup procedure?"

The woman gestured with her hand. "Nothing big, just, you know, start a detonation sequence to collapse the entire facility."

"Darius," Jaxton said, and all eyes focused back on him. "Take Kiarra and leave."

She grabbed Jaxton's free hand and squeezed. "I'm not leaving you here."

He ignored her and kept his gaze on Darius. "Use force if necessary, but leave me and get her out of here."

"No, Jax," Darius answered. "I don't leave people behind."

Jaxton closed his eyes and took a rattling breath. Kiarra squeezed his hand tighter. Jaxton opened his eyes again, but avoided looking at her face, his focus still on Darius. "Kiarra's a Talent. She must be protected."

Kiarra said, "We don't know—"

Darius nodded. "I'll keep her safe."

Darius took her hand, but she called up her fire and heated her hand until Darius released it. She raised her chin a notch. "He was hurt protecting me and I'm not going without him." Kiarra clutched Jaxton's hand to her chest "I won't be dissuaded."

"Darius," the Shadow-Shifter said, "we seriously need to leave. We have five minutes, ten at the most."

Jaxton closed his eyes again and Kiarra caressed his cheek. When he finally opened his eyes, his expression was unreadable. He whispered, "Pet, you're too important to die here. Go. Please."

Kiarra blinked back tears. "You never say please."

Even as the man lay dying, he was trying to protect her. This man would always put her safety above his own.

Kiarra realized she'd finally found someone she trusted with her whole heart, and he was about to die.

"Kiarra, go," Jaxton mumbled before his eyes fluttered closed. His body went limp and his hand fell away from the wound on his neck.

"No," Kiarra whispered as she replaced his fallen hand with her own and put pressure on his wound.

She gripped his shoulder with her other hand and shook it, hoping like hell she could wake him up again. "Jaxton!"

One beat, then another. But Jaxton didn't move.

Darius put a hand on her shoulder, but on instinct, flames appeared on her body and forced him away.

She squeezed her eyes shut and shook her head. She wouldn't—couldn't——leave Jaxton to die.

Think, Kiarra, think. But what could she do?

If only there was a way to heal him enough to move. If there was ever a latent ability needed for a Talent's army that would be it.

The ability to both heal and destroy. Kiarra stilled as she remembered one of the last lines of Thomas Gladstone's journal entry. What if she were a Talent? Then, logically, she should have the power to heal.

She had one last shot, and she was going to take it. She said over her shoulder, "Let me try one last thing, and if doesn't work, I promise to go without a fight."

The Shadow-Shifter huffed, but Kiarra ignored it and placed her other hand on Jaxton's neck.

Please let this work. The only problem? She didn't know how to unleash elemental healing fire.

Thinking back, her negative emotions had helped sustain the wall of fire and the defensive maneuver with Ty's double. Maybe positive emotions would trigger healing abilities, if she had any.

She closed her eyes and concentrated on her positive memories.

Her first feeling of accomplishment when she'd bested Jaxton at the foot of the stairs. Feeling safe in his arms as he'd held her and rubbed her back. His refusal to walk away from her when things had gotten dangerous. His hands caressing her naked skin, his touch setting her on fire. His offer to kill a man simply because he'd hurt her. Jaxton willing to die if it meant she could live.

And most of all, his belief in her abilities and worth as a person.

Warmth filled her chest and radiated down her arms. She imagined Jaxton healthy and full of life, and fixed that image in her mind as she directed the warmth out of her hands and into Jaxton's skin. A few people gasped, but she ignored them and kept her eyes closed. She focused on Jaxton arguing with her, making love to her, working with her on their next DEFEND mission. She wanted all of that. And more.

Jaxton needed to survive so she could tell him, because after this, she wasn't going to share him with any other woman.

He was hers.

As the warmth continued to flow out of her hands, Kiarra struggled to stay upright as her head spun and she wobbled. Opening her eyes as the last of the warmth left her hands, she saw Jaxton's green-eyed gaze right before she passed out.

CHAPTER THIRTY-THREE

Jaxton rubbed his thumb against the back of Kiarra's hand and wished for the thousandth time that she'd wake up. It had been two days since he and Darius's team had escaped the research facility, yet Kiarra remained unconscious.

Remarkably, the bruises on her face and the cut on her lip were gone. If he hadn't seen them heal right before his eyes back at the research facility, he never would've believed it possible.

He still didn't understand exactly what had happened. One minute he'd lain dying, begging Kiarra to leave, and the next he'd been jolted out of unconsciousness to see her glowing a soft orange-red, the exact color of firelight.

He'd been weak from blood loss, his head clouded with pain, so a lot of what had happened was a blur, but he did remember the warmth spreading across his throat, stinging at first, but soon bringing relief. By the time Kiarra fainted, he'd never felt stronger.

If not for Kiarra's stubborn refusal to leave his side, he would probably be dead right now.

Well, that and his latent ability. During the last two days, he'd finally realized why his voice had caused the lights to flicker and the interrogator's ears to bleed. Much like in some of the old *Feiru* legends, strong emotions caused his voice to vibrate.

It wasn't what he would have chosen if given the choice, but being a Screecher was better than being nothing at all. His ability used the vibrations of his voice to incapacitate other *Feiru* and, apparently, could also short out technology. He had yet to try it out on any humans.

He brushed the hair from Kiarra's forehead and smiled, wondering how she'd take the news of his abilities. She would probably tease him about never raising his voice again, just as a precaution. He needed to test the full extent of his ability later and judge if that really was the case. Not being able to argue or raise his voice with Kiarra was not an option.

Especially now, when he had a thing or two to discuss with her.

From what he'd heard, she had gone to meet Gio's people alone, with no backup. Even with her abilities, that was tantamount to suicide. She'd spent fifteen years inside the AMT, and he would never truly try to curb her freedom, but he needed to drill some common sense into her.

Especially as word of her legendary abilities spread.

Speaking of which, he'd expected to hear from Neena or Aislinn by now. Neither one would answer the phone, nor did Neena respond to his dreams. He knew they were busy, probably off locating another Talent, but considering their search would mean nothing if the Fire Talent died, he'd expected some help.

But it wasn't just Kiarra he was worried about; Jaxton didn't know what had happened to Millie. Before Darius had burst into their room back at the research facility, Vanessa had spoken to some people she knew on the inside and confirmed that Millie was no longer there. Some people had said she'd died, while others had thought she'd been sent away. Darius seemed to trust Vanessa's words, though Jaxton had yet to find out why since the pair had disappeared shortly after securing Kiarra and Jaxton in their current location.

Jaxton brought Kiarra's hand to his lips, kissed her knuckles, and willed her to wake up. He needed to find his sister, but he couldn't do anything until he was sure Kiarra would live. He had people searching for Millie in the meantime, but that wasn't enough. He'd lost his brother five years before and he wasn't about to lose his sister too.

He let out a frustrated sigh. Sitting around, doing nothing was not his style. He'd been patient and attentive over the last few days, but it was time to try a different approach with Kiarra. He poked her in the side a few times, and she moved a little. Maybe this would work.

He lightly pinched her hip and ordered, "Get up, lazybones. We've work to do." He rose halfway from the chair and leaned down next to her ear. "Both in and out of the bedroom."

He nipped her ear and Kiarra gave a half-hearted swat before mumbling, "Leave me alone."

Jaxton stilled, and then relaxed. "Never. Now, get up."

His heart pounding, Jaxton waited to see if she would wake up. Kiarra rubbed her head against the pillow, and all of the sudden, he was jealous of an inanimate object.

He needed to touch her.

Brushing her cheek, he murmured, "Please, pet, wake up."

One eye cracked open. "You only use the word 'please' when it's something I don't want to do."

At her words, a rush of warmth went straight to his heart. Until now, he hadn't realized how scared he'd been that his little Fire Talent would never wake up again. Jaxton wanted——no, needed—to hold her in his arms. He swatted her side. "Make room for me."

She looked at him with an unreadable expression before her eyes widened and darted to his throat and back to his face.

"You're alive." She tried to sit up, but she grabbed her head and sank back down onto the bed. "Why am I so lightheaded?"

"Woman, after sitting here for two days, wondering whether you were going to live or die, I'm not going to tell you a bloody thing until you move over so I can hold you in my arms."

She blinked for a second then scowled, although the smile in her voice lessened the effect. "Fine, just this once, I'll do as you say."

Kiarra moved over and held up the blanket in invitation. Jaxton slid under the covers, and as soon as he pulled Kiarra close, his bravado melted away. "Don't ever do something daft like that again, do you hear?"

She rubbed her head against his chest before hitting him with her fist. "You're one to talk. You were bleeding out, right in front of my eyes. If I hadn't been able to heal you…"

Kiarra sobbed and he hugged her tightly. "Sssh, love, I'm here now."

Her tears went straight to his heart, but no matter how much he murmured affirmations, interspersed with kisses to the top of her head, she wouldn't stop crying.

"Can't lose you…too many…people I love…" Kiarra choked out.

Jaxton's hand stopped mid-stroke as he processed her words.

~~*

Kiarra knew she was being an idiot, but once the tears started, she couldn't seem to make them stop. Even with Jaxton holding her close and murmuring reassurances, she clung to him

299

for dear life, afraid that she'd wake up to find it had all been a dream.

He'd almost died, and it was only when she saw him whole again did she realize just how scared she'd been. A lot had been taken away from her over the years, but Jaxton had been the one to coax out her secrets and fears, introducing the concept of trust back into her life. If she lost him, she wasn't sure she could find the strength to recover.

She'd lost too many people she loved in the past; she would fight until her last breath to make sure it didn't happen again.

Her tears were slowing, but it was the cessation of Jaxton's hand on her back and the tensing of his chest under her fingers that finally brought her out of her fit. Transitioning to survival mode, she tried to calm down her emotions. She strained her ears and listened for signs of danger.

Jaxton's heartbeat drowned out everything, so she tried to sit up, but the man's arms were like a steel prison and kept her from moving. "What's wrong, Jaxton? Did you hear something?"

"What did you mean when you said you'd lost too many people you love and can't lose me?"

Had she spoken her thoughts aloud? It was entirely possible.

A vulnerability she couldn't explain gripped her. She hadn't meant to say it, but she couldn't take it back. Plucking at Jaxton's shirt, she hoped he'd understand her silence and let it go. She could barely admit her feelings to herself and she wasn't ready to discuss them with the man in question.

But she knew better. Jaxton attacked everything head on. "Kiarra," he said before leaning back and tilting her head up with her fingers. "Look at me."

Inhaling a deep breath for courage, she met his green-gold gaze. There was no fear, no ridicule, only tenderness. "Yes?"

He stroked the skin just below her lower lip and said, "Tell me what you meant, pet."

She couldn't tear her eyes away from the force of his gaze. Words started coming out before she could stop them. "I-I can't bear the thought of losing you."

He smiled, never stopping the strum of his thumb against her skin. "And why is that, love?"

Love. Not pet, not Kiarra, he'd said "love." The endearment gave her the courage to say, "Because I love you."

He grinned and the transformation knocked the wind out of her lungs. She had trouble focusing on anything but his mouth when he said, "Good, because I'm never letting you go."

His gaze grew heavy and his mouth descended on hers, the playfulness and tenderness from the other night gone. His tongue demanded access to her mouth and Kiarra opened on a groan, snaking her arms around his chest to clutch his shoulders and press her body against his. Between his near-death and the admission of her feelings, she needed to feel his hot, naked skin against hers.

Reading her mind, Jaxton rose to his knees, shucked his shirt, and unzipped his black cargo pants. As he shimmied out of them, her gaze darted to his erection, jutting long and hard from his body. She'd have to ask him to go commando more often.

He ripped open the condom packet he'd plucked from his pants and rolled it down his cock. When he finished, she reached to draw Jaxton down, but he brushed aside her hands to fist the hem of the long black t-shirt she wore and yanked it up over her head. In a flash, her panties were gone too. Jaxton settle his body on top of hers, the weight and heat of his touch sending even more dampness between her legs.

He murmured, "I promise to go slow later," before ravishing her mouth again while he stroked her between her thighs. Kiarra raised her hips in answer, her core throbbing, needing to have him inside her.

He positioned his cock at her entrance, slammed it to the hilt, and she gasped at the feeling of fullness. But she didn't have time to dwell on it before he gripped her breast hard. Kiarra moaned, raking her nails down his back to cup his ass as he thrust into her, over and over. She raised her hips in time to his, wrapping her legs around his waist to allow him to penetrate deeper.

The pressure built, but remained just out of reach. If only he would touch her, but then his hand was pressing and rubbing against her bundle of nerves. After a few more hard thrusts, the world shattered and her sex clenched greedily at his cock. She maintained eye contact, wanting to see his face as he came. Kiarra watched as Jaxton groaned before he stilled, the cords of his neck visible, and she knew he was spilling inside of her.

He soon lowered down, kissing her gently before lying back on the bed and pulling her close. He flicked the blanket over them, and as she listened to the rapid beat of his heart, he kissed her forehead and nuzzled the top of her head.

~~*

Jaxton stroked Kiarra's hip and drew in another deep breath, savoring the smell of her hair. As her fingers played with the hair on his chest, her words echoed inside his head: *I love you.*

After the whole mess with Garrett and Marzina five years ago, Jaxton had never expected to trust any woman enough to care for her more than his own life. But he'd been wrong. When push came to shove, the thought of Kiarra dying had felt like someone had stabbed his heart with a dagger. It was more than the world needing her because she was a Talent. No, the world needed her heart, her stubbornness, her ability to go against incredible odds.

In other words, the world would be a worse place without her.

He hugged her closely, the softness of her breasts against his chest a comfort. There was a lot to be done, many obstacles to tackle in the coming months, but he would be selfish for a little while longer and simply hold the woman he cared about more than his own life.

The words were on the tip of his tongue, but all of the confidence he'd amassed over the years failed him. He was as nervous a teenage boy, aware that a few simple words would forever change his life.

Then he thought about going back to a life devoid of Kiarra's arguments, her humor, her intelligence, and the picture was bleak and lonely.

It was time to step up, time to fight for what he wanted. "Kiarra."

She adjusted her position, tilting her head up toward him, and he tried not to feel smug at her look of contentment. "Hmm?"

He ran his hand up her side until he could cup her cheek. "Before reality intrudes, I want to tell you something." She searched his eyes with her own, the longing in them the final push he needed to say, "I love you, Kiarra Melini." He leaned closer, his breath a whisper. "But only on one condition."

Kiarra blinked. "A condition?"

He leaned in close, a hair's breadth away from her lips, and whispered, "Just be careful not to char off my bollocks."

Kiarra laughed. "We'll see about that. Someone has to keep you in line."

Jaxton rolled her onto her back and pinned her hands over her head. "Did you not hear what I just said, bloody woman?" He gave her a half-lidded gaze. "I love you."

The laughter in her eyes changed into something fiercer. "I love you, too."

Jaxton growled before he kissed her and took his time showing her how much she meant to him.

Epilogue

Several weeks later

Kiarra shifted her feet for the hundredth time inside the car, positive they'd gone more than the necessary ten miles to their destination. She stole a glance at Jaxton in the driver's seat, and without a word, he reached out to squeeze her hand.

His touch helped, but not enough to ease all of her nervous energy. Instead, she focused on something other than their upcoming meeting of doom. "Are you sure no one's following us? We're in the middle of nowhere and pretty easy to spot."

Jaxton raised an eyebrow and slid his gaze to Kiarra before focusing on the road again. "Would I ever knowingly put you in danger?"

"No," she answered without hesitation. "But after recent events, I can't help but be a little paranoid."

He glanced at her again. "I know you're worried about Millie, but she's alive. She'll call us again if she needs our help. As for the rest, Neena and Aislinn have things in hand. Neena ordered us to take two days' rest, and unless you want another scary visit from her, I wouldn't disobey her orders."

"Hmph." Kiarra had almost forgiven Neena for drugging her. The woman had been scarce of late, unwilling to give them much help when it came to controlling her abilities, let alone Jaxton's. Neena had only contacted them to let them know that they would soon be in charge of a new operation.

JESSIE DONOVAN

"I know you're not really upset with Neena," Jaxton said. He squeezed her hand before shifting as the car slowed down to make a turn. "As I've said many times before, don't worry. She's going to love you."

"You're obligated to say that," she murmured, "but I'm not sure I believe you."

Jaxton's hearing was keen. "Well, I look forward to you apologizing to me later, love. We're here."

He pulled in front of a small single-level cottage with bushes and flowers decorating the yard. There was even a garden and two benches off to the side. It was exactly how she pictured the British countryside—slightly aged, but quaint and charming.

Kiarra gave her hair a final run-through with her fingers before exiting the car and joining Jaxton. Even with his arm around her waist, all she could think about were her doubts.

What happens if she doesn't like me? What then?

The front door of the cottage opened and revealed a woman of medium height with hair more gray than brown. The middle-aged woman smiled and walked toward them. When she finally reached them, the mostly gray-haired woman pulled Jaxton down for a hug, her embrace fierce with love. "Aren't you a sight for sore eyes," she said, her voice muffled against Jaxton's chest.

When the woman finally stepped back, she kept a hand on Jaxton's chest and turned her green-gold gaze to Kiarra.

Kiarra started sweating. The time had come.

The woman patted Jaxton on the chest and said, "Aren't you going to introduce me to your lovely companion?"

He placed a hand on Kiarra's lower back. "Mum, this is Kiarra Melini." He gave Kiarra a look of encouragement and continued, "Kiarra, this is my mum, Ellen Ward."

Kiarra put out a hand to shake. "Nice to meet you, Mrs. Ward."

Ellen Ward ignored Kiarra's hand and pulled her into a tight embrace. "Dear, I'm American, and we hug."

Kiarra stopped breathing. Not because she was still adverse to touch, but rather because of the ease of Ellen's acceptance.

Ellen pulled back, keeping her hands on Kiarra's arms. "And call me Ellen, Mum, Ellie, or anything you like that doesn't make me sound a thousand years old."

Kiarra smiled. "Ellen, then."

"Right," Ellen said before situating herself between Jaxton and Kiarra and looping an arm around each of their waists. "Let's have some tea and I'll bring out photos of Jax as a lad." When Jaxton made a sound to interrupt, Ellen shushed him. "I've waited a long time for this day, Jaxton Oliver Ward, so don't you dare deny me this opportunity."

Kiarra leaned forward and saw the resigned look on Jaxton's face; she couldn't help but grin. Ellen Ward was fantastic.

As they made their way up the walkway, Kiarra felt another link tethering her to her past shatter. Even though her future might be uncertain, her gut told her that the Ward family was her family now, too, and she never had to worry about being alone ever again.

Dear Reader:

I hope you enjoyed Kiarra and Jaxton's story. While the next book will focus on Cam and Marco, keep an eye out for Kiarra and Jaxton. They'll be back, along with a lot of the other characters in future books. I love it when authors show us how our favorite characters are doing later on, and I plan to do the same.

This is my debut novel, and I'm grateful for all of the wonderful feedback and honest reviews I've received from readers like you. I'm always curious to hear what you think—both good and bad. You can email me at jessiedauthor@gmail.com or find me on Twitter @jessiedauthor. I really do read every email/tweet I receive, and I try to reply when I can! If you want to receive exclusive content (deleted scenes, short stories, etc.) and updates, you can sign up for my monthly newsletter at jessiedonovan.com.

And finally, I need to ask you a favor. Reviews can be tough to come by these days. You, the reader, have the power to make or break a book, and I'm asking for your help. If you have the time, could you leave an honest review?

Thank you for spending time with my characters. I hope you return to the world of the *Feiru* in *Frozen Desires*, and continue to follow the journey of Neena, DEFEND, and all of the rest. Make sure to turn the page for an excerpt.

With Gratitude,
Jessie Donovan

The story continues with Cam and Marco…Excerpt from
Frozen Desires (AMT#2)

CHAPTER ONE

*"In 1953, the first-born children of Feiru (FEY-roo) mothers were
deemed dangerous by the Feiru High Council. Because these first-
born children have the ability to control fire, earth, water, or wind,
the council passed a law requiring them to be imprisoned at the
age of magical maturity. The council's aim was to keep the Feiru
secret of elemental magic from humans…One of DEFEND's
primary goals is to dismantle the Asylums for Magical Threats'
prison system and to integrate elemental magic users back into our
society."*
—Excerpt from *DEFEND Rules and Regulations*

After what had happened four years ago, Camilla Melini
had never expected to be back in Merida, Mexico.

But DEFEND had sent her here to find one of the Four
Talents—legendary elemental magic users who could both heal
and destroy—and she wasn't about to let memories of that day
ruin her chances of success. As long as she kept her eyes open,
and was careful, she should be able to get in and out of Merida
before anyone from her old life could find her.

And if they did, well, she had a few extra tricks up her
sleeves these days that she could use to try to defeat them.

Cam looked over at Zalika, one of two people that made up
her team, and asked, "Are we finally on the right street?"

Zalika offered Cam the map in her hands. "You try reading
a map in Spanish and see how far you get."

"All I care about is reaching our contact's shop. The sooner we get there, the sooner I can take off this stupid straw thing on my head."

Zalika smiled. "But since the real Cam would never be caught dead in that hat, it's a good disguise."

"I'd rather take my chances if it means I can see properly."

Zalika laughed as they turned the corner. "Jacek is watching our backs, and he'll let us know if he sees anything suspicious."

Jacek was the other half of Cam's team. "He's a good enough lookout, but that's not what I'm worried about."

"You haven't seen your asshole ex or any of the other psychos from your past, have you?"

"No, but that doesn't mean they're not here."

Zalika nodded to the right. "Well, there's the stall. If everything goes to plan, then we should be out of Merida by this evening, and you'll have one less thing to worry about."

She only hoped it would be that easy. "Let's try to be out of here by this afternoon."

Doing the best she could with the brim of her hat hanging partially in front of her face, Cam did a sweep of the area. But nothing seemed out of the ordinary—just street vendors selling food, salespeople trying to entice tourists into their shops, and friends chatting on the street.

Confident that no one was following them, she nodded the all clear to Zalika, and they approached the vendor stall filled with Mexican handicrafts.

Cam glanced over the brightly colored tablecloths, place mats, and purses until she found the section of hand-painted ceramics. Most of the cups and plates featured some kind of flower, but she kept looking until she found a plate with DEFEND's secret symbol subtly worked into the design.

The middle-aged man running the stall matched the picture she'd been given in her assignment file, but to keep up appearances, she asked, "Do you speak English?"

The man smiled. "Yes. Is there something I can help you with?"

Time to use the secret pass-phrase. Cam held up the plate with DEFEND's symbol on it. "My aunt has one just like this in her house, and since she loves it, I'd like to add another one to her collection. Do you have any plates with the same design, but painted in different colors?"

The man replied, "Yes, but my wife tries to hide them away in the back of the store, hoping that I'll forget about them so she can keep them. But if you have time, I can take you to the inside portion of my shop and find the others for you."

The man had used the correct response to the pass-phrase. But in the interest of looking authentic, she looked over to Zalika and said, "What do you think? Can we take a few minutes to look at the other designs?"

Zalika shrugged. "Sure, you've waited for me enough times. Let's check out the other plates."

The man put up a hand. "Give me a second." He disappeared into the door behind him and soon reappeared with a teenage boy that Cam assumed was his son. The man said something in Spanish to the boy and then waved for them to follow him. "Come inside."

Cam took the lead, but right before she reached the door, her instinct told her that she was being watched. She glanced over her shoulder and listened intently with her supersensitive hearing—one of the many bonuses that came with her latent abilities—but came up with nothing. As much as she wanted to find the source of her unease, she and Zalika should be safe enough inside the shop. If someone tried to barge their way in, she had a gun and a knife strapped to her leg under her flowing skirt.

She needed the information this man could provide to get the hell out of Merida and complete her assignment. If she left now, she'd have to linger in Merida long enough to arrange another meeting.

She decided that the possible threat wasn't grave enough to abort her mission. She ducked inside the door, and Zalika followed.

~~*

Marco Alvarez watched Cam enter the shop and breathed a sigh of relief. When she'd turned around, he'd barely had time to hide in the crowd inside the eatery, the one he was using to stake out the vendor stall across the street.

His orders were clear—he was to watch over Camilla Melini and make sure her mission succeeded. The longer he could do it from the shadows, the less of a chance someone would connect them, giving him the advantage of surprise if things turned sour.

Since he'd seen her knock out a shadow-shifter back in the States, he knew firsthand that Cam could take care of herself. But Jaxton Ward—a high-ranking member of DEFEND and his old boss—was either being cautious or knew something that he didn't. Cam was here to explore some Mayan ruins and hopefully find a clue left by a Talent, but he had a feeling that something else was going on. Maybe another group was also searching for the Four Talents.

Whatever it was, watching over Cam and protecting her team was only half of the reason he was back in Mexico. He was also here to hunt down an anti-AMT fringe group that was targeting innocent *Feiru*—and killing them. He was still in the process of collecting evidence, but all Marco knew for certain was that this group had a reach far beyond Mexico.

While waiting for Cam to arrive in Merida, he'd received news that had made his second assignment personal—the same fringe group he was here to investigate had killed one of his cousins down in Colombia.

He clenched his hands inside the pockets of his jeans and tried not to think about how his fourteen-year-old cousin would never grow into the woman she was meant to be. He was determined to prevent other children from dying through no fault of their own. More than enough children already suffered inside the Asylum for Magical Threats compounds simply because they were the eldest child.

He'd started interviewing witnesses last night after the shops had closed, and would interview a few others later. During the day, however, he needed to focus on protecting Cam and Zalika. The owner of the handicraft stall was one of DEFEND's local contacts, and while they didn't think their contact's identity had been compromised, it was always a possibility, especially with the constantly shifting landscape of *Feiru* politics.

He finished the soda in his hand and moved toward the door of the open-air eatery. He needed to find a better place to stake out the stall, one with easier access in case a threat appeared while Cam was inside. But halfway to the exit, a man walked by and knocked him hard on the shoulder. Marco cursed, but the man paid no attention and simply kept on walking.

Marco frowned. It seemed that Mexico, like every other country in the world, had its fair share of rude assholes.

JESSIE DONOVAN

He moved down the street, keeping one eye out for Jacek and the other on the vendor stall. He was just about to browse one of the stalls on his side of the street to keep up appearances when he noticed the rude asshole stop at the same stall where Cam had been minutes earlier. He was about to dismiss it as a coincidence when the teenage boy in charge of the stall started gesticulating wildly.

When the asshole pulled out a gun, Marco cursed, and started picking his way toward the stall as calmly yet efficiently as he could. If he drew too much attention, then the man would probably bolt. He didn't want to chase an unknown enemy through the crowded mid-morning streets of Merida and blow his cover.

But when the asshole started motioning more fervently with his gun, Marco began pushing people out of the way. Despite his apologies, one of the American tourists started yelling at him. The man with the gun noticed, and fled down the street.

Fucking fantastic. Marco ran after him.

They were heading toward the Plaza Grande, the main town square. Once the man reached the square, Marco wouldn't be able to take down the man and question him. There were too many human witnesses, and a fight could attract the *Feiru* authorities.

He wanted to use his elemental water magic to stop the bastard, but Marco wasn't an idiot. The last thing he needed was to be tossed inside an AMT compound where they would drug him out of his mind, and do who knows what to him. He'd never be able to help Cam or his family then.

The tourist crowds started to thin out, and with another turn, the streets were empty. The tops of the buildings surrounding the main plaza were closer, and he decided it was now or never. He lunged for the man.

316

He managed to grab the man's legs, and they tumbled to the ground. But the man rolled out of his reach, and Marco used his arms to lift his upper body and jump into a crouch.

He now stood between the man and the plaza. There was no way he was letting the bastard through, and since they were now alone, with no humans in sight, Marco reached a hand to the west—the direction of elemental water—in case he needed to draw on the elemental water particles in the air to do his magic.

But the man just stood there, not trying to get away or even bothering to attack. Marco knew that inaction could be a tactic, so he kept up his guard, and waited.

Then the man did something Marco should have foreseen—but had overlooked—and crashed through the window of an abandoned house to the left.

Marco grabbed the gun tucked into his waistband under his shirt and crawled through the broken window, careful not to cut himself on the glass. Once inside, he rolled to the side and hid behind an overturned couch that had seen better days. His finger near the trigger, he peeked around the edge, looking and listening for any sign of the man, or anyone else that might happen to be inside the abandoned house.

The coast clear, he inched his way toward the open door in the back of the building. There were footprints in the dirt on the floor, leading toward the back door, but they simply stopped a few feet from the exit. The prints looked fresh, but no one could just disappear into thin air.

But then he remembered. He'd seen it happen once before.

The odds were long, but he could be dealing with a shadow-shifter.

Even with the sun filtering in through the threadbare curtains, the room was half engulfed in darkness. Marco moved to stand in the light near the window and debated using his elemental magic. While streams of water or shards of ice might draw the shadow-shifter out from his hiding place, it would also reveal Marco's abilities to his opponent.

And the last thing he needed was to destroy the cover he'd built up over the last eleven years by using his magic in front of a stranger. Especially if the man somehow managed to escape.

Another option would be to throw something heavy at the first sign of suspicious activity and force the shifter to return to his human-looking *Feiru* form. After what had happened in the States, Marco had learned that a shadow-shifter could only shift once every twenty-four hours. If he could scare the man into shifting back, it would give him a chance to catch and interrogate him.

Deciding to try the latter approach first, he circled around by degrees and checked the shadows for movement, careful to keep his back exposed to the light. Then he saw it—a piece of peeled wallpaper near the ceiling that waved back and forth in the still air.

Marco did a quarter turn away from his target, placed a hand on an old kitchen chair nearby, and swung it around, tossing it up at the spot on the wall where he'd seen the movement.

Right before the chair smashed against the wall, the man emerged from the shadows and rolled to the ground, out of the way. Marco jumped after the man, but the shadow-shifter dashed out the back door and slammed it shut. He heard a screeching sound of something heavy moving across the ground.

Marco pushed against the door, but it wouldn't budge.

The bastard had blocked him in.

Left with no other choice, he made for the broken window he'd come through, and crawled outside.

He made his way around to the back alley, and saw the rusty metal display case sitting in front of the door, but there was no sign of the shifter. After checking up and down the alley, looking into every possible hiding spot, Marco accepted that the man was long gone.

In case the shifter came back with reinforcements, he made his way back toward the street of vendor stalls, careful to take a different route than the way he had come. He needed to find Cam and tell her what had happened.

Thanks to the appearance of an unknown shadow-shifter, he was now going to have to spend more time with Camilla Melini than he'd counted on.

==================

Frozen Desires
Available Now

For exclusive content and updates, sign up for my newsletter at:
http://www.jessiedonovan.com

ACKNOWLEDGMENTS

While writers spend most of their time alone, chained to a desk, the truth is that we wouldn't be able to survive without our wonderful friends and family. I'd like to take this chance to thank them for all that they do.

First and foremost, without Michelle Cuadros, this book may never have happened. She's read my stories since we were teenagers, but when I became serious about writing in late 2008/early 2009, she listened patiently to my ramblings about a 19th century logger in the woods and his encounter with fairies from an underground world. She even read the first early (and clunky) versions of my *Feiru* society. Thanks to her support, those ideas slowly evolved until I had the world you saw in this book. I will be forever grateful for her friendship.

Another person I wish to thank with all my heart is the world's best beta-reader, Wendy Lynn Clark. Her ten-plus pages of enthusiastic comments and questions not only helped fine-tune the overall story, but also helped make Chapter One better than I could've ever imagined. Thanks Wendy!

I also wish to thank Clarissa Yeo of Yocla Designs for the beautiful cover, as well as a shout out to James Archer for not only winning the gold medal for perseverance when it came to wanting a character named after him (he bugged me for six years!), but also for being a great friend who listened to my story ideas despite never having read a romance book in his life.

And finally, I thank you, the reader. I hope you stay along for the ride, into the second book and beyond. The Feiru universe is going to get a lot worse before it gets better, but I hope to make the journey worth your while!

ABOUT THE AUTHOR

Jessie Donovan wrote her first story at age five, and after discovering *The Dragonriders of Pern* series by Anne McCaffrey in junior high, she realized people actually wanted to read stories like those floating around inside her head. From there on out, she was determined to tap into her over-active imagination and write a book someday.

After living abroad for five years and earning degrees in Japanese, Anthropology, and Secondary Education, she buckled down and finally wrote her first full-length book. While that story will never see the light of day, it laid the world-building groundwork of what would become her debut paranormal romance, *Blaze of Secrets*.

Jessie loves to interact with readers, and when not traipsing around some foreign country on a shoestring, can often be found on Facebook and Twitter. Check out her pages below:

http://www.facebook.com/JessieDonovanAuthor
http://www.twitter.com/jessiedauthor

And don't forget to sign-up for her newsletter to receive sneak peeks and inside information. You can sign-up on her website:

http:///www.jessiedonovan.com

Printed in Great Britain
by Amazon